Midshipman Kirk

ALASKA

Langara Island

Rose Spit

Graham Island

Skidegate Inlet

Queen Charlotte Islands

Hecate Strait

CANADA

Cape St. James

Hope Island

FORT RUPERT

Johnstone Strait

Vancouver Island

New Westminster

NANAIMO

Gulf Islands

VICTORIA

ESQUIMALT

Haro Strait

Cape Flattery

Juan de Fuca Strait

Olympic Mountains

Patrol Areas of the Detached Squadron, comprising Her Majesty's Ships
Calcutta and *Porpoise*, during the events related in this book.

Midshipman Kirk

Being the adventures of a midshipman, Royal
Navy, aboard the iron screw corvette HMS
Calcutta, during the 1880s on the west coast of
North America.

by
Ross Westergaard

Horsdal & Schubart

Horsdal & Schubart Publishers Ltd.
4252 Commerce Circle Victoria, B.C. V8Z 4M2

Map drawn by Suzanne Prendergast, Ganges, B.C.
Cover painting "HMS *Malabar* Passing in Royal Review at Cowes",
    by H. Robins, 1882, courtesy of Vancouver Maritime Museum,
    Vancouver, B.C. Painting donated to the museum's collection by Mr.
    F.M. Chapman.
This book is set in Palatino.
Printed and bound by Best/Gagne Book Manufacturers, Toronto,
    Ontario.

This book is dedicated,
with all my love, to my wife, Frances Marie Westergaard.

Canadian Cataloguing in Publication Data

    Westergaard, Ross, 1927-
      Midshipman Kirk

    ISBN 0-920663-16-8

    I. Title.
PS8595.E87M5 1993   C813'.54   C93-091357-4
PR9199.3.W47M5 1993

CONTENTS

Introduction

These yarns were inspired by historical events, and tales and legends of the west coast of North America, in particular British Columbia — along a coast which, to this day, remains windswept and wild. The Russian presence on the west coast is well documented: less widely known is the fact that a British fleet was mobilized, during 1878, against a Russian threat to the Empire "on which the sun never sets."

Spanish sailors explored much of the west coast. Their exploits are commemorated by such names as Cortes, Quadra, Gabriola and Galiano islands, and Malaspina Strait.

Fenians — a group of Irish-Americans plotting attacks on Canada in revenge for supposed British injustices in Ireland — actually invaded Canada in 1866. Two thousand Fenian troops defeated a Canadian volunteer force, and occupied an area close by Fort Erie, Ontario, while in 1871 39 Fenians were clapped into a Manitoba jail, but later released into American custody. During the same period the Royal Navy's Admiral Denman, from his headquarters in Esquimalt, British Columbia, stationed warships off seaports such as Victoria and New Westminster to forestall Fenian attacks. A notorious — if ingenious — promoter named George Francis Train announced in 1869 his intention to raise 40,000 Fenian troops in San Francisco, and invade Vancouver Island by way of a bridge spanning Juan de Fuca Strait. Also, Fenian leaders arranged to buy a primitive submarine from the American inventor, Holland. Professor Holland was apparently never paid — but his submarine vanished. As late as the mid-1880s, reports of Fenian weapons caches in B. C. had the Royal Navy alerted but nothing came of the rumours.

Haida Indians seized and burned the American schooner *Susan*

B. Sturgis (or *Sturges*) after an altercation partly to do with Haida gold; and persistent legends tell of a large Chinese junk seen wrecked on the northern Queen Charlotte Islands, prior to the turn of this century. The "Pig War" of San Juan Island is documented history: an account of the happenings may be read in *Seven Shillings a Year*, by Charles Lillard.

HMS *Boadicea*, 1875 - 1905, was the model for HMS *Calcutta*. Launched in Portsmouth Dockyard, she displaced 3,932 tons, was 280 feet long and 45 feet in beam, with a draft of 23 feet. She joined a miscellaneous fleet assembled at Portland against a Russian threat in 1878, was later on the Cape, and after that had two commissions on the East Indies station as flagship. She went into Class 4 Reserve in 1894 till 1905, when she was one of many ships disposed of by the First Sea Lord, Sir John Fisher.

A few names of friends have, with their permission, been woven into the stories. Midshipman Eric Kirk is derived from my son, Kirk Eric Westergaard, himself a fine sailor, and Lieutenant David Duncan honours my uncle Dave — a gentleman beyond compare.

This is a work of fiction. Other than actual historical events, names as mentioned above and the names of places, any resemblance to real people or events is purely coincidental.

Ross Westergaard, Denman Island

Chapter One

Russian Roulette

"Midshipman Kirk!" The snarling bellow fused steel into the spines of the young officers swaying with the ship's motion, their dark-blue, brass-buttoned uniforms and sea-burnt faces contrasting with the holystoned-white decks. Each of the apprehensive youngsters stared straight ahead as Lieutenant Mudd stumped over to the unfortunate Kirk. Mudd tilted his blotchy face back to glare up at the tall midshipman. "I have been inspecting your journal, Mister Kirk. Your last entry was made a week ago. Well?"

"Yes, sir." Eric Kirk looked through the irate lieutenant, stony features masking his contempt for Mudd. "You see, sir..."

"No explanations, Midshipman Kirk!" Flecks of spittle flew from Mudd's thick lips, to be whisked away by the brisk beam wind. "You'll spend the Dog Watches today and tomorrow bringing your journal up to date, and report with it to me before two bells in the First Watch tomorrow."

"Aye aye, sir!"

HMS *Calcutta*, a ship-rigged iron screw corvette displacing some 3,900 tons, rolled ponderously through the westerly swell off Vancouver Island's rock-scarred west coast, rigging gently creaking, courses and deep single tops'ls stiff-bellied below furled topgallants and royals. Her spindly funnels were, thank goodness, free of the pungent black coal smoke which infiltrated all parts of the ship, leaving soot and cinders.

On the raised quarterdeck, Captain A.N. Whitfeld-Clements, known fondly as "Clemmie" by the ship's company — although definitely not to his face — glanced sharply at the little tableau in the waist. Turning to Commander John Keen, standing beside him and idly tapping a brass telescope against a bony knee, the captain murmured, "I trust you're keeping a weather eye on Mudd?"

1

"Yes, sir." Keen kept his voice low. "He's done nothing outrageous enough to warrant more than a cautionary word from me — as yet."

"Very good." The captain raised his voice, surprisingly gentle for such a massive man, to his normal tone. "We'll exercise the gun crews in the Afternoon Watch, John. Order the engineer officer to raise steam. I want firing practice first under sail, then using the engine."

"Aye aye, sir. I'll have the carpenter break out a couple of empty casks." He paused. "Shall I fall in the Royal Marines for musketry at the same time, sir?"

The captain chuckled. "By all means. Let the bootnecks have some practice, too." Nodding amiably to Keen, he strode forward along the weather side of the quarterdeck, frock coat snapping in the sharp May wind, mind churning with the implications of his newly opened orders.

Midshipman Kirk, mind also churning, but with fear and dislike of Lieutenant Mudd, wondered for the hundredth time if he had blundered by applying for an appointment as a midshipman in Her Majesty's Royal Navy. Then, with the resilience of youth, he shook off the black mood and studied *Calcutta*. He was proud of his ship. Even though she was sheathed with wood and coppered, her frames and shell were built of iron. She carried 14 seven-inch guns — muzzle-loading, but rifled for accuracy — mounted on carriages and slides between decks, plus a pair of carronades fore and aft. Glancing aloft, he watched a trickle of funnel smoke become a torrent as stokers shovelled coal on their banked fires; then he walked forward — "forrard", he reminded himself — moving smartly to forestall accusations of skylarking by the irascible Mudd. Seeing the black look that appeared on his face at the thought of Mudd, a group of off-Watch tars hurriedly shuffled clear of his path.

Kirk leaned well over the rail, ostensibly inspecting the spider-web of rigging under the bowsprit and jib-boom, and watched the figurehead — a carved-oak maharajah, turbanned head resting haughtily against the stem — rhythmically rising and plunging into the "wine-dark sea". Taking a deep breath of fresh salt air, he felt the reassuring solidity of the rubbed teak rail and listened momentarily to the myriad small sounds of a sailing ship under way.

Straightening, the young midshipman turned and looked aft

toward the wheel, grinning to himself as Whitfeld-Clements glanced at the binnacle. The helmsman must have felt the captain's eyes, for he shifted his grasp on the varnished mahogany spokes to steer even more carefully, bare feet firm on the teak gratings and eyes fixed on the luff of the mizzen tops'l. Suddenly a chill shivered along Kirk's back. He'd almost neglected a duty for which even the compassionate Clemmie would have difficulty forgiving him. Marching hurriedly aft — not running, but at a much brisker pace than usual — he mounted the quarterdeck. "Captain, sir," he spoke the traditional phrase, waited for Whitfeld-Clements to turn, then saluted. "Permission to pipe 'Up Spirits'?"

Receiving the captain's nodded assent and a grin from Commander Keen, he saluted again. Catching the cox'n's eye — the petty officer had been watching and waiting for the formality to end — Midshipman Kirk ordered two seamen to belay splicing a hawser, and follow him down the companionway.

An uneven blue line of petty officers and seamen was forming even as the two sailors struggled on deck with the awkward rum cask. They set it down gently at a sharp word from the cox'n, under the thirsty gaze of several score watchful eyes, and the cox'n trilled his call — "Up Spirits!"

And "Stand Fast the Holy Ghost", Kirk thought, irreverently completing the ritual. Standing at ease, hands clasped behind his back, he watched the polished brass words GOD SAVE THE QUEEN winking brightly against the oaken cask, while the hands drew their daily tots.

Later that afternoon, after the captain had expressed his biting displeasure — two full broadsides from each tier of guns had failed to demolish the bobbing casks — Kirk scribbled wearily in his journal, a daily record of all his duties, lessons, achievements and errors. The captain's last remark, directed to "Guns", still rang in his ears: "Perhaps we should stand by to ram, Mister Giles!"

The rumble of gun-carriages and the faintly-heard staccato threat, "Damn my eyes, you'll do better than that or I'll know the reason why!", sliced through the stuffy gunroom air, redolent with damp cotton clothing and oilskins. The gunner, it seemed, was carrying out his promise to exercise the gun crews in the Dog Watches. Kirk grinned wryly in sympathy for his fellow downtrodden, and continued with his scrawled journal: "29 May, 1881..."

Kirk jumped as the gunroom door crashed open and Midshipman Perkins, red-headed, noisy, and an irrepressible prankster, bounced in, shedding wet oilskins onto the already damp deck. Slamming his journal closed — it was only two days behind, now — Eric grinned a greeting as he shoved his hard wooden chair away from the scarred, bolted-down table.

"I say, Eric, Mudd's got it in for you, hasn't he!" It wasn't a question. "All of us have been sculling about a bit with the journals — mine's a week behind — but he keeps singling you out." He blinked owlishly, looking more like a flustered schoolboy than an embryo naval officer.

"Not to worry, Reggie," Eric tried to appear unconcerned. "I should have kept it up to date in spite of Mudd's extra duties." He watched an errant sunbeam flicker through the scuttle and dance momentarily on the deck, before clouds again darkened its source. "I suppose I might have realized he'd check it."

"Well, it's damned unfair," the freckle-faced youngster burst out, his waving arms nearly capsizing the hanging oil lamp, "and if I..."

"If you're wise, Midshipman Perkins, you'll get on with your journal before you're in the rattle, too." The amused voice belonged to Sublieutenant Keith van Dusen, the Sub of the Mess and "Schoolie", responsible for the midshipmen's scholastic efforts as well as decorum in their home, the gunroom. Frowning mock-seriously at the two mids, his face Machiavellian in the gloom, he said quietly, "Don't give Lieutenant Mudd any more reason to ride you, Kirk. He's still not forgotten that episode at the banyan in Fiji."

"But, look here, sub, all I did was trip him when he'd had too much to drink —" ("Again", Perkins interjected) "— and tried to hit that native."

"I know, and if you hadn't, we could well have been stewing in cooking pots the next day — the native was one of their sub-chiefs. But you embarrassed Mudd in front of the other officers, and he'll be a long time forgiving that."

"So I've not got much to look forward to for the rest of this commission," Kirk muttered despondently. He stood and stretched wearily, remembering in the nick of time to duck his head to avoid collision with the deckhead timbers.

"Not necessarily," Perkins piped up. "I overheard Clemmie telling the commander to keep a weather eye on Mudd."

"Your flopping ears and wagging tongue will be waving from the fore t'gallant masthead one of these days, Perkins," warned the sublieutenant. "You clear out and let Kirk finish his journal." He sat down in the gunroom's sole tattered armchair, picked up a book and started reading to show the conversation was terminated.

When the red-head had slunk from the gunroom, cowering in pretended fear, Kirk turned to van Dusen again. "D'you think that the captain knows why Mudd is hounding me, sub?"

Van Dusen glanced at him. "Clemmie doesn't miss much, Kirk. Get back to work." And that was the unsatisfactory — and only — answer he received.

The subject of their short discourse was at that moment recalling his overwhelming joy, two years ago, when an Admiralty messenger had ridden up to the door of his small estate in Kent, horse snorting and splattering spring mud over whitewashed walls. He had ripped open the envelope, then remembered his manners and sent the man 'round to the kitchen for a plate of cold beef and a mug of ale.

"Is it good news, Norman?" His wife had leaned over the hedge, pruning shears dangling forgotten from a gloved hand.

"Yes, my dear," he'd smiled. "Their Lordships have made me a captain, and have given me *Calcutta* — a new cruiser of almost 4,000 tons. I'm to report to Admiralty House at once, and take command within a fortnight."

He smiled again as he remembered his beloved "New House", built by his great-grandfather to replace an older home that had burned to the ground after a chimney fire. Of grey stone was this house, although clambering ivy all but hid it, with red brick chimneys climbing from the slate roof above the timbered second storey. Even though they naturally had a housekeeper, cook and maid, as well as a gardener, groom and stableboy, his wife would let no one but herself tend her roses. Jeb, the crotchety and wizened gardener, muttered at times but would occasionally be seen, when he thought himself unobserved, digging a particularly rich barrow-load of manure in around the rose-bushes. The old man had enough to do, the captain mused, what with a good two acres of vegetables, fruit and berries to tend, as well as disciplining the stableboy's pranks and arguing with the groom as to who was in charge of the stable, the three thatch-roofed outbuildings and the small herd of cattle.

5

A sudden jar as the ship fell into a trough, then recovered, shuddering, brought the captain back to the here-and-now. His wife's shocked face faded from memory as he once more studied his orders, frowning. A fast sloop from the naval base at Esquimalt had come alongside yesterday — a smart bit of seamanship, that — and heaved the orders aboard in a weighted bag.

Skipping the preamble, he read for the fourth time, "... it is therefore assumed that Russia is attempting to obtain a foothold in British North America, to draw attention from her threatening moves toward Afghanistan. The Fleet will not be mobilized as it was in 1878 to meet a similar Russian menace, but you are required to exercise all diligence to ensure that this new plot is unsuccessful. You are warned, however, that provocation of hostilities between Her Britannic Majesty and the Emperor of Russia would be looked upon with great disfavour...."

Although a few Royal Navy captains, among them the notorious Bligh, who was respected as a seaman but detested as a harsh disciplinarian, delighted in keeping their officers and men in a state of mystified ignorance, Whitfeld-Clements was not one of their number. He believed that an informed ship's company was not only happier, but more efficient, so unless orders were secret, every man-jack aboard his ship knew what was being planned.

"Mister Kirk." Kirk trotted up the slanting deck and saluted, a keen wind whipping his face as *Calcutta* slashed through a whitecapped sea.

"Sir?"

"My compliments to Commander Keen, and I'll speak to all officers in my cabin at four bells. That includes yourself and the other snotties." The captain smiled faintly at the term, derived from the habit of previous generations of young midshipmen wiping cold noses on their sleeves. His short, salt-and-pepper beard glistened with salt spray.

"Aye aye, sir." Kirk saluted again, and paced quickly toward the commander's quarters, boots drumming a soft tattoo on the dampened deck.

Calcutta thrashed and vibrated through a short, steep Hecate Strait chop — they'd entered the shallow waters, dividing the mainland from the Queen Charlotte Islands, at daybreak — while the

6

officers assembled, balancing easily on the heaving deck, just outside the captain's quarters. At two sharp double clangs from the ship's bell, Commander Keen knocked once and opened the door, leading them inside. The ship was steaming, her funnels disgorging corpulent billows of black coal smoke. While the captain read his orders aloud, an occasional whiff of smoke drifted in the open scuttles, braced wide to lessen the miasma of too many bodies in too little space. Kirk and his fellow midshipmen, being "below the salt" in the naval hierarchy, stood in a huddled group near a panelled oak bulkhead. There was justice after all, Kirk thought: although the snotties were elbowed to the edges, they received the full benefit of a fresh Pacific breeze through an open port.

Whitfeld-Clements tucked his orders neatly back into a brass-bound folder, then seated himself at the head of his long formal table, motioning his officers to sit down. The midshipmen remained standing. Kirk surreptitiously studied the cabin. Except for his initial welcome aboard, and the occasions when an officer had peremptorily dispatched him with, "My respects to the captain, and...", it was the first time he'd been inside the sanctum. Under polished brass lamps swinging from the deckhead, scattered rugs softened the wooden deck. A glance toward the compact fireplace, glowing with ruddy embers, led his eyes to the carved dolphins supporting the table.... His mind jerked back to attention. The captain was speaking.

"Those are the orders, gentlemen. Your comments, if you please."

The conversation became general, Mudd's growl underlying David Duncan's courteous drawl, Lieutenant Giles' bark, and the engineer officer's amused staccato comments. At the end of a half-hour the captain called a halt. "I see that you're as mystified as I was." He glanced at the silent bevy of midshipmen. "I haven't heard from the young gentlemen. Perhaps you have some words of wisdom, Mister Kirk? No? Then Mister Perkins — I understand that the sharing of knowledge is one of your more endearing traits." Perkins' normally ruddy face glowed deep red as he opened his mouth, but the captain, seeing that his barbed shaft had struck home, looked away with a slight smile, letting Perkins off the hook.

"Very good, gentlemen. Thank you for your attention. We'll simply begin our search and see what develops. Midshipman Kirk, I'll be obliged if you'll remain a moment."

Kirk, stunned, swiftly examined his conscience, but could think of no more than a couple of minor pranks, and those, he told himself a trifle unconvincingly, certainly rated no more than a ticking-off by the sub. The others filed out, one or two glancing curiously sideways at him, and Perkins repressing a mischievous grin with considerable difficulty.

"Now, Mister Kirk," Whitfeld-Clements smiled, "a glass of wine with you. Burgundy or port — or I've an excellent little Madeira?"

"Burgundy, please, sir," answered the youth, more puzzled than ever.

"Good! My own choice." The captain poured from a crystal decanter, then held the stemmed glass to the light, appreciating the colour. They drank; the captain with gusto, Kirk with relief that he wasn't, apparently, in for a dressing-down.

"Now to business." The captain seated himself on a leather sofa, waving the midshipman to an adjoining chair. "I understand that you speak a little Russian. Is that correct?" He stared quizzically at Kirk.

"Uh — yes, sir. But only a few words. I understand more than I speak, because, uh, I had a Russian nanny..." His voice trailed off.

"How did that come about?" The captain raised his voice slightly as a pair of boots thudded past on the quarterdeck overhead.

"My parents, sir." Kirk gained confidence. "My father was a merchant captain. He made several voyages to Russia, and brought back a Russian family he found starving near the docks. The husband sailed with him as a sort of purser and translator — he was an educated man, sir, but had made enemies in the nobility. His wife stayed with us as my sister's and my nanny."

"And you chose the navy rather than a merchant career?" The captain frowned slightly. "Why was that?"

Kirk steadied himself as the ship rolled deeply. "My father told me, 'Half-pay's better than no pay', sir. There were times when he was left with less than wages after settling accounts. He finally sold his shares in the barque and bought a farm."

Whitfeld-Clements chuckled. "I see. The sailor's last refuge. And the Russian family?" His calf-length boots, gleaming softly as he crossed his legs, caught Kirk's eye. Gulping, he realized suddenly that the boots must be worth the equal of six months' pay for a midshipman.

"Oh, they're on the farm too, sir." He recovered himself and laughed. "They wouldn't leave my parents. Andrew is the farm manager. He taught my father how to play chess, and they sometimes play an evening game at the local pub, while nanny and mother complain."

"Andrew?"

"Actually Andrevitch, sir, but my father said he was tired of trying to wrap his tongue around the name." Kirk cut the remark off short, suddenly realizing that he was on the verge of his great failing — being too loquacious in the presence of his seniors.

The captain waited for him to continue for a moment, before remarking, "Well, young man, you have an interesting background. It may yet be of some help to your naval career."

"You mean if we meet any Russians, sir?" Kirk tried to appear alert, but the lack of rest while writing his journal was beginning to tell.

"Yes." The captain reached over his chair back to a short bookshelf, picking out a thick volume. "Here's a Russian lexicon. Study it well, and pay special attention to words with a naval or military connotation. Thank you for your company, Mister Kirk. We'll have a chat again."

"Thank you, sir." The midshipman lurched to his feet as the captain rose.

When Kirk turned to leave, bending his head to avoid the low beams, the captain added quietly, "Don't be concerned about your journal, Eric. I've personally examined and passed it." Despite the young man's weariness, his eyebrows quirked in surprise at being addressed by his first name. He'd heard the captain call Commander Keen "John", and had heard him address a lieutenant by his given name once or twice, but a midshipman? Never!

When Kirk entered the murky gunroom, he was pounced upon by the four other snotties, smothering him with curiosity. Even Sublieutenant van Dusen, temporarily discarding his carefully cultivated aloofness, joined in with a cautiously-phrased question.

"Wait a moment," Kirk yelped. "Let me put the captain's book away!" Setting it carefully on a shelf, he nonchalantly leaned against a bulkhead and scanned his questioners with a superior eye. "All that Clemmie wanted was my advice on a small matter, and for me to..." His voice rose to a shriek as a drenching pitcher of tepid water cascaded over his head and dripped down his back.

"Let that be a lesson to you, wart!" Setting the pitcher on its hanger, van Dusen looked pleased with himself and the other midshipmen roared with laughter at the discomfited Kirk.

HMS *Calcutta* reached down the rocky, reef-infested west coast of the Queen Charlotte Islands, all plain sail set in the Force 5 westerly, rolling easily in the swell. On deck and aloft, seamen tended to their ship's well-being — splicing, overhauling buntlines, cleaning and painting. On deck the sailmaker had found a sunny spot to wield his palm and needle on great folds of bulky canvas, out of the way of bare-footed "matlows" soogieing the deck with holystones and "bibles". In the maintop, a lookout, quid in cheek, scanned the empty horizon unceasingly as he and the mast swung in huge, elliptical arcs.

Derek Giles, the first lieutenant and gunner, had the deck. He paced monotonously fore and aft — 14 paces forward, turn about, 14 paces aft, turn about — telescope under arm and eyes restless. From his post just abaft the helmsman's slightly raised platform, Kirk glanced over at Giles regularly, wanting to be ready the moment he gave an order. The lieutenant's mouth opened and Kirk took a half step — but it wasn't for him. A crisp word and a lifted eyebrow summoned the gunner's mate to the quarterdeck.

The petty officer, as round as a bass drum, with a gravelly voice to match, doubled up and fell into step beside Giles. "Sir..."

Kirk eavesdropped unashamedly on the conversation. Since the captain's derisive remarks about the ship's gunnery, some ten days past, Giles had doubled the pressure on his crews. Without changing his pace or so much as glancing at the gunner's mate, he snapped, "The lashings on Number Two port gun were badly frayed when I inspected them this morning."

The petty officer was unfazed. "Gun crew overhauling them now, sir," he rumbled. "I set them to it straightaway."

"Very good. Keep an eye on that crew — they've a tendency to be slack. Make sure the gun captain knows I mentioned it."

"Aye aye, sir." The petty officer nodded, saluted, and strode forward, grizzled white beard bristling in the wind.

10

"Deck there!" The voice shrilled down from the maintop. Kirk was instantly alert as Giles looked aloft. A fiddler in the waist stopped playing in mid-note, with a screech like a wounded tomcat, and small groups of off-Watch sailors broke off yarning or mending clothes to likewise peer up at the lookout.

"Sail ho! Two points to looard. Looks like a barque beatin' up toward us, sir."

"Mister Kirk!" Giles didn't wait for an answer. "My respects to the captain, and there's a ship in sight. Then get back here and get aloft with a telescope."

Within seconds Kirk had delivered his message, received an acknowledgement, and was back on deck to report. Wordlessly the lieutenant handed him a folded brass telescope and jerked a calloused thumb at the rigging. Heart pounding, Kirk stuffed the instrument into a deep pocket, clambered into the weather main shrouds and began the laborious climb up the shuddering ratlines. From below, Derek Giles watched impatiently until the midshipman reached the tiny platform and the lookout moved over to make room. Four double clangs — eight bells — marked the change of the Watch, but Kirk ignored the formal minuet of changing duties on the deck far below.

He nodded at the seaman, recalling his name — Tidball — with an effort, as he wrapped an arm around a shroud and shook open the telescope. Focussing it with some difficulty — the mast was swaying widely — he brought the distant stranger into sight. "Right you are, Tidball," he murmured, then called down, "It's a barque, sir — still hull down."

"What colours is she flying, Mister Kirk?" The captain had arrived on deck, still buttoning his coat, and Lieutenant Duncan now stood beside him and Derek Giles.

"None hoisted, sir," Kirk shouted, "but if she holds her course she'll pass close by. She's closing fast, sir."

He heard Tidball ostentatiously clear his throat, and looked at the sailor questioningly. The lookout muttered through his beard, hardly moving his lips, "She'm hoistin' colours, sir."

Kirk whipped the glass to his eye again, and squinted. Sure enough, the barque's black hull had lifted above the grey horizon and, as he watched, a bright splash of colour broke out at her gaff, sharply defined against the bank of low rain-clouds hovering over

Cape St. James. "She's Russian, sir!" He screamed. "Just now hoisted her colours."

"Very good, Mister Kirk," the captain shouted. "You may come down now."

When Kirk reached the deck, puffing a little, Whitfeld-Clements was giving orders to the gunner. "Have the guns loaded and ready to run out, Mister Giles, but don't open the gunports without orders."

"Aye aye, sir." Giles walked swiftly to the after companion and slid down it, almost losing his balance as a bigger-than-usual sea made *Calcutta* lurch. As Kirk listened to rumbles and low shouts from the 'tween decks, indicating that the 12-pounders were being made ready for action, the captain turned to him.

"Midshipman Kirk, have the drummer beat to quarters."

Pulse pounding with excitement and the possibility of imminent action — his first — Kirk trotted forward and passed the order to the Royal Marine sergeant, a gnarled veteran of a score of skirmishes and battles throughout the far-flung reaches of the empire. Although he treated Kirk's exhilaration with amusement, the echoing rattle of the drum soon brought men running and tumbling from all parts of the ship, and a billow of smoke from the funnels showed that the stokers were feeding their banked fires.

"What do you intend to do, sir?" Commander Keen asked with a touch of trepidation; the captain was not noted for inviting questions. "We'll be abeam of him in an hour or less."

Captain Whitfeld-Clements sniffed the fresh breeze. "That depends on the action he takes. We'll keep the weather gauge however, in case he's less than friendly."

Their vision was suddenly obscured as a dense, stifling cloud of funnel smoke rolled down, caught by a caprice of wind. It whipped away quickly, and they silently watched the barque beating toward *Calcutta*, until a scant three miles of white-flecked ocean separated the two.

"Silence on deck, there!" Lieutenant Mudd yelled at a group of whispering seamen. "Master-at-Arms, take those men's names!"

Whitfeld-Clements suddenly turned to the third lieutenant, David Duncan, Officer of the Watch. "Tell the engine room to stand by, David, then furl all sail."

"Aye aye, sir." The patrician officer spoke quickly to the seaman standing by the polished brass telegraph. The instrument's commanding jangle was muted by Duncan's shouted orders, then by the pounding of bare feet over the deck as seamen cast off halyards and raced up swaying ratlines.

"Well done, Mister Duncan. Less than three minutes! Signal the engine room for half-speed ahead."

"Aye aye, sir." The deck vibrated gently as the screw bit into the water, and a churning wake appeared astern.

"Yeoman, hoist 'Heave to. I am sending boat'." The captain turned to Commander Keen, "You'll go, John. Take Midshipman Kirk with you to examine her documents, and have the boat's crew issued cutlasses." Signal flags snapped crisply from halyards as the commander waved to Kirk and dashed forward.

Whitfeld-Clements watched the approaching barque closely. Minutes passed. Kirk tumbled into the cutter, taking his place in the stern-sheets as the crew settled on thwarts. Commander Keen stepped into the swaying boat last, in keeping with the tradition that the senior officer is last into a boat, and first out. A double line of seamen waited at the falls as the bo's'n awaited an order to lower. The barque showed no sign of heaving to, or even acknowledging the signal. Kirk glanced at the captain. He was biting his lip. As Kirk watched, he saw the captain visibly come to a decision. "Mister Duncan," he roared. "Manoeuvre to keep the weather gauge, and run out the guns!"

"Aye aye, sir!" David Duncan issued a series of crisp orders. Muted slams and booms echoed below decks as gunports were triced up and guns run out. Kirk unbelievingly watched the barque sail unheedingly on, a half-mile astern and to leeward of *Calcutta*, as Duncan handled the man o' war to maintain a commanding position.

"Bring the ship to starboard, Mister Duncan." The captain stalked forward, "Mister Giles!"

"Sir?"

"Put a shot across his bow. Close."

"Aye aye, sir."

Calcutta heeled to port as she turned, the cutter swaying out. "Fend off, you men," snapped Kirk, then recalling the commander's presence, "By your leave, sir."

A crash and a cloud of acrid smoke forward preceded a water-spout less than half a cable's length off the Russian's jib-boom.

13

Pandemonium was instant. Men scurried up the Russian rigging, petty officers belabouring them with rope's ends, while officers on the poop shouted and gesticulated angrily at the British ship.

Slowly, clumsily, the Russian's royals and topgallants were furled, while her main yards swung slowly aback to heave her to. The captain turned to Lieutenant Duncan, "Dead slow ahead. Lower the cutter."

Within minutes Kirk was steering the dancing cutter through sun-flecked water toward the barque. Within seconds, it seemed, they were alongside and he was scrambling up the ship's side behind Commander Keen, closely followed by cutlass-waving seamen, leaving two boatkeepers bobbing in the cutter.

Captain Whitfeld-Clements watched through his telescope as the Russians closed about the small group, then saw a cutlass flash as the seamen aligned themselves along the bulwarks, while his two officers disappeared below with a handful of Russians.

Kirk, scrambling up the ramshackle boarding ladder grudgingly lowered for them, drew a sharp breath as he followed Commander Keen over the splintered wooden rail, and was instantly sorry. The stench of unwashed bodies from the Russians crowding the British sailors turned his stomach, even in the brisk breeze. Conditions aboard any one of Her Britannic Majesty's men o' war were far from ideal, but none stank like this! A twinge of — fear? — no, more like apprehension, ran down his back as the brutish Muscovites shuffled nearer, and he rested a hand on his midshipman's dirk. At a quiet command from Keen, Kirk turned to the seamen clambering monkey-like up the ship's side and over the rail.

"Form line along the ship's side," he ordered crisply, "no talking, and don't let the Russkies crowd you." Catching a glimpse of a frayed halyard overhead, he moved swiftly from under.

A grossly fat, thickly-bearded man pushed through the milling sailors, spitting curses and orders. Reluctantly the men gave way, shambling back to their duties. Followed by a group of Russian officers, their rich, if dirty, uniforms in stark contrast to the sailors' rags, he approached the British party.

"I am Petroffski," he announced thickly, his breath sending a wave of garlicky fumes across the intervening space, "official interpreter. This is..." One by one he introduced the captain and officers to Commander Keen, ignoring Kirk after a single contemptuous stare.

Gradually Kirk's ears made sense of the accent, so very different from Andrew's and nanny's. As he picked out words and phrases from the officers making remarks to one another, he studied Petroffski. Ornate jewelled rings studded the interpreter's fat fingers, and a ruby earring gleamed dully through greasy locks. His concentration was jarred by Commander Keen. "They want me to go below, Kirk. You had best come along." He followed the motley group down a companionway, along a short, dark and fetid passage, into what was apparently the master's cabin.

A rumpled, unmade bed occupied one side, while a clutter of charts with cabalistic markings lay scattered over a tabletop sticky with, he surmised, spilled drinks. Here the sour smell was less remarkable, but the air was so stale as to be nearly unbreathable. A glance at the green-tinged brass ports confirmed his conclusion that they hadn't been opened for weeks, if ever. A sudden clatter of broken English recalled his duty, and he sidled nearer the table. Gradually the squeaks, timber-groans, creakings and other ship-sounds faded from the midshipman's awareness, as he concentrated his full attention on understanding muttered Russian comments, and surreptitiously studying a coastal chart. With a muttered "Thank you", he accepted the log tossed casually to him by a Russian officer and pretended to study it, while keeping ears sharpened on an understood scattering of Slavic chatter.

Calcutta moved slowly through the water with bare steerage way on, matching the barque's drift. The captain studied the other ship closely, noting her six guns per side — they appeared to be 12-pounders — and the fact that the Russian was riding higher in the water than would be normal for an honest trading vessel. He pointed out her shallow draft to Duncan, remarking, "It seems that we may have had a fortunate interception, David. Ah, here comes the boarding party now."

The Russian officers waved as the cutter pulled away, then the barque's sails were shaken out and her main yards sheeted home. As she gathered way her ensign fluttered down in salute, waited for the warship's acknowledgement, then rose again jerkily to the peak of her gaff.

"Have the cutter hoisted in, Mister Duncan. Send Commander Keen and young Kirk to me as soon as they're aboard." He leaned over the side to watch the cutter being hoisted in, then headed for

15

his cabin, saying over his shoulder, "You may stand down the engine, David, and set sail as soon as the cutter's lashed down."

A double knock on his door preceded the entrance of Commander Keen and Kirk. The commander was smiling.

"We caught them out, sir," he reported. "Kirk didn't let on that he spoke their language, and was able to gather enough of what they said amongst themselves to put the lie to their false log."

"Well done! Tell me about it, young Kirk — but I'm forgetting my manners. Sit down, sit down, gentlemen. Ashley," the captain called his steward, hovering nearby, "bring a decanter of wine and glasses. Quickly, now."

"Well, sir," Kirk began, "I studied their log, but pretended to be mystified by it. There was an officer aboard who spoke a little English — of sorts — so while he interpreted for the commander, I stood back and listened to the others chattering among themselves."

"Their plans were well laid, sir," Keen interjected. "If Kirk hadn't been along they'd have pulled the wool over my eyes." He paused. "They had a cock-and-bull story about having been blown far south by a spring gale, while searching for the sealing fleet to pick up a cargo of skins."

"I see," murmured the captain. "That would have explained why they were riding high in the water. Now then, what did you overhear while Commander Keen was being told this?"

"They've established a fortified community on the mainland coast, sir," Kirk piped. "It was difficult to gather much without appearing to be eavesdropping, but I understood that there were two small ships, both armed, and a garrison of about 500."

The captain sipped his wine, and Kirk, grateful for the intermission, took a large gulp. Studying the cabin's contents with curiosity, he compared the heavy-legged, ornately carved teak table, curtains, baroque lamps and sideboard with the Spartan austerity of the gunroom. His resolve to pass his lieutenant's examination at the first opportunity was reinforced. Suddenly realizing that he was being addressed, his eyes snapped from the polished mahogany writing desk to the captain, who regarded him amusedly.

"Prefer this to the gunroom?"

He blushed. "Yes, sir."

"All in time, my boy. Took me 19 years to get here."

Kirk added, and mentally quailed; he could spend another 16

years as midshipman and lieutenant before getting a cabin such as
this. Longer if he failed his examinations. The captain was speaking
again.

"You said a garrison of about 500, Kirk. Five hundred soldiers
— or 500 in total?"

"I can't say, sir. My Russian isn't good enough to get every
word, so I concentrated on remembering only the essence of what
they talked about. But I think I located the fort's position, sir —
they'd left a chart on the same table where I examined the log, and
I think that I spotted the place. The barque, by the way, sir, is the
Koryak of Okhotsk."

"Good!" Whitfeld-Clements pushed himself to his feet, Commander Keen and Kirk levering themselves up with alacrity as the
senior officer stood. The captain rolled open a chart on the table, and
placed sand-filled canvas weights at each side to prevent it re-roll-
ing. "Now show me where you think this place might be."

The chart's smell reached Kirk's nose — a fresh aroma of paper
and ink, in contrast with the ripe, pungent odour of the tattered gunroom chart used for practice in navigation — as he carefully ran a
finger down the light-blue coastline. The paper even felt new and crisp.

"About here, sir," Kirk pointed. "It's located in a hidden inlet
behind an island. The Russians were snickering because we could
sail right past and not see it — or if we did come in, we'd be trapped
and their guns could blow us out of the water."

Commander Keen leaned forward. "Perhaps a cutting-out expedition to seize the ships, sir?" Anxiety tinged his voice, Kirk noticed; the
commander had, according to lower deck rumour, been passed over
twice for promotion. Unless he was commended for some act of gal-
lantry, he was likely destined to retire as a commander.

The captain shook his head. "No. I'd want to have a look at the
place first. That's all the information you could gather, young Kirk?"

"Yes, sir." A vagrant thought plucked at the back of Kirk's
mind, but didn't quite reach the front. It bothered him, but
Whitfeld-Clements hated imprecise answers.

"You did well. You may go, now."

"Aye aye, sir." The midshipman bent down to pick up a parcel
wrapped in white sailcloth. "The Russian captain sent this for you,
sir — some caviar and vodka, I was told."

"All right, Mister Kirk. Thank you."

17

Colonel Count Nikolai Mikhaloff, hands on hips, surveyed his command through a monocled eye as aides and junior officers fawned nearby. The three, ten-foot-high log palisades of the rectangular enclosure were complete, sharp points ready to impale anyone attempting to scale them. A vertical rock cliff forming the fourth wall tossed back the echoes of hammers and saws as sweating soldiers levered the sixth and last cannon into place on its raised log platform. Five other muzzles already jutted menacingly through piercings in the inlet-facing fortress.

Against the south wall long rows of conical white tents were pitched, starkly contrasting with the trampled ground and the once-blue mountain stream carrying sewage sluggishly to the harbour. The sergeant-major's thundered commands racked the stillness as bear-skinned Imperial Guards marched and countermarched past the spindly lookout tower, and a smell of cooking meat drifted skyward from a rough hut.

Satisfied, the colonel growled and turned, elbowing an aide aside as others hurriedly shuffled out of his path. They followed the burly figure into his large, if crude, headquarters, then stood shifting from foot to foot, awaiting his decision.

"It's up to the diplomats, now," he finally rumbled. "If they can convince those slippery bastards in London and those Canadian peasants that we've held this territory for decades, we'll cause enough confusion to keep the British parliament fussing and fidgeting for months. Then we'll march into Afghanistan with only a few squadrons of Lancers to oppose us!" He cleared his throat raucously and spat on the dirt floor. "Our Cossacks will make short work of them." He snorted and spat again, then seized a bottle and poured a tumbler full of glass-clear vodka. As he tossed it down in two huge gulps, an aide asked apprehensively, "When will the diplomats begin, Your Highness?"

The colonel swivelled, surprised at the temerity of the man initiating a discussion, then condescendingly replied. "The *Koryak* must return to Okhotsk, load more supplies and a troop of Cossacks, then come back here. When she returns to Mother Russia, her captain will report that all is in order, and the diplomats will begin their conniving."

"So this effort could still fail?" The speaker blanched as the colonel's face darkened in fury. Mikhaloff lashed out with an open hand,

18

smacking the doubter's face with a pistol-crack. The man reeled and fell to his knees, face torn and bleeding where the colonel's massive gold ring had lacerated his skin.

"Get this treacherous bastard out of my sight," Mikhaloff snarled, his face purple. As the stunned underling half-crawled, half-stumbled out, the colonel glared at those remaining. "Does anyone else think we can fail?"

A raven's querulous squawk was all that broke the tense silence while the colonel's red-rimmed eyes shifted from man to man. "No? Good! Put that useless traitor to work shovelling shit with the latrine detail!"

HMS *Calcutta* lay quietly at anchor under the blistering sun, awaiting the overland scouting party's return from their search for the Russian outpost. Captain Whitfeld-Clements paced the quarterdeck, slapping at the occasional mosquito wafted out from the narrow cove's rocky, tree-lined shore. The ship's company remained well forward or below decks, out of his now-irascible sight.

All bells and pipes had been ordered belayed, as well as any other noise which might serve to alert any possible Russians. Petty officers padded silently from man to man at the change of the Watches, gun crews stood by their loaded and run-out cannon, boarding nettings were slackly rigged, and cutlasses were stacked in tiers along the rails, polished steel winking savagely in the sun.

A bush at the water's edge twitched, the movement reflected in the still water. A slim figure stepped into view and whistled softly: Lieutenant Giles, followed by Midshipman Kirk and two seamen. In seconds a boat was skimming toward them over the translucent lagoon.

The captain stood impatiently by the entry port as the cox'n parted the nettings to allow them to sidle through. Giles came first, then Kirk, the seamen stopping to help trice up the boarding nettings again, while the boat's crew followed.

"They're here, sir," Giles murmured to the captain, "only about two miles distant."

"Good. You and Kirk come below to report. Mister Mudd, see that these two seamen are issued tots of rum."

The captain led the way to his quarters, their footsteps reverberating like pistol shots in the hushed ship. He waved them to seats, and listened intently as Giles and Kirk described the formidable encampment, running his hand along the polished oak arm of his chair.

"Right, gentlemen," the captain said crisply, "tell me everything you saw and heard. Smartly if you please."

Giles and Kirk looked at each other. Giles said, "Go ahead, mid, you're the one who kens their lingo."

"Well, sir," the midshipman began, "from what I could hear when we crawled up on the cliff overlooking their fort, and from what we actually saw, the officer in command is a colonel in the Imperial Guards — and he seems to be both feared and disliked. They appear to be sure that the fort won't be discovered, but if it is, that their mounted cannon and soldiers could wipe out any attackers. There's a lot of drill and spit-and-polish, but the sentries seem to be more interested in looking smart than keeping a good lookout. There should have been a post on top of the cliff, but we saw no sign that anyone but ourselves had ever been there."

"We felt, sir," Giles interrupted, "that if an overland party, perhaps disguised as Indians, could make its way to the cliff, they could throw down boulders and fire-bombs to destroy the buildings."

Kirk twitched excitedly in his chair, unable to restrain himself. The captain smiled. "Yes, Mister Kirk?"

"Sir, if the party carried on with gunfire afterward, the ammunition store could be blown," Kirk jabbered excitedly, "and the attack would be blamed on natives!" The captain opened his mouth, but Kirk, unseeing, stood up and continued, "And then, sir, while the cliff attack diverts their attention, the cutters could slip up on the anchored ships under cover of dark, cut their cables and set them on fire too!"

The midshipman suddenly realized that he was lecturing officers vastly his senior in age and experience, and sat down quickly. "I beg your pardon, sir — I was carried away."

Whitfeld-Clements' expression momentarily reminded Kirk of a certified ship's surgeon receiving anatomy lessons from a witch doctor, but then the captain suddenly laughed. "That's all right. Occasionally a youngster's viewpoint is like a breath of fresh air. However," he sobered, "don't make a habit of it, Kirk — some officers would have you perched on the masthead like a lonesome seagull for interrupting like that!"

Deciding that his best path was to say little, Kirk sat very still and nodded solemnly.

"As I was about to say, we might arrive the next day, as though attracted by the smoke." The captain rubbed his bearded chin for a moment, "But how do we get them back to Russia? We can't be sure of success even if we try to save one of the ships."

"Sir," Kirk said hesitantly, "we could leave them enough rations, perhaps ship's biscuit and those two casks of salt meat that smell, to last them until their supply ship returns."

Both the captain and commander impaled the midshipman with cold eyes. The captain spoke. "You failed to mention the supply ship, snotty! You'd better tell me all that you know, and quickly!" The captain's eyes narrowed and he stabbed Kirk with a steely gaze.

Kirk was abashed, and showed it in his glowing cheeks. "I'm sorry, sir. It's an unforgivable oversight." He stammered, "It's the *Koryak*, sir — the barque that we boarded off Cape St. James."

Commander Keen removed his cap to rub his ever-so-slightly balding head. Kirk stared. Keen *never* removed his cap — even to go to bed, some of the snotties said.

"Well, young man," Whitfeld-Clements pronounced deliberately, "your omission might have been serious — but the *Koryak* won't bother us. She can't possibly get back in less than six weeks, and if she's bound for Okhotsk, it could very well be August before her return. Very good, gentlemen, that'll do for now. I must make plans."

Captain Whitfeld-Clements was issuing last-minute orders to the group of officers, petty officers and ratings clustered in the ship's waist, doing his best not to smile at the incongruous sight. Their faces were darkened with a foul-smelling concoction brewed by the bo's'n in his paint locker, several wore feathers stripped from unwary gulls, and all flaunted bright red stripes emblazoned across their foreheads or cheekbones.

The sailmaker had excelled himself with costumes; a Haida, Tlingit or Tsimpsean might have doubled up with laughter, but the jackets and imitation bark kilts or trousers bore more resemblance to Indian garb than to "pusser" issue of the Royal Navy.

Kirk paid close attention to the captain's words, trying not to glance at Commander Keen, who had rigid ideas about what constituted proper dress for seamen. At present the commander stood withdrawn slightly from the motley group, staring sadly into the sea. Kirk thought his appearance was akin to a staunch Presbyterian minister at a cannibal picnic.

"You all understand, now," the captain cautioned. "Not a sound until I drop the first grenade — then you will all whoop and scream and yell as though you were an Indian war party, and start throwing boulders and grenades onto the buildings." A general nod of assent rolled along the assembled heads, and somewhere a timber creaked as if it too agreed.

"When the cutter parties hear the noise," he continued, "Mister Mudd's boat will slip up on the ship anchored farthest out, cut her cable and set her afire. Mister Duncan's party will board the other, chasing the ship's company overside and slashing the running rigging. I want this ship left intact to carry the Russians home." He paused for air, looking sternly at the camouflaged assembly, then, "Midshipman Kirk will take command of the shore party if I fall. Similarly Midshipman Perkins and Sublieutenant van Dusen if Lieutenants Duncan or Mudd are struck down."

He turned to Keen and Derek Giles, unhappily waiting close by, in uniform. "You have your orders, Commander Keen. There's to be no attempt at rescue should we fail and be captured. Proceed directly to Esquimalt and report to the commanding officer there."

The ragamuffin crews clambered over the rail into the whaler and two cutters lying alongside, Captain Whitfeld-Clements steering the whaler for shore. The time was eight bells of the second Dog Watch — eight p.m.: one and one-half hours till sunset, and ample time to get into position before darkness blanketed the forbidding coastline.

Keen and Giles watched the two cutters, silent with muffled oars, pull around the point and out of sight, arrowing ripples on the calm, steel-blue water the only sign of their ghost-like passing. Ashore, the captain's party had disappeared into the forest, and the whaler was returning to the warship. Apprehension hung heavy on the still air as a dull red sun lowered to the horizon, first twilight, then gloom settling over the cove. A light breeze sprang up, whispering soft arias in the rigging as the ship swung with the change of tide.

Although the Watch had almost its full four hours to go, no one went below. Those on duty silently kept lookout, or fidgeted restlessly with their weapons until a muttered oath from Lieutenant Giles stilled their movement. Others listened quietly or stood in twos or threes whispering speculatively. In the heads, an ordinary seaman broke wind thunderously, and was at once hissed into sullen silence.

The stillness was obtrusive as the small British force huddled uncomfortably on the rocky bluff overlooking the Russian compound, their darkened faces glowing dimly in the flickering light from scattered campfires. Only isolated snores from the tent-rows, the soft sand-padding of sentries and occasional raucous laughter from a log structure directly beneath them disturbed the blanket of silence.

The captain stood, his salt-and-pepper beard incongruous against his warpaint. Motioning for silence, he shuffled cautiously to the cliff's edge, and gently tossed a grenade. Skilfully thrown — or luckily — it plunged down the smoking tin chimney, just as a door suddenly burst open and a drunken Russian officer staggered out. He stood unsteadily, one hand on the doorframe, urinating on the sand until a crashing blast of crimson fire obliterated both him and the moist patch on the ground.

Kirk shrieked blood-chillingly as a storm of rocks, grenades, boulders and fire-bombs descended on the fort and sleeping soldiers. Shots blazed like fireflies in the gloom; startled sentries yanked haphazardly at triggers. Doors and tent flaps flew open and groggy soldiers lurched out, pulling on trousers or ludicrously hopping single-footed in attempts to pull on boots and run simultaneously.

Pandemonium became rampant. Fires crackled, then belched out in dragon's roars as log buildings took flame. Roofs collapsed inward, their cedar shingles blazing upward in crackling explosions. Men staggered aimlessly looking for tangible enemies, loosing off musket-fire into the blackness, and sprawled bodies testified mutely to the undisciplined frenzy of indiscriminate shooting.

Whitfeld-Clements and his crew yelled, screamed and hooted as they sweated to lever boulders over the cliff, and pitched a furious fusillade of rocks and grenades down at the terrorized Russians. They froze momentarily when an entire building, tongues of fire licking from its seams, lurched ponderously into the air and dissolved into its constituent logs in a great blurt of hissing flame, smoke and thunder.

"Their powder magazine, d'ye think, sir?" Kirk shouted, sweat streaking his painted cheeks. "Captain, look there!" He pointed.

A burly bear-skinned officer, giant among the cowering troops, scampered madly through the blazing destruction, sabre-lashing furiously at any unlucky enough to be in his deranged path. A twisted trail of twitching, screaming bodies, and some obscenely still, marked his route among the carnage. He suddenly stopped, threw up his hands and collapsed, crumpled over a smouldering log. His sabre splashed crimson into the sanitation ditch, and a soldier mouthing unheard curses lowered his smoking musket.

Kirk ducked as a bullet whined past his left ear, slipping on a wet rock and cracking his elbow viciously. As he involuntarily moaned with pain, another bullet ricocheted from a boulder and spun humming into the distance, and yet another slammed into a sailor standing close by. The man screamed, whirled and fell, blood spurting from a torn thigh. The captain, exuberant with the joy of physical action, looked 'round in the flickering light and saw the wounded sailor. "Get here, Kirk!" he yelled. "Tear a piece of cloth off and bind his wound. Quick now."

Kirk knelt. His elbow forgotten, he ripped a long strip of cloth from his jacket. Two other "Indians" joined them, holding the injured man down as he thrashed and screamed.

" 'Ere, myte," one muttered, opening a canteen and tipping it gently to the man's mouth. The sharp odour of rum pierced the air. The captain glanced sharply at the donor, but said nothing as he and Kirk hurriedly slashed open the pant leg.

"Pour a little of that in the wound," he ordered. When a trickle of the dark fluid had been dribbled into the oozing gash, he wrapped the cloth around the man's leg and tied it tightly. "We'll withdraw now, Mister Kirk," he said curtly. "You two men help this one back. Gently, mind you."

As the thin file of painted men started to vanish into the whispering woods, Kirk touched the captain's arm. "Look, sir."

In the bay, a reddish glow rose, higher and higher, illuminating the spars and hull of a drifting ship, then faintly lighting a more distant one. Thin shouts drifted over the water, accentuated by shots and the clang of steel.

"Good," said the captain shortly. "No time to waste. Get forrard, Mister Kirk, and lead us back."

A tremendous explosion halted them. Turning to stare, Kirk saw a huge, twisting pyre of flame reach skyward, sending embers and twists of flaming canvas high in the air, while burning chunks of ragged timber floated sizzling and smouldering over the calm water. The captain nudged him, not unkindly. "Get on with it, Kirk. There could be a Russian patrol on its way up here right now!"

Slipping and sliding on moss and dew-damp rocks, face whiplashed with stinging twigs and branches, Kirk led the naval contingent back through a tarry blackness made lighter only by diminishing flames from the Russian encampment. Whitfeld-Clements, bringing up the rear to ensure no one went astray, felt the thrill of battle giving way to fear that his boat crews might have suffered harm and that the moans of the injured man might yet attract a roving Russian patrol. The line slowed, then stopped. Men awkwardly crashed into those ahead as a warning "Easy!" was passed back in hoarse whispers. Suddenly a blue flare blazed in the gloom ahead, and the men saw water shimmering only a few yards down-slope.

Aboard the ship, only the creaking of rigging and the soft slap of the running tide past the anchor cable broke the silence as anxious men waited out the interminable minutes. Commander Keen paced the deck with short, quick steps, and blurred bunches of sailors murmured quietly in the soft dark.

A sputtering, short-lived blue flare shattered the invisible shoreline's gloom. "Quickly there," Lieutenant Giles' voice pierced the dark like a stiletto, "Away whaler!" Oars were creaking as his last word fell on eager ears. Five minutes, and the "war-party", dirty, scratched and torn, most grinning from ear to ear, stood on deck, while a sling was hurriedly rigged to sway up the wounded man.

Careful, tender hands lifted him from the sling into a stretcher and hurried him to sick bay, the aroma of rum suddenly strong on the air. A light rain had begun falling, muting the excited babble of questions from officers and ratings. The captain quickly hushed the noise. "Belay that gab! Go below and tell your stories — and keep them short and quiet. Those on Watch keep your eyes peeled."

Midshipman Kirk shivered suddenly, not only from the release of tension. The just-realized awareness that the bullet which had crippled the sailor — Adams? — could just as easily have hit him, in his first action, was shocking. He made a mental note to stop by the sick bay to check on the man's condition in the morning, although judging from the smell of rum, he'd be in no pain.

"How was it, sir?" asked Keen as the excited mob dispersed.

"Excellent! We took them completely by surprise. Kirk here," the captain smiled at the midshipman, white teeth gleaming as a waning moon blinked through a layer of cloud, "let out a warwhoop that would have done justice to a Zulu, and then we poured grenades, rocks and boulders down on the roofs. When we left the entire fort was ablaze, with Russians running and firing in every direction in absolute panic. I saw an officer — may have been the colonel himself — laying about him with a sabre, without the slightest effect on his troops. Except to get himself shot in the back," he added soberly.

"Did you hear the explosion, Commander Keen?" Kirk asked. "That was the fort's magazine exploding. And directly after it, one of the ships blew up."

They turned as the forward lookout called a soft challenge, "Boat ahoy."

"Aye, aye," came the reply, "stand by — we've a couple of wounded on board." One cutter slid alongside, the second appearing wraith-like out of the mists astern. With rattles of blocks and the rhythmic pad of bare feet, both boats were hoisted inboard and nestled groaning in their chocks.

Sublieutenant van Dusen peered through the gloom, then, locating the captain, strode quickly over to him to report.

"The attack was successful, sir. We set the ship afire and then she blew up. Mister Mudd's missing, sir." The young officer's face didn't reflect particular sorrow. "He went back aboard just before the ship blew up, to make certain the fire was going well," van Dusen hesitated, "and he didn't have a chance, sir. We lay off and waited, but he must have been right in the middle of the blast. Two ratings slightly injured, sir — one burned, one with a cutlass slash."

"Very good, sub. Well done. I'm sorry to hear about poor Mudd." The captain turned to Lieutenant Duncan, standing dripping nearby into a puddle of water on the deck, his aristocratic poise only slightly lessened by the soggy clothes clinging damply to him. "Did you have time to bathe, Mister Duncan?"

Duncan grinned, "It was involuntary, sir. We'd chased the crew over the side — they didn't seem disposed to put up any sort of a struggle — and were engaged in cutting her sheets, braces and halyards when one of her officers attacked me. He must have been asleep below. Fortunately, young Perkins tripped him as he charged at me, but he succeeded in tumbling both of us over the rail. I could swim, he apparently couldn't. Poor chap went down like a stone."

The captain interrupted, "There was no indication that they suspected that you were anything but natives?"

"No, sir. They were completely taken in, so far as we could tell."

"Splendid!"

Duncan continued, "After I swam to the main chains and climbed back aboard, we cut her tiller ropes and slipped her cable. The tide was flooding, so she should have nicely grounded herself by now, sir."

"Good!" Whitfeld-Clements exclaimed. "Everything came together nicely. A fine evening's work. There's an hour yet before the tide turns to ebb, Mister Giles. I believe that it's your Watch?"

"Yes, sir."

"Very good. Leave the boarding nettings triced up. Weigh and sail with the tide. Have the engine room keep steam up, and heave to just within sight of the Russians' position — the fires will help you."

"Aye aye, sir."

Captain Whitfeld-Clements sighed as he blotted the ink, then picked up his handwritten report, scanning the time-honoured phrases: "I have the honour to report..." his eyes skipped over the familiar words, stopping only at pertinent sentences. "...Led by Lt. Roger Mudd, who was unfortunately lost in action...fort destroyed by fire and one ship blown up....commendation to Midshipman Eric Kirk...interpreted....Slt. van Dusen...took command..." He set down the papers, as an aroma of cooking drifted through his open scuttles. The hands must be having breakfast. He reached for the congealed remains of his ham and eggs — how Ashley had managed to preserve them he'd probably never know — and stuffed a forkful into his mouth, chewing without relish. A pot of steaming tea sat on the sideboard. Ashley must have padded in while he was writing the report. Gratefully, the captain poured a thick white mug full of the hot liquid, and felt the warmth permeating his body as he sipped.

He glanced at the papers again. Tomorrow there would undoubtedly be more to write, if he were still alive to do it after the meeting with the Russians. He grimaced. They might have recovered their morale and be spoiling for a fight. No sense worrying about it now; he shrugged into his coat and went on deck, enjoying deep breaths of the fresh salt air.

Commander Keen came to him as he stepped onto the quarterdeck, "Good morning, sir."

"Morning, John. I see that the Russkies are still smouldering." He peered at a pall of dirty grey smoke obscuring the rugged shores.

"Yes, sir. Been blazing all night, I'm told."

The captain looked aloft. *Calcutta* was bowling along under tops'ls and topgallants, a fresh south breeze driving her at a good six knots as she plunged and heaved, tossing rainbows of spray under the bright sky. He took another deep breath, watching his sailors working cheerfully on deck. One danced a few steps of a hornpipe as he ran forward carrying a coil of line. He smiled at Keen. "Nothing like a little action to wipe out the doldrums in the lower decks, John."

"Right, sir. We've a happy ship, but today they're downright merry! Does 'em good to break routine occasionally."

"Yes... well, John, we'd better hear what the Russkies have to say. Stand in to shore. Have the engine room stand by, then furl all sail and use the screw when we're two miles off. Have a man in the chains with a deepsea lead — no point in going aground after a successful action. Call me before entering the cove."

"Aye aye, sir."

"And send van Dusen and young Kirk to my cabin, if you please. We'll need an acting lieutenant to replace poor Mudd — which will have to be van Dusen — and a subbie for the gunroom to keep the midshipmen in hand. D'you think Kirk'll be suitable?"

"Yes, sir. He's a good lad — if a bit harum-scarum — and he showed his worth with the Russians."

A diffident knock was tapped at the door, which opened as the captain called, "Come in." Eric Kirk and Keith van Dusen, hair neatly combed, uniforms obviously newly brushed and shoes hurriedly shined, entered uncertainly. Whitfeld-Clements swung in his

28

chair, stern-facedly staring them up and down, then smiled. "Stand easy, gentlemen. Mister van Dusen, there's a lieutenant's vacancy in the ship's establishment, because of Mister Mudd's loss. You are now an acting lieutenant, with seniority of today's date," the captain grinned suddenly, showing white, even teeth above his beard. "Provided, of course, that you pass your examinations at the appropriate time!"

The new lieutenant grinned back, "Even Lord Hornblower almost failed his examination, did he not, sir?"

"Yes — but your circumstances may not be the same. His Lordship's examination was during wartime, fighting the Frogs, and I understand that had much to do with his success." The captain turned to Kirk, standing nervously to one side, "And you, Eric — can you keep the gunroom in line?"

"Sir, I don't quite..."

"Come now, mid, with Mister van Dusen promoted, there'll have to be a sublieutenant, or the snotties will tear the ship to pieces! You've done quite well on this cruise. As of now, you are Sublieutenant Eric Kirk, and Sub of the Gunroom Mess. Both of you had best see the commander regarding your new appointments. Carry on now, and my congratulations." The captain stood, shook hands with both, and was interrupted by a short, sharp rap on the door. Midshipman Perkins' thatch of flaming hair inserted itself through the opening. "Commander's respects, sir, and we're two cables away from the Russian cove."

The captain was surprised. He realized suddenly that the deck under his feet had been throbbing for some time. He dismissed the two young officers, and said abruptly to Perkins, "My compliments to Commander Keen, and I'll be on deck directly. I'll have the guns loaded and run out forthwith."

"Aye aye, sir!" The boy was gone, his feet slamming on the teak deck.

As the captain came on deck, blinking slightly in the transition from gloom to daylight, he heard the chant of the leadsman, "No bottom! No bottom with this line." He looked about. The ship was approaching a narrow inlet, shadowed on the north by a granite cliff rising vertically from the restless surf, partly concealed by a mounded island overgrown with towering cedars to the northwest. As they neared the inlet, it opened wider and wider, revealing a calm estuary.

"Dead slow," he ordered. The telegraph clanged a repeat of his order, and the deck's vibration lessened. They were passing the island now, a spacious cove opening up, and tendrils of wood, and other, smoke wrinkling their nostrils.

"Stop engine." Again the telegraph jangled and the vibration ceased. They stared at the catastrophic wreckage ashore: smouldering heaps of rubble, dismounted cannon lying drunkenly half-buried in the sand, dozens, no, scores of soldiers wandering aimlessly, everywhere smoke rising lazily from the charred remnants of buildings, walls, towers and palisades. A small brig lay at anchor with shoddily dressed sailors working listlessly in her rigging, while her officers uninterestedly watched *Calcutta* approach. "Take command, Commander Keen. Keep the guns bearing on the beach. Load the carronades with grapeshot and cover the brig. Sub-lieutenant Kirk!"

Kirk pounded up to the captain. "Sir?"

"Tell off 20 men for the cutter. Pistols and cutlasses. We'll go ashore immediately."

"Aye aye, sir!" Kirk ran forward, shouting.

As the cutter raced beachward, a few Russians straggled toward the water's edge. "Keep your eyes in the boat, there," Sublieutenant Kirk warned as the bow grated on sand. The bowman leaped over the side to plant the sand anchor, and Captain Whitfeld-Clements followed him, a trifle clumsily.

As he splashed through the shallow water, the captain snapped at the men without turning his head, "Stay in line behind me, and keep your hands off your weapons!" To Kirk he said more softly, "We'll behave as though this were an ordinary visit. Stay beside me, boy — I'll no doubt have need of your services."

Kirk carefully observed the ragged group of Russian officers trudging toward the British party, spurts of sand masking their boots as they slapped at the clouds of sand-flies swarming outside the sanctuary of the smoke. The leader drew himself up haughtily, and in passable English, asked, "Whom have I the honour of addressing?"

The captain spoke shortly. "Captain Whitfeld-Clements, of Her Britannic Majesty's Ship *Calcutta*. And you, sir, are..?"

The officer saluted with a half-bow, "Major Count Ivan Smirzki of the Imperial Dragoons. Acting commanding officer since our colonel was murdered during an Indian attack last night."

Kirk glanced sideways at the captain to see his response. His eyes narrowing sharply, Whitfeld-Clements was curt, "What are you doing here, major? This is British territory." Kirk gave a quiet command as the Russians, hearing the hostile tone, moved about uneasily. Twenty seamen instantly put their hands on cutlass hilts. The Russian movement ceased.

"We were bound for Okhotsk," the Russian's voice became ingratiating, "returning from a South American expedition to aid allies of our emperor, when a terrible storm drove our ships in here. For days we had no idea where we were, and when the gale abated, we were fortunate enough to find this little harbour, where we crept in to repair our damaged ships."

"I see. And the fortifications?"

"Only for protection against savages, captain — in vain, as you can see as the murderous brutes got through!"

"Where's your other ship, Major Smirzki?"

"Burned by savages," the other said bitterly, "with most of our supplies. It was only because our brave sailors drove them off that we have the *Potarkin* left." He indicated the brig with a wave as the other Russians smiled sheepishly at the two Royal Navy officers.

Kirk choked down a laugh, emitting a strangled cough. The captain turned to him, "Surely you're not laughing at the misfortunes of our fellow sailors, Mister Kirk!"

"Sorry, sir. Must have swallowed a mosquito."

"Very well." The captain returned to the Russian. "Have you buried those killed in the attack, Major Smirzki?"

"Yes — this very morning."

"I suggest that it would be dangerous for you to remain any longer, then. The savages are no doubt aware that you're defenceless now, and may be planning to come back — perhaps even tonight."

Kirk turned to the seamen. "Take your hands off those cutlasses, men. Can't you tell that these people are no more than distressed seamen?" He let one eyelid droop slowly as he barked out the admonition, interrupting the Russian reply.

"What can we do, Captain — uh — Whitfeld-Clements?"

"Get your men embarked. I'll give you enough food and water to get you to a Russian port, and then tow you to sea." He turned to the sublieutenant, "Go aboard and make arrangements to have the supplies taken to the brig, Mister Kirk. I'll leave it to the com-

31

mander's discretion what and how much he sends, but get started at once. I want to be away from here within two hours."

"Aye aye, sir!" Kirk, trying to stop his nose from curling at the stench of smouldering wood, cloth, and other things not to be thought about, singled out a boat's crew for the cutter, leaving eight seamen with his captain. As he shoved off, he heard the captain tell the balance of the British sailors to spike the guns and see that the fort was completely razed.

Aboard the man o' war, Kirk passed on the captain's wishes to Commander Keen, then awaited further orders. Leaning against the rail, he watched the brig's boats pull into shore to embark the straggling lines of Imperial Guards, tongue-lashed by Russian officers. The clang of spikes being hammered into cannon touch-holes echoed off the cliff, as the brig's boats scuttled across the bay like four-legged water spiders.

"Mister Kirk, go ashore and tell the captain that the brig's supplies have been sent." Commander Keen had caught him day-dreaming. Kirk straightened with a jerk, snapped a quick salute, "Aye aye, sir!", and summoned his cutter crew.

On the beach, he stood aloof for a moment as Major Smirzki approached Whitfeld-Clements diffidently.

"All of my men are aboard, sir. We will be ready to be towed out as soon as your generous orders to provision us have been carried out."

The captain glanced at Kirk, who stepped forward and again saluted. "Commander Keen's respects, sir, and all the supplies have been sent to the brig." He stepped back.

"Very good, Mister Kirk." He looked at the Russian officer, his eyes narrowing. "I shouldn't be surprised if I were ordered to make regular patrols of this area, Major Smirzki — merely to aid in the peaceful settlement of this part of the coast, of course."

"Of course," the Russian hurriedly agreed.

"It would be most distressing should anything happen to disturb the excellent relationship we have had with the tribes," continued Whitfeld-Clements remorselessly, "and, of course, anything to impair the friendly relations between Her Majesty's government and the Emperor of Russia."

"I quite agree, Captain Whitfeld-Clements." There was no stumbling over the name this time.

"Then, sir, allow me to escort you to your boat."

32

Calcutta smashed through the North Pacific rollers under fighting sail, courses and tops'ls only, with the crew standing by the guns. She was, warily, three miles to windward and slightly ahead of the *Potarkin*, as the brig settled on course for the Sea of Okhotsk. The captain and a few officers closely watched the Russian vessel, while petty officers guided seamen flaking the towline fore and aft for drying before it was re-stowed below decks.

"Put the ship on course for Esquimalt, Mister Giles," the captain didn't look away from the brig. "I doubt that we'll hear from those people again. I shouldn't like to be in that major's boots when he returns to Russia — I understand the penalty for failure is exile into Siberia!"

"Aye aye, sir." Giles cupped his hands to be heard above the crisp wind wailing through the rigging, "Hands wear ship!" As men scurried to sheets and braces, and the ship's jib-boom swung across the leaden sky past the brig, sails filling with hollow booms, *Calcutta* broad-reached for Juan de Fuca Strait.

The captain added, "Warn the lookouts to be alert. I don't think that the Russkies will try anything, but we'll take no chances."

Giles, his hands full with the manifold tasks of getting the square-rigger balanced so that rudder and sails complemented each other, gasped, "Aye aye, sir," as the captain went below.

"Gentlemen, don't get up," said Clemmie, guest of honour in the wardroom, as he pushed back his chair with a squeak. "The meal was delicious and the company excellent. I beg you to excuse me for a moment, Mister President — I've been remiss."

"Certainly, sir," Commander Keen, President of the Wardroom Mess, looked puzzled as his captain disappeared through the door.

He returned in less than four minutes, bearing a parcel which he carried to the foot of the table. "Perhaps, Mister Vice, you'd care to apportion these." The captain ripped the paper open, "I can think of nothing more fitting than to toast the Russian defeat in their own vodka!" He flourished the bottle, letting the paper wrapping fall to the deck, "And to temper the vodka with their own caviar!"

Kirk, his tarpaulin jacket rattling as spatters of cold rain ricocheted off it, pondered the past eventful days as he stood Watch with David Duncan. What would have happened if the Russians had captured the "Indian" raiders? Or if *Calcutta* had missed the *Koryak* — or if.... He shook his head. What was done was done, and they'd won. His mind drifted idly as he scanned the dark horizon. He wondered if his father and Andrew might be strolling down the hedgerows toward the George and Dragon, and made a mental note to look up the time difference so that he'd know what the hour was at home.

Unconsciously he grinned, remembering how he'd been taken for a pint with them before joining *Calcutta*. Villagers had nodded and winked as they touched caps in greeting — "Evenin', Squire" — and a bevy of village girls whispered and giggled as he had tried to keep his voice deep and manly, like his father's rumble and Andrew's slow, thick speech. All too soon they had passed the dozen or so cottages, front doors at the dusty street and thatched roofs drooping so low that his shoulders brushed, and entered the dimly lighted inn, redolent of the fumes of tobacco, sweat, manure and ale.

"A pint each for Andrew and me," his father had boomed, "and a pint for my sailor son who's goin' to sea with the Royal Navy!" Scanning the eight or nine smocked farmhands and villagers relaxing with their pipes and pints, he added to the grinning innkeeper, "And, Ben, take a pint to each man-jack here. 'Tis not every day a man's son goes to sea as a Queen's officer!"

David Duncan noticed Kirk's face. "Pleasant thoughts?"

The younger man smiled. He liked Duncan. "Yes, sir." He explained in a few words.

"Well, youngster, one might say that what we've done in the last while has assured their right to stroll to the pub for some time longer."

"Yes, sir." Kirk found the lieutenant's remark a little obscure, and resolved to give it more thought later on, but the sound of laughter from the wardroom distracted him as the ship rolled through the windswept night.

34

Chapter Two

And Pigs Might Fly

Eric Kirk stood by the main chains of his anchored ship, staring fascinated at the crumbling log stockade surrounding Fort Rupert, on Vancouver Island's thickly forested northeast coast. A good 18 or 20 feet high, he guessed, since only the roofs of the buildings inside were visible, and at least a hundred feet on each side — maybe 150. He switched his gaze to the decrepit Indian village sprawled in a semi-circle above the beach, just outside the fort's walls. Must be almost abandoned, he thought: most of the cedar walls were crumbling, and only a few figures could be seen listlessly watching either the ship or the dusty double row of sweating sailors ashore passing bulky coal-hampers into waiting boats. He coughed as a vagrant breeze swirled coal-dust off the deck, filling his nostrils; after working four full hours in the midst of the grime, he had no wish to taste more of it.

Moving aft, he continued his survey of the decaying fort. Bastions poked sagging roofs from above the weathered gates and corners of the stockade, several cannons jutting rusting muzzles from gunports. Only a solitary plume of smoke rose from a stone chimney, despite the chill air, and an indefinable feeling of approaching dissolution permeated the area.

"How'd you like to be posted here for a few years, Eric?"

He turned to face Lieutenant Giles. "Not much, sir. I was just comparing it to where we were last week."

"New Westminster? Now there's a thriving town! Board streets, even right up the hills. New buildings rising every day, sternwheelers heading upriver, engineers building roads.... It's alive, where this place" — he sniffed — "has long since seen its day!" He pointed his nose toward the beach and sniffed again, "The stink from those clam shells is enough to make a hog retch!"

Kirk was emboldened by Giles' friendliness and apparent willingness to talk. "Why are we coaling here, sir, instead of..."

"A shilling a ton, that's why — and I'm damned if it's worth a penny more!" The new speaker was Lieutenant Bullen, panjandrum of the engine room. He continued, slapping dust from his grimy coveralls, "Damned stuff's been mouldering in a leaking shed for years, and I'll be damned lucky not to have spontaneous combustion every day and twice in the damned Dog Watches!"

Giles laughed aloud at the engineer's vehemence, while Kirk grinned inwardly at the unusual profanity. After a moment Bullen joined in the laughter. "A penny-pinching Admiralty can't pass up a bargain — even if bricks'd burn better!"

Kirk's mystification showed in his face, and Bullen chuckled again. "Damned place started off as a coal mine, then the HBC bought it for use as a trading post, and when they left, their factor — chap named Hunt — bought it and he's selling off everything piece by piece. That's why we're here. He found a hundred tons of coal in a tumbledown shed and offered it to the admiral for a shilling a ton. Less than a tenth of what it costs at Nanaimo or Esquimalt. About what it's worth, too," he added as an afterthought.

"You look puzzled," Giles looked at Kirk quizzically.

"What's 'HBC', sir?"

"Hudson's Bay Company," Giles told him. "Been in business since before 1700. Some people swear the letters stand for 'Here Before Christ'."

"There's the last of it coming off, thank God!" Bullen interjected. He rubbed a grimy finger along the rail, lifted it and showed Giles the ridge of coal-dust it had accumulated. "You'll have the hands cleaning ship till well after sundown to get rid of this."

Giles nodded ruefully, then straightened to attention, Bullen and Kirk following his lead, as Commander Keen hurried toward them.

"Have the boats hoisted in and put all hands to cleaning ship as soon as the last of the coal is stowed, Mister Giles. Leave the gig alongside, but have it hosed and scrubbed in case the captain wants to go ashore."

"Aye aye, sir." Giles trotted off, his boots grinding grittily with each pace.

Keen turned to Bullen. "Have steam raised for eight bells in the Morning Watch."

"Aye aye, sir." Bullen hesitated; engineers were still not quite accepted as "real" officers in many parts of the navy, then he asked diffidently, "Could you tell me where we're bound, sir? Just so I'll have an idea of the coal..."

"The captain will speak to the ship's company this evening. But for your own information" — he glanced at Kirk — "and keep this to yourself, Sublieutenant Kirk, we will be proceeding to Haro Strait to patrol the boundary."

Captain Whitfeld-Clements surveyed his officers, petty officers, ratings and Marines, drawn up on deck by divisions. "Stand the ship's company at ease, Commander Keen."

When the order had been carried out, the captain raised his voice. "There will be no shore leave here. The Indians of this village, called Kukultz" — he pronounced it carefully — "have a reputation for unfriendliness, so that on several occasions in the past warships have been dispatched to restore order. We sail in the morning for San Juan Island, to patrol the disputed boundary area. It is likely that we will encounter an American naval vessel, so I caution you now to behave with utmost circumspection. Our nations are at peace, fragile though that peace may be, and I want no man of this ship's company to shatter it! A war almost broke out in 1859 — just a little more than 20 years ago — because an American shot a pig owned by the Hudson's Bay Company! Carry on, Commander Keen." Turning shortly, he stalked aft, paying no attention to the commander's shout:

"Close up, duty men. Go below the Watches."

The captain called Midshipman Perkins to his side. Although a brisk wind was whining through the rigging, whipping billows of oily black funnel smoke away to leeward where it rolled greasily along wave-tops before reluctantly dissipating in spray and mist, his voice carried.

"My compliments to Lieutenant Bullen, and he is making excessive smoke."

"Aye aye, sir," the youth piped, saluting quickly and darting for the companionway. He was back in moments, closely followed by a red-faced engineer officer. Making every effort to appear not to be listening, Kirk caught a few phrases before they became wind-shredded. "Coal, sir!... No better than slate.... Mostly ash and clinkers...."

From the corner of his eye Kirk glimpsed Bullen and the captain, now equally high in colour, exchanging stiffly formal salutes before turning in opposite directions and walking stiff-legged away.

Taking discretion to be the "better part of valour", as Lieutenant Duncan had once cautioned him, Kirk moved unobtrusively to the lee rail, leaving the captain alone on his traditional weather side. Sharp strokes on the ship's bell startled him: seven bells in the Afternoon Watch — he had only half an hour to go. He looked in a now-practised sweep, up and through the maze of masts and yards with neatly furled sails sketching arcs against the low clouds, the tracery of shrouds and halyards, sheets and braces, then let his gaze fall to the damp decks, unconsciously noting that every hand was busy. His attention drifted to leeward toward the land.

Since the fresh southeast breeze was blowing almost directly toward them, the captain had elected to steam. His course laid them close along the coast, only a mile or two offshore. The low-lying land, rising steeply in half-obscured mountains to the westward, looked rich, and he could faintly discern chimney smoke from scattered farmhouses, although mist, combined with *Calcutta*'s funnel smoke, made it hard to see. Kirk was glad he'd studied the chart before the captain's altercation with Mister Bullen: he had no wish to approach his irascible commanding officer at this time. He recognized the wide indentation in the land as the shallow head of Baynes Sound, leading to the Courtenay River, and the two islands they were about to pass between as Denman and Hornby — both named after British naval officers. A solitary figure bending over on Denman Island's long, curving beach — digging clams? Kirk wondered — straightened up and waved briefly before continuing his labours. Glancing quickly at his captain, the young officer returned the greeting just as eight bells was made.

Three days later, relations between the captain and his engineer had thawed. The engine room was on standby status, and the ship was rolling gently along Haro Strait with all plain sail set, under a warm, cloud-studded sky. Most of the officers were on deck, listening as the captain gave a thumbnail summary of the "Pig War".

38

"It seems that the Canadian-American boundary along the 49th parallel made sense, but at that time it was thought that there was just one large channel separating Vancouver Island from the American mainland. Only when it was found that there were two channels, with numerous islands, did the dispute arise. We claimed that the boundary should pass through Rosario Strait, closer to the United States; the Americans argued that Haro Strait was the natural route. Both sides established garrisons on San Juan Island, on our port side" — he pointed at the rocky-shored, green island the ship was passing — "after the pig incident I mentioned earlier. The British camp was there," he pointed again, "in a bay sheltered by a smaller island, and the American camp was nearer the southern tip of San Juan Island."

"How was it finally settled, sir?"

The captain glared at the irrepressible Perkins. "I was about to discuss that, snotty, if you don't mind waiting!"

The midshipman shrivelled into his uniform as the captain continued, "Arguments went on and on between the governments, but an actual breakout of hostilities was prevented by the common sense of local commanding officers on both sides, naval and military. Finally, since they were unable to reach agreement, the matter was referred to Germany's Emperor Wilhelm — and in 1872 he backed the American claim, choosing Haro Strait."

Even Lieutenant Duncan appeared puzzled. "If those have been American waters for ten years, sir, then why are we...?" He left the question unfinished.

"Officially we are merely cruising. A courtesy American flag will be hoisted as soon as we cross the boundary, and we will exchange dips with any American-flag vessel we encounter. Unofficially, I want a sharp lookout kept for any signs of unusual military activity — for reasons which I may or may not explain later."

The ship slid along Haro Strait past Cattle Point in the light airs, a jaunty Stars and Stripes fluttering from the fore topgallant masthead. Passing Lopez Island, the captain ordered a northerly course set along Rosario Strait's blue-rippled waters. Seamen off-duty relaxed in the warm sun.

"Sail ho!"

"Where away?"

"Ahead, sir — p'int t' loo'ard, mebbe five mile off, sir." Acting Lieutenant van Dusen turned to the messenger. "My respects to the captain, and there's a strange ship in sight."

He leaned back to yell at the lookout, "Can you make her out yet?"

"Aye, sir — she's a steamer. Looks like a gunboat, sir. I c'n see cannon on deck."

The captain arrived on deck in time to catch the last exchange. "Hmmm — I had hoped..," he clamped his lips firmly shut.

"Deck there! She's a Yankee, sir. I c'n see 'er colours now," the lookout bellowed.

"Very good," murmured the captain. "Mister van Dusen, you may now demonstrate your seamanship. Shorten sail and heave the ship to."

By the expression on his face, van Dusen would cheerfully have changed places with a stoker at that moment. However, an order is an order, so with hardly more than four or five seconds for thought, the young man began shouting commands, with the captain watching, frozen-faced.

"Signal, sir," announced the yeoman. " 'What ship?' "

"Make the response, yeoman, and return the query." The captain shifted his feet slightly.

Folded signal flags streamed up the halyard, to be broken out by a flick of the yeoman's wrist when the topmost was close up to the block. An answering rainbow broke out at the rapidly nearing steamer's yardarm.

"USS *Growler*, sir. She's signalling again. 'Am sending boat'."

"Very good. Commander Keen," — the second-in-command had come on deck, squinting in the sunlight — "I suspect it will be her captain who will be coming. Have the side manned, and see that the appropriate honours are given. Oh yes — have the Royal Marines' fifes and drums play 'Yankee Doodle' or some such tune as the boat nears, then the side boys will pipe the officers aboard."

As the American boat neared, van Dusen raised his voice over what he considered the hideous rattling and squeaking of the Marines' music, "Boat ahoy!"

The response was instant. *"Growler!"*

"It's the commanding officer, just as I thought," muttered Whitfeld-Clements. "I'll greet him at the brow."

Bo's'n's calls wailed as the American officers climbed slowly up the accommodation ladder hurriedly rigged for them. Glancing past the bobbing gig, the captain saw the gunboat — a sidewheeler, he noted with some surprise, must be stationed only in protected waters — lying cautiously off his starboard quarter, where *Calcutta* could bring no guns to bear. *Growler* had her own gunports unfastened: he could see them moving slightly as the steamer rolled in the low swell. Moving forward with a smile as the first American officer stepped aboard, touching his cap in salute, he said warmly, "Captain Whitfeld-Clements, Royal Navy, commanding HMS *Calcutta*."

The visitor replied shortly, "Commander Jabez Werner, USS *Growler*. What are you doing here, captain? These are United States territorial waters."

"Of course, captain. I had hoped to encounter an American man o' war, so it gives me great pleasure to welcome you aboard." He turned to the *Calcutta* officers standing at attention with the ship's gentle motion. "May I introduce my officers? Commander John Keen, Lieutenant David Duncan," he went along the row quickly.

The American, faced with the choice of answering courtesy with rudeness or emulating the British captain's politeness, chose the latter. He smiled, although tightly, "My executive officer, Lieutenant-Commander Dawson, and my gunnery officer, Lieutenant Westfall."

Hands were shaken, greetings exchanged, and the atmosphere became noticeably less tense. "Perhaps Lieutenant Westfall would care to inspect our armament? After a drink in the wardroom, of course. Lieutenant Giles is our gunnery officer. Lieutenant Giles, would you...?"

"Certainly, sir." Giles grinned at his opposite number, "Care to come along with me?"

"Mister Kirk, take the deck, if you please. My compliments to Mister van Dusen, and I would like him to join the other officers in the wardroom. Since it is almost six bells, and time for tots to be issued, perhaps — with your permission — your boat's crew would care to join in?" As Commander Werner thawed further, nodding, the captain called, "Chief Petty Officer Warfield, please detail a boatkeeper for Commander Werner's gig, and invite the boat's crew to partake in 'Up Spirits'. Head of the line, if you please." Turning back to the American officers, he said, "Now, gentlemen, I have rather a good cellar, if I might induce you? Good! Commander Keen, would you be kind enough to summon my steward and then join us?"

With the four officers comfortably seated in the captain's cabin, and Ashley creakily setting out glasses on the sideboard, Whitfeld-Clements cheerfully asked, "What is your preference, gentlemen? I have an excellent burgundy, some quite passable Madeira and port, a claret which is just reaching its best, or if you fancy something with a bit more authority, may I suggest a Plymouth gin or Navy rum?"

When the two commanding officers had selected burgundy, and the others had opted for rum, the captain opened the conversation. "Your health." He sipped, then leaned forward. "You were asking my purpose in these waters, captain. Rest assured that I have no intention of re-opening the Pig War!" He grinned widely. "No — my purpose is merely to exercise my officers and ship's company, and if time serves, to pay an official visit to an American community. I trust that this meets with your approval?"

Commander Werner cleared his throat. "Yes — by all means. I was somewhat surprised, you'll understand, to encounter a British warship here — particularly in view of the fairly recent animosities. But, by all means, continue your cruise."

"I thank you. Now, may I request a further favour on your part?" As the American's face darkened with suspicion, he hastily added, "That is — your permission to anchor in a nearby suitable cove, and for you and your officers to join us for dinner this evening?"

Werner's face cleared. "It will be a pleasure, sir! At what hour would you care to receive us?"

With details settled, the captain pressed another drink on his guests, and conversation settled into naval reminiscences before they took their leave.

As he saw them over the side, again with side boys and the Marines' fifes and drums, Whitfeld-Clements judged, from the flushed faces of the boat's crew and a pungent aroma of rum, that Warfield had been more than usually generous with the tots.

The evening's dinner and ensuing party welded relationships. The ship's cook had been sent ashore with orders to buy a pig —

"An appropriate meal," the captain murmured — and somehow the galley staff had been able to tenderize the tough old porker. Portions were distributed to all messes, so that even the newest-joined boy seaman got a taste, and mouth-watering smells of roast pork drifted through the ship. When the gathering at last broke up, close to midnight, the captain invited Commander Werner to his cabin for a nightcap. While pouring, he asked casually, "Have there been any rumours of Fenians stirring up trouble in this area, Jabez?" They were now on a first-name basis.

Werner thought for a moment. "Not recently, Norman. Of course, they're always up to something, but since O'Neill tried his invasion of Canada across Lake Erie, and was forced to surrender to one of our gunboats — the *Michigan*, I believe it was — nothing much has been heard except for the usual rumblings and stirrings." He thought for a moment, "I did hear something about a group of 'em in San Francisco — but nothing about what they were up to."

"Well, not to worry. A final toast, Jabez — may politicians some day acquire the sense of sailors, so that another Pig War never happens!"

The American raised his glass. "I'll drink to that, but I'm doubtful — politicians might gain common sense, and pigs might fly!"

Captain Whitfeld-Clements looked thoughtfully at his admiral. "No, sir. Commander Werner is an honourable man — although I was hoping to encounter an officer of somewhat higher rank. When he told me that he knew little of the Fenians, I believed him — and I've heard nothing since to change my opinion."

Admiral Brown grunted. "Very well, then. We can't go chasing down every bloody rumour that floats past — but I'm still wary of that gang of Irish renegades!" He changed the subject. "So the Fort Rupert coal was no bargain?"

"No, sir! We had two incidents of spontaneous combustion, and burned twice as much coal as usual to get less speed."

"That's unfortunate. There's more coal like that here and there. But if it's no good, then I'll tell the Admiralty there's no sense in being 'penny wise and pound foolish', and we'll take no more of it." The admiral suddenly smiled wickedly. "However, captain, there's a novel change in store for you — from plots to plunder, one might say."

In response to the captain's obvious puzzlement, he laughed aloud. "Your new orders originate on high." He handed the captain a thick brown envelope, heavily sealed with red wax bearing a deeply embossed crown imprint. "Let me know on your return if you sighted any golden galleons, captain — and fare ye well!"

"Mister Kirk!" Kirk started. He had been glooming over having been on Watch during the whole of the Americans' visit, and having just barely managed to spear a morsel of the gunroom's roast pork allotment before the midshipmen gobbled it all. He snapped back to the present. The captain, standing near the taffrail, watched him quizzically.

"Sir?"

"My compliments to the commander and Lieutenant Bullen, and I'll be pleased to see them in my quarters forthwith."

"Aye aye, sir." Kirk started to turn away, but stopped when the captain continued speaking in a somewhat lower voice.

"Do you read your Bible, Mister Kirk?"

Taken aback by the question — Clemmie was not noted as a religious man and had even been heard to mutter about missionaries "messing about with the natives" — the young officer stammered, "N-not often, sir."

"Well, Mister Kirk, I suggest that you look up Kings 10, Verse 11, Old Testament. It will give you a hint as to our orders — and might cheer you up somewhat."

Later, having thumbed laboriously through the tattered gunroom Bible to find: "And the navy also of Hiram, that brought gold from Ophir, brought in from Ophir great plenty of almug trees and precious stones", Kirk was again accosted by the captain.

"And what did you think of my Biblical suggestion, young Kirk?"

Kirk had in fact been wondering about his meaning, but the captain's query required an immediate response, right or wrong. "It seems to indicate that we're to search for a treasure trove in the South Seas, sir."

The captain chuckled. "Very perceptive, Mister Kirk, very perceptive. But you're off course by some 16 points." He walked aft still chuckling to himself, "Off course by 16 points!" leaving the young officer wondering.

Chapter Three

The Roving Spanish, Aye!

Acting Sublieutenant Eric Kirk, Royal Navy, of Her Britannic Majesty's Ship *Calcutta*, pulled the tiller to port as he said quietly, "Oars." The whaler's crew, following the stroke's timing, rested on their oars, the dripping blades tracing bubbling patterns in the rippled water as the boat lost way.

Kirk looked around, half wishing that someone else had been placed in command of the whaler. He grimaced at the thought of his studies, getting further and further behind with his new duties as Sub of the Mess. The memory of how he and the other midshipmen used to badger van Dusen returned to taunt him, and he heartily wished, sometimes, that he could revert to the carefree life of a snotty, with the spectre of examinations for sublieutenant far off in the misty future. Now, he was likely to be summoned before a Board whenever one could be convened, to confirm his promotion. Or, conversely, to return him abruptly to the rank of midshipman. He brought his mind back to the present with a conscious effort, his eyes searching the shore.

Ahead, alders and cedars grew to the water's edge, leaning outward and softening the harsh outline of the mossy granite shore. Behind, mountains rose precipitously, stark against the greyish sky, the evergreen growth ceasing as abruptly as a tonsured monk's. Tendrils of smoke curled and twisted indolently upward in the still air, hanging over the low plateau between ocean and mountain range. The men, weary after days of steaming and rowing, searching in vain for the elusive treasure, sniffed hungrily as the aroma of roasting meat and baking salmon tantalized their appetites.

"Give way." Backs arched as oars bit into the sluggish current, and a burble grew under the bow. Kirk steered for a logbound beach, one of a score of similar landing places he'd explored in the past days, watching over the side for treacherous pinnacles of rock.

45

"Not likely they Spanishers left anythin' worth findin' after all, is it, sir?" asked the petty officer pulling the stroke oar.

"I don't know, Petty Officer Peebles," Kirk answered slowly, reluctant to, even by inference, criticize his captain. "It'll be a long search though — of that I'm sure!"

A sailor swore as a black fly bit deeply, slapping at the tormenting insect and simultaneously catching a crab with his oar. "Pipe down there, Boodle," Peebles snapped with a deferential wink at Kirk. "Just 'cause I addresses a word or two to Mister Kirk don't mean for the whole crew to engage in repartee!"

"Oars," said Kirk, grinning to himself at the discomfited seaman, then, "Hold water, port, give way, starboard."

The 27-foot whaler spun in her own length, a few fathoms from shore. "Toss oars," and the whaler, losing way, gently grounded on a gravel bottom. "Boat your oars. Make her fast, bows."

The heavy, clinker-built boat lurched as the bowman jumped on to the sloping, bouldered beach with a squelch of waterlogged sand, and trotted toward a clump of bushes, painter in hand. Kirk stepped over the gunwale, wincing as his laboriously polished seaboots sank into the salt water, and splashed up to shore, feeling pebbles through his soles.

HMS *Porpoise*, Commander Ira Knight, had scarcely rejoined *Calcutta*, when new orders had arrived from the Admiralty. Again, Eric Kirk and other officers were to see the captain wearing an unusual, for him, puzzled expression. As the small squadron lay alongside the Esquimalt jetty he, following his accustomed practice, called the officers of both vessels into his cabin.

After seeing them settled, he said, "Gentlemen, again I must confess to being at somewhat of a loss. Their Lordships have sent a most unusual and highly confidential signal — I'll read you the pertinent parts."

Kirk, enjoying the privilege of being seated with the officers for the first time, hearkened closely as Whitfeld-Clements cleared his throat and continued. "I'll not trouble you with the preliminaries....'Studies have indicated that a large amount of gold, silver and precious jewels was brought northward from Mexico in about 1778, for the purpose of buying the alliance of the Indian nations. When Captain Quadra's ship, the *Sonora*, was found to be nearly unseaworthy and his crew suffering from scurvy, the treasure was hidden in a cave, and its location entrusted to a chief whose name has not survived, in order that the treasure might not be lost should the vessel succumb to the perils of the sea'."

"Long-winded blighters, ain't they?" whispered Clarence Gosling, midshipman aboard HMS *Porpoise*. Sublieutenant Kirk merely turned and glared at the youngster from his new and exalted rank.

Whitfeld-Clements continued, " 'Quadra did not return, but in 1787 Captain Jose Martinez attempted to recover the treasure. He met British trading ships in Nootka Sound, seized them and confiscated their cargoes. This high-handed act so nearly caused war between England and Spain that Martinez fled, and it is assumed that the treasure still remains hidden'." He again cleared his throat. "If you'll bear with me a moment more...'You are therefore requested and required to proceed with your squadron to' — I'll not read out the latitude or longitude — 'and use your best endeavours to recover this treasure which now lies on British soil. Upon recovery, the treasure is to be conveyed to His Excellency the Lieutenant-Governor of British Columbia, in the city of Victoria, and you will thereupon deliver it to him and hold your squadron at his disposal'."

The captain surveyed the faces, some curious, others calculating or bright with interest and anticipation. "You'll keep this information to yourselves until after we sail. Both ships are to be ready for sea by the day after tomorrow, and will sail on the morning tide. Commander Knight, I will issue you written orders."

"Yes, sir."

The officers left one by one, ducking under the beams. As if on cue, speculative conversation began the moment they were out of earshot of the captain, who, with Commander Keen, was studying a chart in the dimness relieved only by the overhead skylight.

"Like looking for a needle in a haystack, sir."

"It is, John. Not only that, but so much could have happened in a hundred years. The natives may have forgotten it, traders may have found and taken it, or even a landslide may have buried the entire cave!"

"Or the Indians themselves may have removed it to another location, sir. As I recall, Spain didn't make a large number of friends in these waters."

"True enough. Nevertheless, my orders are explicit." The captain laid a tanned finger on the chart. "We'll proceed here under steam, leaving *Porpoise* to come along under sail. There are one or two places I want Commander Knight to investigate en route."

"And when we arrive, sir?"

"I'll make that decision later. At the moment I believe that a cutter and the whaler, under command of the sub and one of the midshipmen — the lads can take turns — will be sent to scout out the area after we arrive."

"Make noise, men," said Kirk. "We don't want to startle these people." They clumped onward, slapping at mosquitoes, talking and whistling. Kirk stopped suddenly, causing his next in line to bump. He waited, then strode boldly if a little nervously into the clearing, hand upraised in peace.

Just ahead, a number of Indian warriors, Tlingit, he thought — this was supposed to be their country — clustered around cooking fires. Slowly they ceased their converse and turned to face the intruders. Women tending the baking fish and roasting haunches of meat drew back behind the men, clutching their little children to them. Other youths moved beside the men, while tots peered curiously from behind mothers' skin robes. Kirk grinned at one peeking toddler, and received a shy smile in return.

" 'Ere, you lot," the petty officer growled quickly, "pass me all yer 'baccy, an' laugh while yer doin' it. Mister Kirk'll see yer done right by, won't yer, Mister Kirk?"

"Right, Peebles," Kirk said gratefully, accepting the proffered pouches of pipe and chewing tobacco in both hands and making a mental note to commend the petty officer to the first lieutenant for his quickness of thought.

He marched forward over the dusty ground, skirting a cluster of intricately woven baskets, and halted in front of a tall, heavy-set man, obviously of high rank, Kirk thought, judging from his great dignity. The young officer silently laid the gifts on a flat rock, then stepped back, waiting.

The chief bent, gingerly brought the tobacco to his nose, and sniffed. He smiled, turned, and waved forward another, shorter native, who emulated his actions.

48

"Bueno, senor!" The chief's face contorted as he mouthed the unfamiliar words. He stepped toward Kirk, hand upraised, calling quietly over his shoulder. Women walked forward shyly, bearing wooden platters of smoking meat and fish, a few younger ones exchanging glances with the sailors.

"Take it, men, and nod and say 'thankee' as you take it and by God, keep yer eyes and hands off the women or I'll have yer guts fer garters!"

Kirk grinned at Peebles' savage orders, then turned to the chief and smiled broadly. Using his small knowledge of Spanish, he said plainly, "Buenos dias, senor."

The sachem nodded politely, signalled Kirk to follow, and led the way to an ornately carved cedar-log lodge, stooping as he entered.

Before he went inside, Kirk beckoned to Petty Officer Peebles. "Stay here, PO, and see that the men behave."

"Aye aye, sir. The first one o' these bastards as takes 'is pecker out'll have it sewn to 'is bootlaces!"

Inside the gloomy lodge, smelling of woodsmoke and hides, the chief and six warriors sat down with their feet in a hollowed-out trench several feet across, facing a smouldering fire. Kirk sat facing them, attempting to keep his smoke-reddened eyes from watering. He drew his midshipman's dirk, which he still carried, and sketched a passable drawing of *Calcutta* on the earth floor; then, straining his linguistic abilities to the utmost, said, "My barco."

The Indians nodded, and muttered softly among themselves as the chief waited for more. Kirk drew another, smaller ship, and looking earnestly at the chief, said, "Barco of Spain."

They looked puzzled. He waved an arm to signify a long passage of time. "Long time ago. Many moons." The puzzled expressions grew deeper.

He raised a hand, palm forward, to ask the tribesmen to remain seated, then stumbled to the opening and stooped through, blinking in the sudden light. "Petty Officer Peebles."

"Sir?" Peebles trotted over, swallowing as he came.

"How could I describe the passage of time without speaking their language?"

"Well, sir — I dunno." The petty officer looked around for inspiration and his face brightened. "Look, sir, at th' moon." He pointed at the orb, faintly visible in the morning sky. "Draw that, sir, or a whole bleedin' fleet o' them, an' show them what yer drawin'.'"

"Good, Peebles, I'm obliged." Kirk spoke with the pomposity of youth, knowing that he sounded like an old admiral with gouty feet as he did so. Peebles grinned, returning to the cooking fires, and the younger man blushed as he caught a glimpse of the grin. He returned to the conference with a new humility.

Bare feet pounding over the scraping of fiddles, with shouts of encouragement and laughter, showed the popularity of the hornpipe contest. Commander Keen, well aware that a week at anchor could set even the jolliest bluejacket's teeth to grinding, had devised antidotes.

First was a fishing derby. Three leading seamen, working with the armourer, had made up hooks and line enough for everyone. Able Seaman Lazarus Jenkins had been declared undisputed winner after dragging a flailing 40-pound halibut over the rail. The fish not only won Jenkins the prize — two shillings and an extra tot of rum — but provided a meal for the lower deck the very next day. Small arms practice followed, with the crackle of musketry echoing from the nearby cliffs; then cutlass swinging, rigging races, and now the hornpipes.

Captain Whitfeld-Clements grimaced as a heavy thump shook dust from the deckhead, interrupting his questioning of Acting Sublieutenant Kirk long enough to wink at the younger man and direct a softly-barbed remark to Commander Keen. "Keeping the ship's company happy is a worthwhile endeavour, John, but not at the expense of my sanity!"

"Sorry, sir," the commander shrugged as another thump reverberated through the cabin, "but the men are in good spirits, and practically the only cost is a few shillings and extra tots for the winners."

The captain nodded. "Fact. Well, Kirk, so the Indians realized that you were interested in an ancient Spanish vessel. What about the treasure cave?"

Kirk looked straight at the captain, "Sorry, sir. The chief knew only a couple of words of Spanish — about the same as me — and one of his councillors understood a bare half-dozen phrases in English." He grinned. "The rest of the conversation was sketches in the dirt and sign language."

"You found nothing, Perkins?" The captain turned to the red-headed midshipman.

"No, sir. I talked to seven groups of natives, and not one of them had any notion what I wanted."

"I see. You were fortunate then, Kirk."

"Yes, sir," Kirk agreed. "Chief Kitlup is apparently one of the hereditary chiefs and a direct descendant of some chief who had contact with Spaniards." He hesitated, "Occasionally they'd seem to understand me, sir — I'd draw a cave and a sea-chest in the dirt, and they'd look at each other and nod — then their faces would become blank again." Kirk opened his mouth to say more, but suddenly recalled — with horrifying clarity — lecturing his seniors in tactics during the Russian encounter. He closed his lips with an almost audible smack.

The captain closed his eyes for a moment, expecting Kirk to continue, but the only sounds were the eternal creaking of the ship's timbers and a soft howl of wind in the rigging. He felt a small glow of approval: the new sublieutenant was learning. "Anything else of importance, Mister Kirk?"

"No, sir, except —" Kirk hesitated, then blurted, "except sometimes when they seemed to understand me, the chief or one of his councillors would point at my head, then shake his."

"I see. No telling what they meant." He was silent for a few seconds, then, "Commander, I'll go ashore myself in the morning to try my luck. Have your whaler alongside at four bells in the Forenoon Watch, Mister Kirk. Perkins, you may as well come along with your cutter."

"Sail ho!" The faint cry filtered through the light rain and mist which shrouded *Calcutta* in the open anchorage. A short exchange of shouts, then Acting Lieutenant van Dusen knocked and entered, standing at rigid attention. "*Porpoise* just hove in sight, sir. Six miles southwest, close-hauled. Tide's ebbing, sir. Four hours till low slack."

"Very good, Mister van Dusen." The swarthy officer saluted and left, a bustle of ship-noises entering the cabin as he opened and closed the door.

"Captain, sir," Kirk stumbled over his words as Whitfeld-Clements raised an interrogative eyebrow. "The men — that is — gave up their tobacco." Briefly he explained about Petty Officer Peebles' order, and his helpful suggestion.

"Oh, very well, then. Tell the purser that he's to issue the men replacements from his stores. Nothing extra, mind you."

"Thank you, sir."

"Now — four hours till slack water, and a light breeze. I don't expect we'll see Commander Knight until dawn. He's a daring seaman, but no fool, and I don't expect he'll chance putting his brig aground in the dark." He sniffed the air, "Particularly if the usual fog sets in overnight. Very good, gentlemen, I won't detain you further." He picked up a book and sat down next to a scuttle as they quietly filed out.

A low, clammy mist was fighting a losing battle against the morning sun as the whaler, with Midshipman Perkins' cutter close astern, pulled up to the pebble beach.

"One man to a boat," growled the captain. "Lie off and wait for us. Lead the way, Mister Kirk."

The lanky young officer pushed his way through alders and thorns, holding branches so his captain didn't receive a whiplash across the face — which could effectively delay any promotion for some years, Kirk thought to himself — trailed by the captain, Midshipman Perkins, Petty Officer Peebles and 14 ratings.

"Avast, Mister Kirk," breathed the captain as they broke through onto the flats. He stood silent, staring in some awe at the imperious totem poles glaring haughtily down at the puny humans. His eyes flickered to the massive log longhouse and skin tents, to the handsome, proud men and women watching the strangers without fear or unease, and to the immense dignity of the burly chief awaiting them at the head of his councillors.

Without turning, he said, "Have the gifts ready, Petty Officer Peebles," and advanced toward the waiting group. Halting a bare six feet away, he swept off his cap and bowed courteously. Chief Kitlup, not a trace of emotion crossing his aquiline features, returned the bow.

"The musket, Peebles." The captain reached behind him without taking his eyes from the chief, and brought his hand forward bearing the weapon. Silently he handed it to Kitlup, who stoically inspected the musket and handed it to a councillor without comment.

Impasse. Captain Whitfeld-Clements and Chief Kitlup faced each other in not unfriendly silence: silence broken only by birdsong and a few dogs yelping in the distance.

Suddenly the stillness was shattered, like a china plate dropped on a tiled floor. The chief and councillors stared, chattering and pointing excitedly. The captain spun around. Midshipman Perkins had removed his cap to surreptitiously mop his sweating forehead, and his flaming red hair glinted in the sun.

The chief's facial muscles strained as he smiled, and grunted painfully but plainly, "Bueno. El Rojo!" He made a signal to four husky tribesmen, then strode toward the nearby slopes, indicating with a wave of a bronze arm that Whitfeld-Clements and the two youths were to follow.

Skirting boulders, trudging in line behind the chief, the party slowly climbed a pebbled, dusty trail until the village below was toy-sized. Kirk noted with a faint feeling of superiority that the captain was beginning to puff heavily, and that the back of his neck was reddening. Then the younger man almost crashed into his senior officer's back as the chief abruptly halted.

At a guttural command, the four warriors knelt and began clearing brush from the face of a rock bluff. While they did so, the chief grasped Perkins' arm, pulling him to the front. As the last of the greenery was wrenched away, a tiny cave, no more than two feet wide, was revealed. Whitfeld-Clements began to speak, but the chief imperiously waved him to silence, and pushed Perkins toward the entrance.

There was nothing else for the midshipman to do. The redhead, wincing slightly, fell to his belly and crawled into the dark hole. Only moments passed before his dusty boots, then his legs emerged, followed by his cobwebbed body and head. A dull scraping, then a triumphant grunt, and the midshipman was crouching outside the cave, bending over an ancient chest. He straightened with an effort as the chief gave another order. The warriors took hold of the chest, swinging it easily to their shoulders, and the chief strode down-slope. At the village again, sailors and Indians alike gaped at the long-hidden container until the chief, now grinning widely, shouted a command. Drums thumped monotonously as warriors, women and children assembled, laughing and talking. Then the feasting and dancing began.

Cheers and shouts of farewell echoed over the deep green water as the war canoes, plunging in the heavy chop with spray wisping from tall stems, turned back to shore. Chief Kitlup, resplendent in an old uniform presented to him by the captain, raised an arm in aristocratic farewell as Her Britannic Majesty's Ships *Calcutta* and *Porpoise*, under all plain sail, rigging festooned with seamen, stood out to sea.

A gun boomed in final salute as the screw corvette and brig squared away for the passage to Esquimalt. In his cabin, Captain Whitfeld-Clements discussed the treasure recovery with Commanders Keen and Knight. "It was a good thing we had young Perkins along," he said, "otherwise we could be searching for weeks yet."

"How's that, sir?" asked Knight. "All I know is that I lay there all morning, as you ordered, with guns loaded and run out, and then suddenly there's a great hullaballoo and you come out like a ruddy Oriental potentate at the head of a fleet of war canoes!"

The captain laughed. "I'd surmise that Quadra's lieutenant, or whoever entrusted the treasure chest to Kitlup's ancestor, was redheaded. Whatever else was forgotten in the mists of time, the red hair was remembered. A superstition grew that some day a redheaded sailor would return to claim his chest, so El Rojo, 'The Red One', became a legend."

"That explains why they'd point at young Kirk's head and shut up like clams, then, sir," Keen interjected.

"Right. Kirk did a fine piece of work, but his fair hair effectively forestalled success. If Perkins hadn't removed his cap at a propitious moment, we might never have found the treasure."

"We could have found it, sir," Knight muttered grimly. "A little persuasion of the right kind..."

"I'll have none of that," the captain said sharply. "We want these people to be our allies, not enemies! They're noted for their readiness to fight — and how would you feel about having to report that you'd lost your ship to them?"

Knight mumbled something indistinctly, which the captain chose to ignore. "Now, gentlemen, I have reports to write. If you'll be kind enough to heave the ship to, John, Commander Knight can return to *Porpoise*."

Calcutta and *Porpoise* lay at anchor in the quiet Esquimalt roadstead, the stillness broken only by a shifting breeze in the shrouds, pounding of caulking mallets from the naval dockyard,

and distant hammering from the town. The captain waved his written report gently to dry the ink, his mind absently wandering the
more than 300 miles of unpredictably sunny or savagely weather-
stricken coast, along which they had sailed and steamed with the
ancient treasure chest. Hundreds of shadowy, cliff-lined coves and
twisting fjords penetrated the inhospitable shores, any one of which
could have concealed the Spanish hoard. They were lucky to have
discovered it, he mused, although his success would bring him but
small credit at the Admiralty. Failure, on the other hand... he shook
his head, clearing the cobwebs away. Two North West Mounted
Policemen, under command of a fiercely mustached corporal, had
taken the trove for delivery to the lieutenant-governor's residence,
and glad he had been to see the last of it! His Excellency in person,
a roly-poly gentleman with an effervescent wit and a passion for
gardening, had come briefly aboard to examine the chest. His aide,
a scion of the nobility to whom the captain had taken an instant dislike, had been sent ahead with a request for "no ceremony", a
request of which he all too obviously had disapproved.

Lieutenant Giles thrust his ruddy, homely face through the open
door, jarring his captain's deliberations. "Boat coming off, sir. Looks
like H.E.'s aide."

The captain sighed. "Very good, Mister Giles. See to the proper
ceremony and bring him to me when he's aboard."

"Aye aye, sir." Giles withdrew, and a few minutes later was
replaced by an army captain, dazzling in the scarlet and brass of the
Grenadier Guards. He came, almost condescendingly, to attention
and saluted.

"His Excellency's compliments, sir, and he'd be most gratified if
you'd wait upon him at your early convenience." The plummy, upper-
class drawl, strained through a drooping mustache, unaccountably
irritated Whitfeld-Clements, as the aide continued, "I have a boat and
carriage waiting, sir, if you'd care to accompany me."

"Thank you, captain. I'll take my gig ashore." Raising his voice
— needlessly, he knew, for Giles would be waiting close by — he
called, "Mister Giles!"

"Sir?"

"See the captain to the entry port, then tell the sub to have my
gig lowered immediately." He swung his attention back to the army
officer. "I will meet you at the landing stage in 15 minutes."

The lieutenant-governor, rubicund face wreathed in smiles and portly body quivering with suppressed laughter, welcomed Whitfeld-Clements and Kirk as the buggy clattered to a dusty halt. "Run along, Captain Puffington," he bubbled. "I'm certain you have guards to inspect or offenders to flog or something equally military."

"Your Excellency," Whitfeld-Clements said carefully, uncertain of how to take this Falstaffian nobleman, "May I present Mid — uh — Sublieutenant Kirk, the officer who actually found the treasure."

"The treasure! Oh, of course, of course." He grabbed one of Kirk's hands in both of his own and peered short-sightedly at the young man. "Come along, come along with us, young man — to see the fruits of your labours!"

Seizing their arms, he bustled them along a dimly-lit hallway festooned with frowning portraits of long-departed dukes, earls and lesser nobility. An armed guard jerked to sudden alertness, stamped to booted attention and with a clatter of accoutrements, presented arms as Her Majesty's representative unceremoniously pushed open a massive panelled door. In the centre of a parquet floor sat a glowing oil lamp on a low table. Below it rested the chest, flaking bits of rust and leather forming a horizontal aura around it. The windowless room stank darkly of mustiness and decayed leather.

"Open it, young man!" Kirk felt himself gently urged forward. Kneeling beside the decrepit artifact, he gingerly lifted the lid. A whiff of foul air oozed out, a rusted hinge parted with a dull clunk, and the lid fell askew with one battered edge resting on the polished floor. Kirk stared at the heaped jewels covering gold plates... then looked more closely. He picked up a handful of the glittering baubles, letting them run through his fingers. Slowly realization broke upon him, and a wry smile crossed his face as he looked up at his two seniors.

"They're only beads, sir." He got to his feet, dusting his knees.

"Precisely!" The lieutenant-governor chuckled. "What's treasure to some...", he left the sentence unfinished as Whitfeld-Clements bent, picked up some beads and allowed them to trickle through his hands like a gemstone waterfall. The peer too reached in, pulled out a sheet of copper, crusted green with the patina of ages, and looked at the naval officers.

"Copper and beads," Whitfeld-Clements choked out. "Precious to the Indians, but..."

"Exactly," laughed the peer of the realm, and linking arms once more, the three men walked out of the room and down the portraited hall, leaving the sentry staring and the ancient chest gaping open.

"...and so," Kirk wrote, "it all turned out to be quite worthless, which the captain said was just as well, as if it actually had been gold, the Spaniards probably would have demanded it back, causing no end of trouble. Oh, I found out why Commander Keen is sometimes so unhappy. His wife and baby boy were lost some years ago while taking passage in an East Indiaman which disappeared in a typhoon. We all like him and wish we could help, but he keeps himself bottled up and doesn't talk to anyone about it. Lieutenant Bullen, who is usually so jolly, almost wept when he told me the story...."

Chapter Four

An Assault by Night

Eric Kirk and Clarence Gosling, stumbling slightly on the rough wooden sidewalk, partly due to a slight excess of wine, partly because of drifting mists obscuring occasional puddles of light from the few flickering streetlights, came to a halt and hearkened. Scattered buildings loomed darkly on either side, while behind them a dimly-lit tavern spilled a low rumble of sound into the cool night. Somewhere a horse's clip-clop masked the rattle of wagon wheels, but elsewhere all was silence, except...

"I heard something," Gosling whispered. Kirk nodded — then, realizing his gesture couldn't be seen, grunted an affirmative.

"There it is again," Gosling's voice was louder. "It came from that field..."

A shrill voice slashed through the gloom. "HELP!" and was muffled instantly as though by a rough hand over a mouth.

The two young officers pelted toward the sound, stones and pebbles rattling underfoot. "Hold on — we're coming!" Kirk yelled as they plunged into a tangle of weeds and bushes. Ahead, a white blur resolved into two prone figures as Gosling shouted, then tripped and sprawled headlong into a patch of thistles. One of the shapes rose and bolted into the darkness. Kirk heard a muttered "Fuckin' barstards!" as it vanished into the surrounding forest, with a crash of breaking branches and more indistinguishable curses.

As he knelt, Kirk's nostrils were assaulted by a blend of sweat, cheap perfume and cheaper gin. His eyes widened to see a female form, naked from the waist down, drunkenly thrashing as she tried to pull her skirts over her — as he could now see — full-blown nudity.

More thrashing as Gosling's blurred figure stamped clear of thistle-barbs, muttering as he joined his friend, then quieting as he peered down at the fumbling, swearing woman, now on her knees.

"Goddam bugger," she grumbled slurringly, "promishes me gin, then tries ter..." She glanced up at the two. "But yer gennelmen, ain't yer, sirs? Won't one o' yer gimme a hand up?" She tittered coyly, sending another waft of gin-breath aloft.

Silently Kirk extended his hand, immediately seized by sweaty fingers as the woman levered herself up, then stood swaying.

"Where do you live?"

"What happened?" Kirk and Gosling asked simultaneously.

"Goddam bugger," the woman repeated, "promised me gin, then — but you gennelmen'll take me home, won't yer?" She leaned toward Gosling, clutching his coat as she lost her balance, and they swayed in a momentary drunken ballet.

Gradually the two shuffled the babbling female toward the gravelled street, Kirk not knowing whether to be grateful to, or curse, the full moon that had broken through the clouds, lighting their path, but at the same time making them visible to any passers-by. Slowly her story emerged. She was "in service" as a cook, and had been out for an evening stroll before retiring, when she had been accosted by "a sylor 'e wuz, but 'e be'yved like a gennelman until..." who invited her for a drink.

She had drunk "jus' one small gin — well, mebbe two", and had invited the sailor to escort her home. On the way, she had felt the necessity to answer a call of nature, and had asked her escort to wait while she disappeared into the bushes "fer a minnit".

"I wuz barely finished, when 'e follers me in, knocks me down an' ups me dress an' pulls out his great tallywhacker an' I yells bloody murder an' then you gennelmen comes chargin' in like," she hiccupped politely, "a coupla knights in armour."

Her voice had risen as she stumbled along the road, each hand firmly grasping one of the officers' arms.

"How much farther —" Kirk had begun, when he was rudely interrupted.

"Nah, then — what's all this?"

"Oh, God," Clarence Gosling muttered as their way was blocked by a burly figure topped by a police helmet.

A flurry of explanations ensued, all three talking at once until the constable waved them majestically to silence and bent forward. "Is it you agyne, Meg? Ah, so 'tis. Well now, you young gentlemen had best come along o' me while I tyke the lydie 'ome."

Their objections were dismissed with a frown and a suggestion that they might prefer "a stroll t' the stytion house t' explyne it t' the sarjint."

Ten minutes later they were disconsolately standing behind the policeman as he, one massive hand supporting Meg, tapped a brass, lions-head knocker illuminated by a matched pair of brass carriage lamps.

The door swung wide, allowing a flood of lamplight to flow past the black-and-white-clad maidservant who stared out, gasped, then turned to shriek.

"Ow, mum — it's Meg agyne with a couple of sylors!"

The constable touched his helmet deferentially to the hawk-nosed but not unattractive woman who suddenly filled the doorway. "What is it this time, Higgins?" she demanded imperiously, pearl necklace trembling in outrage against her imposing bosom.

"Your cook agyne, mum — found 'er with these two sylors, 'ere."

"We are naval officers," Kirk began, "and..."

"So much the more disgraceful!" she snapped. "Take their names, constable. I will speak to their commanding officer in the morning!" The door slammed shut. Meg, snuffling, scuttled 'round the side of the house and disappeared.

Acting Sublieutenant Kirk, Officer of the Day, stood by *Calcutta*'s brow, unhappily observing the Watch on duty scrubbing the decks. Turning to look astern at *Porpoise*, also secured alongside the jetty, he saw Clarence Gosling chivvying groups of seamen hanging overside on stages, touching up the ship's paint.

"Morning, sub." Kirk jumped to attention and saluted Commander Keen.

"Good morning, sir." He hesitated, then plunged. "Sir — I'm in some trouble. Not my fault, but..." he floundered.

"Spit it out, young man," Keen said quietly.

Kirk swallowed, then poured out the tale of the previous evening's happenings as Keen listened intently, nodding from time to time. "And," he finished, "the lady's going to complain to Cl — to the captain this morning."

Commander Keen lowered his voice. "I'll have a word with him immediately. He may want to hear it from you — and he'll possibly want young Gosling here, too. Carry on, sub," Keen turned, walking aft quickly, but carefully avoiding the barefooted sweepers sloshing buckets of water about the decks with cheerful abandon.

A couple of hours later, after "Colours" had been piped and the ship's company had dispersed to duties, shore leave or off Watch below decks — the captain hadn't appeared on deck yet, which set Kirk to both wondering and worrying — a dust-cloud rolled along the dirt road leading to the jetty. As an open carriage pulled by a matched team of greys came to a stop, his spirits fell. One of the passengers was the lady addressed by the constable as "Mum".

Summoning his messenger with a glance, Kirk walked to the brow to await the inevitable, almost missing the fact that the driver had jumped down to assist two ladies from the carriage.

As the women, fashionably gowned, each shielding herself from the morning sun with a light green parasol, picked their way daintily toward the ship, the young officer openly studied them. One was much younger and though obviously related to, lacked the autocratic nose of the older. In fact, Kirk caught himself musing, her nose was pert, and her mouth equally saucy. However, they were climbing the brow so, keeping his eyes with an effort on the older lady, he saluted, "Good morning, ma'am. May I help you?"

"I am Mrs. Jeremiah Willoughby. I wish to speak to your captain." She studied him more closely, and her voice harshened. "Are you ...?"

Kirk interrupted. "Yes, ma'am." He turned. "Messenger," he said, unnecessarily loudly, "My respects to the captain, and there is a Mrs. Willoughby wishing to see him."

The two visitors and Kirk stood near the rail in unwilling company, ship noises added to by the impatient tapping of the older woman's umbrella on the teak deck. Trying to avoid Mrs. Willoughby's cold gaze, Kirk let his eyes rove in every direction but hers. Sailor after sailor, glancing curiously at the little tableau, had his eyes fixed by the young officer, and hurriedly returned to his work.

Kirk's eyes met the younger woman's, just a girl, he suddenly realized, as though a spark had leapt between them. His mind, in the split second before he looked away, registered dark hair, brown eyes, and a hint of a smile? on her very! attractive features. Unfortunately, his eyes met Mrs. Willoughby's — like a clash of ice-cold cutlasses. Unable to shift his gaze, he felt a freezing shiver roll down his back but was saved by the appearance of Captain Whitfeld-Clements, with Commander Keen at his side.

Curtly answering Kirk's salute without otherwise showing awareness of his presence, the senior officers introduced themselves and led the ladies aft. Kirk exhaled the deep breath he had held since crossing glances with, as he unconsciously thought, "the Willoughby Witch!"

Leaving the messenger at the brow to warn him of anyone approaching, Sublieutenant Kirk attempted to put his problems out of mind by busying himself about the deck, managing, in doing so, to thoroughly disrupt the work being carried out. Luckily, he missed overhearing the "Fuckin' young jumped-up snotty!" hissed by one old hand.

With no more seamen to disturb, he returned to the brow and stood looking outboard, telescope under arm, and allowed himself to lapse into daydreaming of home — always a dangerous pastime, since lieutenants were notorious for pouncing at the first hint of a far-away look on a junior's face. Thoughts of his family drifted past, then home, fishing with his father and Andrew, then to a neighbouring farmer's twin daughters, Jane and Janet MacKenzie. Their father was a dour Scot, who wore his kilt winter and summer, but their mother had liked him and had often invited him over for scones and "tae".... His reverie was shattered by an insistent voice, "Mister Kirk, sir. Sir!"

Suppressing a start, Kirk turned to the impatient messenger and, as he had seen Lieutenant Duncan sometimes do, lifted, more or less successfully, an interrogative eyebrow.

"Sir! Captain's compliments, and 'e wishes to see you an' Mister Gosling at yer early convenience. I'm to go to *Porpoise* fer Mister Gosling."

Kirk felt the now-familiar chill crawl down his back, but kept a still face and retreated into the naval officers' catch-all phrase, "Very good — carry on." The short, youthful seaman, who must be younger than himself, Kirk realized, doubled down the brow as a light spatter of summer rain drummed over the deck, barely wetting the drying wood.

Almost too soon Gosling marched over the brow, tossing a smarter-than-usual salute to the quarterdeck. Lieutenant Giles strolled over to the pair before they had a chance to speak, and grinned. "I'll take over the brow while you're below — you randy young buggers!"

Kirk, somewhat against his wishes, involuntarily grinned, then looked at Gosling. "Well, shall we get the situation straightened out?"

The two walked aft in step to the captain's quarters. Kirk rapped twice, then, in response to a barely discernible "Come in", turned the latch and entered.

Captain Whitfeld-Clements and Commander Keen, seated on one side of the huge table, were smiling at the two ladies as Ashley, the captain's venerable steward, poured tea. Only one of the guests returned a faint smile; Mrs. Willoughby's features were contorted with a mixture of anger, disbelief and doubt.

Kirk and Gosling, caps tucked under their arms, came to attention just inside the door. Kirk, senior to Midshipman Gosling, spoke. "You wished to see us, sir." It was not a question.

"Yes, gentlemen," the captain said softly. "Mrs. Willoughby and Miss Geraldine Willoughby, may I introduce the young officers who rescued your cook from an assault?" His voice rose during the last seven words, as if to drive them indelibly into the women's minds. "Sublieutenant Eric Kirk, HMS *Calcutta*, and Midshipman Clarence Gosling, HMS *Porpoise*." Not waiting for an acknowledgement by either of the newly introduced parties, he carried on forcefully, speaking directly to Kirk and Gosling.

"Commander Keen has related the circumstances — as you told them to him — of yesterday evening to Mrs. Willoughby, and I feel certain that but for one or two details, the matter can be closed." He turned to the women, "Sublieutenant Kirk was instrumental in resolving a search for lost relics of the Spanish presence in British Columbia, and was complimented personally by His Excellency the Lieutenant-Governor."

With an inward grin, Kirk saw the Willoughby Witch's expression slowly change. She smiled, with a visible effort, tightly at him. "My daughter and I are delighted to meet such distinguished officers."

"Charmed,"

"Honoured," the two responded, sensing rather than hearing the sarcasm.

"I will speak severely to my cook," she said, pushing her chair back and standing before anyone could move to pull it back, "and now we bid you good morning."

Kirk, moving more swiftly than the others, captured Geraldine Willoughby's chair, eased it back as she stood, and received a quick smile, which vanished instantly as her mother frowned.

When the ladies had been seen into their waiting carriage — not without a few lascivious looks from seamen on deck — and had driven away with a spiral of dust curling from carriage wheels and the trotting horses' hooves, the captain turned to Kirk. "Two questions, Mister Kirk. Did you see the man who attacked Mrs. Willoughby's cook at all clearly, and if so, was he a member of either of our ships' companies?"

"No, sir," Kirk shook his head forcefully. "All that I saw was a blur disappearing into the woods —it was very dark, sir. He swore something at us, but I don't think I'd recognize the voice again."

"And you, Mister Gosling?"

"No, sir." Gosling ruefully touched a finger to his bruised face. "I tripped and slid face-first into a patch of thistles."

Commander Keen smiled. "First things first, eh Gosling?"

"Yes, sir."

The captain frowned slightly at the interruption. "Very good then, gentlemen. I think you did well, considering the circumstances —although you might have been more forceful with the constable." He grinned suddenly with a flash of white teeth in his tanned face. "The incident is closed. That is, unless Mister Kirk, of course, wishes to further a new-found acquaintance!" Leaving the younger men stunned by his perspicacity, he headed back to the ship followed by Commander Keen. Neither chuckled aloud, but Kirk, still holding a half-salute, noticed their shoulders trembling ever so slightly with suppressed laughter.

Three days later the squadron put to sea, westward through misty Juan de Fuca Strait, then northwestward off the perilous western coast of Vancouver Island. Caught up in the tense, demanding, though monotonous routine of a man o' war at sea, Kirk forgot about the matter, except sometimes at night, when Geraldine Willoughby's face, with its quick flashing smile, would drift past his weary eyes. Occasionally, a memory of his momentary sight of the cook's naked buxom body would come erotically to mind, and he'd wonder dreamily what Geraldine would look like without her clothes.

It was in such a situation that he was caught out. "Mister Kirk. Mister Kirk!" The irritated voice penetrated his daydream and he was shocked back to the here-and-now to find Commander Keen glaring at him.

"Sir?"

Ignoring the helmsman and standby, who were all too obviously paying undivided attention to steering the ship, Keen leaned against the binnacle and murmured harshly, "I expect an instant response when I speak to an officer, Mister Kirk."

"Yes, sir." Neither Keen nor the captain had patience with lame explanations.

"Very good. The captain wants to see you in a half-hour, at four bells."

"Aye aye, sir."

Captain Whitfeld-Clements, studying a chart spread out on his cabin table, felt his mind drifting off as he ruminated about Kirk and the attraction the girl — Geraldine, was it? — had for him. Young Kirk would have a problem with the mother, who obviously nourished a dislike for sailors and the navy. Perhaps he could find out why.... He recalled meeting his wife-to-be, at a garden party given by baron what's-his-name, with the perfume of flower-beds and tiny fragile teacups and delicate little cucumber sandwiches and hovering servants discreetly offering the gentlemen small glasses of brandy, while in the background the Scottish gardener glared sourly over the hum of conversation at the harm being done to his lawns and rockeries.

She had floated into his vision, daringly mocking him, since they hadn't been introduced. "Not having brandy, lieutenant? I thought all naval officers began their day with a drink."

He had flushed and stammered, but had, he remembered with pleasure, retained his wits enough to seek out his hostess, who, fortunately, enjoyed playing Cupid, and wangle an introduction. The remarks he had so carefully rehearsed vanished like gunsmoke in a gale when the young lady smiled at him, off-handedly remarking, "I wondered how you would arrange to meet me — but since sailors have 'a girl in every port', I imagine that you have had a great deal of practice." The baroness had discreetly disappeared, smiling, as he had fumbled for words, and all that he could later recall of the talk was the girl's name: Beatrice.

A subdued knock shattered his musings. Hurriedly composing his features, the captain called, "Come in", and Lieutenant Duncan and Kirk entered, ushered by Commander Keen.

The captain studied Duncan's and Kirk's faces silently for a few moments, as the two stood at attention, shifting their balance with the ship's easy motion. *Calcutta* was under all plain sail, rolling and pitching gently in the low westerly swell. Finally — to Kirk it seemed like a quarter-hour had passed — the captain waved a weary hand at the widespread chart. "Look at this, David." His glance swung to Kirk. "You too, sub."

As they moved to the table, somewhat puzzled, the captain nodded to Commander Keen. "Perhaps you'll explain the situation, John."

"Aye aye, sir." Keen took two long steps, then laid a hard brown hand on the chart, covering a good third of Vancouver Island's west coast. He grinned shortly at Duncan and Kirk. "Our successful expedition to recover the Spaniards' brassware has led to further ramifications," he stopped, seeing Kirk's quizzical look.

" 'Ramifications', Sublieutenant Kirk", he explained, "may be likened to further developments — possibly differing slightly from the original. At any rate, information has been received by the powers-that-be about more old Spanish artifacts —" he moved his hand gently on the chart, "somewhere in this area. Our orders are to investigate and bring back anything of value. The captain," he dipped his head deferentially in his commanding officer's direction, "wishes you to take the cutter and a whaler and thoroughly explore any likely-looking coves or inlets we pass. Commander Knight will also be dispatching a whaler."

"Explore thoroughly but not exhaustively," the captain interjected, a peevish note in his voice. "I don't want the ships' companies dawdling about with their fingers up their bums while you two are rollicking about in the boats! Damned shore-side," he stopped short. "I beg your pardon, but I'll say it regardless. Damned shore-side official ink-wallahs think we have nothing better to do than chase down idle tavern rumours while the ships' routines go to Hell in a hand-basket!"

Kirk felt shocked. His captain's temper was always a touchy thing, but profanity! He couldn't remember when he had last heard Clemmie swear.

For the next ten days Kirk and David Duncan, in their respective boats, had their boat crews pull laboriously up a dozen steep-sided, twisting fjords and inlets, while Gosling did the same a few miles north. Unending hours of hand-blistering rowing, scrambling up rocky shores through thorns and nettles, forcing paths through tangled trees and over treacherous deadfalls, two-thirds of it in mist or drenching rain, the remainder harassed by clouds of whining insects under a merciless sun, would have tried the patience of far more cool-headed men than Royal Navy Jack Tars. Audible tooth-sucking, mumbled complaints and slow responses to orders became common.

Even the infallibly cheerful Petty Officer Peebles lost his easy manner, going so far as to snap at his officer, "How much longer does the captain want us to carry out this 'ere charade, sir?" when they were out of earshot of the others.

Kirk sympathized with the petty officer, but realized the near-insolence needed bringing up short. "Watch your tone, Petty Officer Peebles!" He left it at that.

"Aye aye, sir." It was more a groan than a response. When the two crews clambered wearily aboard that evening, leaving the boats secured to the boom, Kirk sought out Lieutenant Duncan. "Sir — my crew is," he hesitated, then blurted out the story.

"I know," Duncan grimaced. "My crew's the same. We can't initiate orders, but — I'll talk to the commander." He grinned sourly. "If our men are this sulky, young Gosling's are most likely in a state of near-mutiny!"

"Deck there! Sail ho!"

Duncan looked at Kirk whimsically. "We may just have been reprieved."

Midshipman Perkins, entrusted as Officer of the Watch while the ship was at anchor, tilted his head back to shout. "Where away — can you make her out?" His attempt to deepen his voice was partly successful; only on the word "out" did it rise to a cracked treble.

"Aye, sir — it's *Porpoise*, close-hauled an' beatin' up t'wards us!"

67

The captain, Commander Keen, and several more officers and ratings, lured by the shouts, straggled on deck.

"Be a couple of hours before she gets near enough to send a boat," David Duncan murmured to Eric Kirk. "I'm going below to freshen up as soon as I report the day's doings — and I suggest you do the same."

Commander Knight clambered through the entry port, puffing heavily, as Perkins saluted. Lieutenant Youngberg followed closely behind, skipping nimbly to one side as Knight leaned back over the rail, his portly body forcing him to crane his neck in an ungainly manner in order to see his boat crew.

"Lie off and wait for me," he ordered brusquely, "and keep silence in the boat!"

"Aye aye, sir," curtly the reply sliced through the gathering dusk. "Shove off, bows! Give way, port. Hold water, starboard." A few seconds elapsed, the only sounds water gurgling past the whaler, and creaking of *Calcutta's* rigging, then faintly, "Way 'nuff! Boat yer oars."

Commander Knight stamped over to Whitfeld-Clements. They exchanged salutes and a few quiet words, then the captain led the two commanders and Lieutenant Youngberg aft to his quarters.

The cool night was as black as Stockholm tar when they emerged. Commander Keen called to Lieutenant Giles, "We'll get under way, Mister Giles. Have the hands weigh anchor as soon as the engine room has steam up." He turned, straining to see as his eyes slowly became adjusted to the dark. "Is that you, David? And Sublieutenant Kirk? Perhaps Commander Knight will allow Lieutenant Youngberg to tell you his tale." Knight grunted a grudging assent as Youngberg walked over, carefully stepping around or over unfamiliar articles of ship's gear. His face mostly in shadow — the few lanterns served more to emphasize the dark than to dispel it — he began.

"The mid fell down a rock bluff day before yesterday. Nothing broken, but he's in sick bay with a hundred bruises and scratches, so I took the whaler out yesterday and today. Found the remnants of a log fort, maybe Spanish."

"Or Russian?" Kirk interjected. "Maybe there were more than the one we..." he stopped, abashed at letting his tongue run away again, when he thought he'd broken the habit. "Sorry, sir."

Youngberg, only slightly annoyed, continued. "Maybe Spanish, maybe Russian — could be Chinese for all I know. It was late in the day when we saw it, and since it was high up on a cliff, I didn't go ashore. I buoyed the location — these damned cliffs all look alike — and reported to my captain."

"How's young Gosling feel?" asked Duncan. "Not to change the subject, but did you give him the news?"

"Oh, I told him," Youngberg laughed, "but the way he felt, all that he said was 'I'm glad that you'll be scaling the cliff, not me!' At any rate, the upshot was that we reported to your captain, and we'll all have a look-see tomorrow." He lowered his voice. "Am I right in thinking he'll be just as happy to see this search over and done with?"

"I believe so," said Duncan, leaving further explanation for another time.

Two whalers and a cutter crawled spider-like up the cliff-walled, watery canyon, outflowing wind raising a short, steep chop. Rising in silvered arrowheads as bows plunged into troughs, the water was transformed into wind-driven spray which drenched every man aboard. The boats were laden with "brass", as one sailor had whispered before being quelled with a sharp look from Petty Officer Peebles. Lieutenant Duncan's cutter was under the captain's critical eye; Commander Keen rode gloomily along in Kirk's whaler, while Knight's irritable presence ensured an uneasy silence in Youngberg's boat, leading the others as the commander fumed and grumbled through the slowly dissipating mists.

Within two hours Youngberg spotted the oar he'd left anchored; the boats were pulled into the shelving gravel beach and three seamen detailed as boatkeepers. The three petty officers loaded their rifles, a precaution ordered by the captain, as Kirk warned Adams, the "Queen's Hard Bargain", "It's a rising tide, and you'll have to keep moving the boats in, so don't wander away."

"Aye aye, sir," the man rumbled. Kirk looked at him doubtfully: the seaman had the attention span of a gnat, but... he was loyal. "I be keepin' an eye on them other buggers, too, sir," he added earnestly, jerking his pigtailed head at the other boatkeepers.

Looking back as he hurriedly scrambled after the rest of the party, Kirk glimpsed Adams comfortably seated, back against a boulder and smoke curling aloft from his pipe. The subbie grinned to himself, thinking that no self-respecting mosquito would venture into those foul-smelling fumes.

A half-hour of slipping and stumbling along an animal trail — "Deer, I hope," the captain remarked cheerfully, "but possibly bear, so you petty officers keep your weapons ready" — brought them to a crumbling, moss-strewn stockade, surrounded by overgrown, rotting stumps. With the captain leading, they pussy-footed gingerly over the fallen gate, and stopped to stare. Inside there was nothing. No sagging buildings, no remnants of gardens or wells, not so much as a rusty saw or broken musket barrel. Nothing. The log walls might have dropped from the sky into a rain forest, and been left to time's inexorable decay.

"Well," breathed the captain, "someone built it — only to abandon it...."

"Indians?" Keen suggested.

"You riflemen keep your eyes peeled, dammit," Knight snarled. "Whatever happened here could happen again!" Dirt crunched under boot-heels as sailors quickly turned to look about, but there was nothing except wind in the cedars and occasional slaps at the maddening mosquitoes.

"Make a sketch of the fort's interior," Keen ordered Lieutenant Duncan. "You can do a second one looking up from the beach."

"Quickly, David," the captain added, "and we can catch the ebb."

"I've thought about it much, Your Excellency," Whitfeld-Clements stated forcefully, leaning forward in the commodious leather armchair, "and I suspect that whoever built the stockade was an outright fool!"

"And why?" The lieutenant-governor sipped his port, eyes sparkling. "Be sure you get this down, Scratch," he ordered his secretary, perched on a stool behind a tall rosewood lectern.

"Several things, sir." Now that he had made the decisive statement, something like punching his fist through a glass door, the captain leaned back, feeling the soft leather close comfortably around his back. "No commander in his right mind would situate a fort high on a cliff, with no water supply and the access limited to a practically impassable goat-trail!" He snorted, "I'd like to have seen them trying to manhandle so much as a six-pounder carronade up that cliff."

His Excellency stared unseeingly at the ruby-coloured drapes surrounding huge leaded-glass windows, musing aloud, "But it did command the sea approach."

"That it did, sir," the captain agreed, sipping his port and inhaling its bouquet appreciatively. "However, an Indian attack — such as we made on the Russians — would not necessarily have come from seaward. In fact, a large enough war-party could have surrounded the stockade, held the defenders inside until they were either starving or half-mad from thirst, then massacred them as they tried to break out. Or," he added thoughtfully, "enslaved them. A considerable amount of prestige, I believe, accrued to any chief with white slaves."

"I see. Well — whatever happened, it all took place too long ago to be of concern to us now. On to more interesting matters! I'm holding a levee next Thursday evening — on the lawns if the weather is favourable, otherwise in the grand ballroom. Her Ladyship greatly enjoys these events," he grimaced, "and she — I, too, of course — would like you and your officers to attend."

"With pleasure, sir." The captain saw an opportunity. "May I enquire if a Mister and Mrs. Willoughby will be attending?"

"Willoughby? Willoughby — Scratch?"

"Captain Willoughby is at sea, sir, but Mrs. and Miss Willoughby have indicated they will be present." The secretary glanced at his employer, "May I speak further, sir?"

"Certainly. Have at it, man!"

"Captain Willoughby was retired from the Royal Navy in the rank of commander, sir. The family, 'tis said, holds some animosity toward the navy for its refusal to award him the customary promotion to captain on retirement. He has since become quite successful in trade, owning one brig — which he captains — and shares in two schooners."

"Now that your question's been answered, Norman, it's your turn," the peer chortled. "Spit it out, captain! Not thinking of a fling with la Willoughby, are you?" He pounded his teak desk in sudden glee, sending papers and an inkwell skittering across the top.

"Not bloody likely, sir!" The captain's vehemence lifted the lieutenant-governor's eyebrows, then Whitfeld-Clements grinned at his own fervour. "In fact, sir, Sublieutenant Kirk — whom you may recall, is the one..."

Sublieutenant Kirk, in his Number One uniform (of superfine Pilot Cloth, said the label), hastily exhumed from his sea-chest to dispel the sharp aroma of camphor, looked around appreciatively at the festive lawns. Japanese lanterns dangled swaying from branches; glittering brass lamps gleamed from sconces recessed into a seven-foot granite fence behind rosebeds, and wavering flames from ornate candelabra illuminated whitely draped tables. Each table was loaded with food and drink, and presided over by a steward, several of whom, Kirk noted, were Chinese, each clad in maroon livery and great hauteur.

Captain Whitfeld-Clements and his officers had arrived en masse, but had immediately dispersed to mingle with other guests. Kirk's eyes were busy. Elegantly-gowned women with elaborate hats perched atop even more elaborate hairdos, and wreaths of pearls resting comfortably on daringly low-cut bosoms, chatted archly with scarlet-tunicked, tight-trousered infantry officers. Here and there spurs jangled, reflecting candles' gleam as cavalry officers shuffled polished boots.

Civilian "aristocracy" — ship-owners, wealthy traders and civil service panjandrums — in velvet-lapelled formal dress, conversed earnestly or gaily while a string quartet, secluded in an arbutus grove, strove desperately to be heard over the undulating babble of conversation and tinkling of crystal.

Kirk jumped as his arm was seized and a cheery voice, fortified by a whiff of brandy, exploded in his ear. "Aah! Sublieutenant Kirk, is it not? Doughty discoverer of Spanish gold! Good!"

Snapping his eyes toward the speaker, Kirk realized it was his host. "Ohhh — yes, sir — I mean Your Excel ..."

"Never mind that balderdash, my young bravo! Come along now. There are people I want you to meet." He strode away. Kirk went with him, willy-nilly, as the peer's hand was still firmly clutching his arm. A half-step behind the exuberant lord, Kirk became aware they were heading toward a trio: an army officer and two ladies. One was Geraldine! His mind in a fog, he scarcely heard his host speaking.

"Ah, Mrs. Willoughby! How pleased you could come. May I introduce my young friend and protege, Sublieutenant Eric Kirk,

Royal Navy, of Her Majesty's Ship *Calcutta*? Eric, Mrs. Jeremiah Willoughby and Miss Geraldine Willoughby, and of course you have already met my aide, Captain Puffington."

A confusion of "How d'ye dos" and "Charmeds" was cut through by the Witch's suddenly cordial contralto. "I have had the delight of meeting Mister Kirk — how pleasant to see you again." She extended her gloved hand and Eric, abruptly inspired, bowed to touch his lips to it. Straightening, he saw a flash of pleasure in her eyes as he turned to take Geraldine's hand.

"Now, captain, I'm sure that Mrs. Willoughby has not yet tasted our chef's smoked salmon nor the '69 Madeira, so let us older ones leave the youngsters to themselves. I'm certain that a naval officer of Eric's repute" (my first name — from a lieutenant-governor! Eric thought, trying hard not to show his surprise) "can be trusted to see Miss Willoughby safely home later on. Mrs. Willoughby, your arm." Stilling the woman's instinctive protest with a risque comment about a notably rakish cavalry officer a short distance away, he led Mrs. Willoughby and his aide off.

Fumbling for words with which to present himself to the girl as a witty, dashing sailor with a classical appreciation of the arts, Kirk was forestalled by a gentle squeeze on his arm. "I've been hoping that we could meet ever since I saw you on your boat."

"Ship," he corrected automatically, then his innate reserve crumbled and they began chattering like old friends.

The evening passed as swiftly as a summer squall. Keeping a weather eye open for Geraldine's mother, he asked, half expecting a rebuff, "May I see you home, Miss Willoughby?"

"Of course you may! And since we've been Mistering and Missing each other all evening, don't you think you might try calling me Geraldine?"

The two said good-night to their hostess, who cheerfully told them to "Run along now, children, and do come back to see us some time soon." Blessing the good fortune that had made him save some money, Kirk handed Geraldine into one of the hansom cabs waiting patiently by the gates.

"Where to, sir?" asked the elderly cabbie, inhaling a pinch of snuff and sneezing as his passengers settled cosily on the narrow seat.

Kirk paid the cab off at the Willoughby home, tipping the driver lavishly and realizing as he did so that he'd have to hike back to the ship. As he escorted Geraldine to the front steps, where the door was opened instantly by the same alert maid he'd previously encountered, he asked hesitantly if he might call on her again.

"I should be very angry if you did not!" She flashed her quick smile and vanished into the house.

Immersed in a warm flood of exhilaration, the young sublieutenant began the lengthy trek back to *Calcutta*.

"Evening, sub. Did you enjoy the reception?"

Kirk jerked his head around, trying not to appear startled. He had just exchanged a very few words with van Dusen, Officer of the Watch, and had seen no one else on deck but for the sentries and messenger. Commander Keen had materialized from the shadows cast by the entry port's flickering lantern.

"Uh — yes, sir," he stammered momentarily. "The lieutenant-governor was most cordial and ..."

"So I noticed," Keen chuckled. "And you saw the young lady home to her mother's satisfaction?"

"I believe so, sir." Kirk regained some of his aplomb.

"Good," the commander grinned, "and now, sub, how would you, for a change, like to become a bobby?"

Disconcerted by the sudden change in subject, Kirk hesitated. "A policeman, sir? I don't ..."

Keen took him off the hook. "As you should know, the American national holiday is a fortnight away. Victoria's chief constable asked the squadron to supply patrols to assist in quelling any Yankees who, shall we say, over-celebrate, and the captain has agreed to the request. You and young Perkins will each take 30 ratings, a petty officer and a leading seaman and report in turn to the police station. See me in the morning after Divisions and I'll give you the details." Keen smiled, "Good night, young fellow."

"Good night, sir." Kirk shuffled below, wondering what could possibly happen next.

Chapter Five

Gawd — Save — Oireland!

Special duty! The commander had even smiled when he'd laid this job on, as though he'd done a favour. Kirk's expression was unsmiling and a trifle severe, as befitted an acting sublieutenant in the Royal Navy, but his mind was churning furiously. No studies again!

Thumping and crashing, the tiny Royal Marine band marched and counter-marched across the parade square, bugles blaring "Heart of Oak" as the White Ensign was slowly, with great dignity, hoisted and the halyard secured. "So come cheer up, my lads, 'Tis to Glory we steer!" the words rang through Kirk's head while he watched the flag rise.

There — it was up, and the band was marching off, to the tune of "Liverpool Lou". He snapped his hand smartly down from the salute and turned about, blinking at the morning sun.

"Division, stand at — ease! Stand easy." The 30 ratings and Petty Officer Peebles relaxed. "As you know, today is July 4th, the American holiday. Our orders are to assist the police force to maintain order. There are many Americans in Esquimalt and Victoria," Kirk grinned, "a number of whom think that Vancouver Island should be a part of the United States."

The young officer stiffened. "Division!" he barked; the men resumed the "At Ease" position. "Ho!" and they came to attention. "Petty Officer Peebles!" Peebles, anticipating the call, doubled around the division, tiny spurts of dust puffing from under his polished boots.

"Sir."

"Divide the division into three patrols of ten. I will take command of one squad, you and Leading Seaman Blake will take charge of the other two. We'll march to the quay and take three whalers across the Inner Harbour to Victoria."

"Aye aye, sir!"

Parts of Victoria were in an uproarious state. Shouts, snatches of maudlin song and shrieked laughter, punctuated with exploding firecrackers and the occasional shot, rolled and crackled over the normally peaceful harbour as the boats eased alongside a float.

"The police department will issue truncheons at the station a few blocks up Water Street," said Kirk quietly to Peebles as the seamen made the whalers fast, then formed into fours. "Detail four of your best men to take care of any troublemakers on the way. I'll blow my whistle if they're to take action. We want no general melee."

"Aye aye, sir." The petty officer spoke to four bluejackets, shifting men so that the selected four were in one file. He called the men to attention, marched up to Kirk and saluted. "Division ready to move off, sir. Special detail fallen in as ordered."

"Very good, PO, carry on. Right in fours, right turn!" Kirk placed himself at the division's head. "By the left, quick march."

Victoria's streets were an anomalous mixture of the frolicsome and sedate — staggering miners and trappers in dusty buckskins and the occasional tipsily dignified remittance man jostled and reeled along wandering board sidewalks, brushing elbows with morning matrons apprehensively shopping for the day's groceries. A bubble of silence accompanied the infrequent helmeted policeman or scarlet-jacketed mounted policeman passing by, bursting when they had vanished into the distance. Cheers and jeers greeted the sailors, but only once was Kirk forced to halt while his special detail up-ended a vituperous drunk into a convenient horse-trough, to the accompaniment of mixed applause from bystanders.

Carriages full of gentry clattered past, billows of rolling dust in their wakes obscuring the rows of false-fronted frame structures. From second-storey windows desultory bawdy invitations screamed down as strumpets hawked their wares or shrieked stridently at the sailors. When at last he halted his men before a dusty brick building marked "Police", Kirk felt he'd already been through a battle.Truncheons issued, he gave final instructions for patrol areas, concluding, "Assemble here at six bells of the Afternoon Watch. Midshipman Perkins' division will then take over, and we'll return to the ship. Carry on."

As he led off his own patrol of ten seamen, Kirk studied the city with some interest. Unlike many of the coastal communities he had seen, Victoria's streets were wide, about 60 feet, and were mostly macadamized, fringed with wooden footpaths. Many substantial warehouses and offices, solidly built of brick or stone, lined the waterfront, though as the patrol moved away from the city's centre at Fort and Government streets, the construction changed to frame. Most had concrete or brick foundations, and, he noticed, there seemed to be a busy tavern or public-house in every block. In the distance Kirk saw a parklike area, heavily treed with a high knoll in its centre. "Beacon Hill Park, that is," he was told by a passer-by, who hospitably offered a drink from a flat brown bottle, "an' over there," he waved an arm, "that pile lookin' like a stack o' bird cages, is the govermint offices an' the courthouse."

The day passed like a clipper ship in the Roaring Forties; good nature reigned and Kirk's main problem was fending off drinks pressed on him by convivial citizens. When he and his party returned aboard in mid-afternoon, he reported to Lieutenant Duncan, Officer of the Watch.

"There were a few incidents, sir," and he related the early morning horse-trough dunking, "but in general, except for a few private fights, people were enjoying themselves." He grinned broadly, "Especially since the Americans were buying drinks for anyone who'd stand still!" He sobered, "I did hear rumours about 'Fenians' — whatever they are — planning something dramatic, but nothing else." He shifted his feet unobtrusively. Standing watches aboard ship did little to prepare feet for long patrols over city streets and board sidewalks, to say nothing of splashing through ankle-deep mud on the outskirts.

"No trouble with the men?" David Duncan smiled. "With that lot of defaulters, I expected you to spend half the time chasing your own division!"

"No trouble, sir. They conducted themselves very well." He hesitated. He'd been wondering how to broach that very matter for a good part of the day. "In view of the fact that they did behave well — and seeing that their leave is stopped, sir —" the young man hesitated again, "do you think they might have a short run ashore?"

"I'll speak to the commander. Carry on."

Petty Officer Peebles intercepted Kirk by the main hatch. "Any leave for the men, Mister Kirk?"

"I spoke to Lieutenant Duncan, PO, and he said that he'd have a word with the commander. The captain's at Government House."

"Fenians," murmured John Keen, sipping his gin and tonic. "I thought that the movement had died in 1877 or '78 along with O'Neill."

"O'Neill, sir?" Duncan raised an eyebrow. "The name's a bit familiar, but I can't quite place the man."

Keen put his glass down, carefully setting a piece of paper underneath so as not to stain the mahogany. "John O'Neill, David. A renegade Irishman turned American, who led several raids across the Canadian border to redress," the commander laughed shortly, "imagined wrongs in Ireland. Pack o' ne'er-do-wells, actually." Commander Keen glanced at Duncan searchingly. "Thought you'd have heard of him, or the Fenians. Didn't your family own land in Ireland?"

Duncan paused in his answer until a squad of lead-footed Royal Marines had stamped overhead, and their sergeant's hoarse bawling had stopped echoing. "Yes, sir. And still do. But as a younger son, one loses track of the estates and their trouble...." He let the words trail off, then, "The service, sir, requires enough of a man."

"I suppose so," Keen, who would never be troubled with estates or an excess of money, said. "This O'Neill moved to the American west before he died. I don't know if he sired a son, but he had time to incite any Irish around him to some sort of deviltry — and I don't like this rumour that young Kirk passed on." Keen paused as the Marines' boots pounded on the deckhead again, shaking the cabin. "I'll send a messenger to the captain telling him about this. Have the boarding nettings rigged, David, and double the Watch after sunset."

"Aye aye, sir. What about Kirk's division?"

"Oh, let them go ashore. But they're to be back aboard by midnight without fail, or Lord help them!"

"Aye aye, sir." Duncan turned to go, then halted as a thought struck him. "Shall I have the gun crews stand by after sunset, sir?"

"No, I don't think we need to go that far, David. The captain may decide to do more when he comes aboard, but for the meantime, keep a good lookout for canoes or pulling boats. If the Fenians are going to try anything, it may well be a boarding party."

Her Majesty's Ships *Calcutta* and *Porpoise* lay quietly at anchor in the gloom, reflected bonfire-lights flickering over the still harbour as the day's celebrations, and celebrants, simmered down. Tidal currents rippled and chuckled past anchor chains; anchor lights cast a dull glow over decks becoming damp with evening dew, while the doubled lookouts whispered or peered quietly at their posts.

"Clang-clang, clang-clang, clang-clang!" Kirk jumped as the quartermaster made six bells of the First Watch — 11 p.m. — and Lieutenant Giles yawned. Reddening slightly at the quartermaster's grin, Kirk straightened his back and swung his telescope around the dark harbour. Only one more hour, he thought, and van Dusen would relieve him. It had been a long day. His hard, confined berth seemed as attractive as a pasha's canopied, scented chambers. A blurred object swam into focus and he steadied the glass on it.

"Boat coming off, sir," he said clearly to Giles. "Shall I challenge?"

"Yes," Giles answered shortly, bringing his own telescope to bear.

"Boat ahoy!"

"Aye, aye." The response was sharp.

"Aye, aye," muttered Giles. "Officer aboard. What officer? There's no officer ashore except young Perkins and he's not due back until midnight."

Kirk ran to the rail. "Keep your distance, there," he shouted. "Lay off and identify yourself!"

The rhythmically swinging oars didn't miss a beat. Tiny whirl-pools marked the boat's path as a voice called back, "Message from the lieutenant-governor, sir."

Kirk frowned. Was that a brogue? Hard to be certain, and the boat was indistinct in the rippling water. He yawned. Giles would take care of it; all that he had to do was be there for the next hour, looking alert even if he was asleep on his feet. He moved to the other rail, casually searching the murky harbour. A muffled splash tossed up a puddle of phosphorescence, and he looked harder, then jumped and yelled to Giles:

"Boats, sir! Closing in on us!"

Giles' head snapped around as he screamed, "Beat to quarters!" He shrilled his silver whistle and roared out, "All hands on deck! Repel boarders!"

Shouts erupted from the nearby boats as secrecy was abandoned, and shots blossomed redly in the darkness. Cutlass-armed seamen pounded up the companionways and on deck.

"Mister Giles. Grapeshot from the carronades." The captain had rushed to the quarterdeck. "Mister Duncan, drop shot into their boats as they come alongside." The decks came alive with shouting men and muzzle flashes as the small Royal Marine contingent returned fire.

"Look out!" A hulking figure swayed clumsily on the boarding nettings, then tumbled back with a choked gurgle as Keith van Dusen's sword flashed silver, then red, in the dim light. Kirk ducked as a massive boarder swung a cutlass at him, the blade sssss'ing as it sang past his ear. Stumbling, he dropped his sword and his opponent raised his weapon for another slash. A large shape materialized beside him and the intruder fell with a thud.

"Thanks, Peebles," he managed to gasp as he recognized the petty officer.

"Don't mention it, sir," Peebles sniffed. "From th' stink o' this one he's been rollin' about in his native bogs." Lifting the unconscious unknown without effort, he parted the nettings and dropped the man overside. A scream and splintering crash followed. "Appears the lad stopped by th' boat on his way to bathe," commented the petty officer unfeelingly, turning with Kirk to attack another of their assailants, who dropped his club and fled.

Surprise lost, the boarders evidently realized that they had little chance against the disciplined defences of the ship. Three sharp whistle blasts heralded a retreat; the attackers fled for their boats helter-skelter, leaving an inanimate body sprawled on the deck. Kirk, the red rage of battle slowly leaving him, noticed with surprise that he was shaking uncontrollably, and though his body was soaked with sweat, he was suddenly chilly. He heard, as through a fog, the captain bawling, "Take that one prisoner — that one at least."

As the hubbub on deck stilled, a sailor shouted, "Boat ahoy!" At the call, a dim figure stood in the stern-sheets. "*Porpoise*! Don't fire — we're coming to help."

Moments later Commander Knight scrambled through the entry port, puffing and blowing like a beached whale — and looking much like one, Kirk noted. Fat men were supposed to be jolly, but Knight had a dark repute for severe discipline throughout the squadron.

"I cleared lower decks and came to help as soon as the attack was reported," he puffed. "Not soon enough, I see." He looked grim, "My Officer of the Watch will have some explaining to do."

"Boat ahoy!"

"What now," Whitfeld-Clements exclaimed, "more help or more attackers? Find out, if you please, Mister Kirk."

Kirk strode to the rail, his hammering pulse almost normal, and opened his mouth to shout but was too late. "Hold yer fire — we're comin' to help!"

Kirk turned to the captain. "It's the liberty party returning, sir."

"Damn my eyes!" Commander Keen exploded, "I thought nothing short of an earthquake would get them back before midnight."

A burly sailor walked up to Kirk, rum fumes preceding him, dragging a limp and dripping figure. He saluted unsteadily, "We found this 'ere sunnava whore floatin', sir, an' thought you might like a look at 'im."

"Thank you, Adams." Kirk looked at the captain, "Shall I have the prisoner put in cells, sir?"

"Yes. And the other one. Have them kept separate, so they don't have a chance to talk."

"Aye aye, sir." Kirk saluted and suddenly noticed his right sleeve was dangling loosely from his shoulder. He whistled to himself. That cutlass slash must have been a lot closer than he'd thought! Oh, well — it had missed him. "Master at Arms," he called, and as the "Crusher" came doubling up, said, "Put these two in cells." He added the captain's edict to keep them separate, then, foggily, stumbled down to his berth and collapsed across it, fully dressed.

Acting Sublieutenant Eric Kirk, with a petty officer and two armed seamen, stood guard outside the opened door to the captain's cabin. Commander Keen poked his head out, "Come in, Kirk. We may need your story."

Removing his cap, the young man entered and was at once ordered by the captain, "Open that scuttle, sub." Whitfeld-Clements touched his nose. "The effluvium of this one's a bit much." The previous night's boarders stood slumped, wrists and ankles in chains. Kirk eyed them curiously. They were rumpled and unshaven, and one had an eye blackening above stained, gaping teeth.

Kirk flipped the clips and swung the port open, then stood silently, watching and listening. Early morning sunlight glanced through the skylight, sending rays glinting and dancing over chairs, desk and bulkheads as the ship swung. Chief Petty Officer Warfield, massive against the carved legs of the formal dining table nested against the starboard side, glared at the shackled felons from under a bandaged forehead.

One of the Fenians, as they'd claimed to be, moved his battered lips as though rehearsing a speech, then muttered eloquently, "Youse limeys ain't gettin' nuthin' outa me." The stench of his breath expanded through the cabin as he continued, "O'Neill's gonna do fer youse when the boat..." He suddenly shut his mouth, the action uncannily reminiscent of a clamshell, when the second Fenian glared at him with a throaty growl.

"Have the two of them taken ashore under guard, Mister Kirk," the captain ordered politely, "and turned over to the police. I imagine that they'll be deported."

Kirk motioned to Warfield, who brusquely shoved the two through the door. As the sublieutenant followed them out, he heard the captain say quietly to Keen, "You were right, John. O'Neill enters into this somewhere — it must be a son or close relative who's behind it."

"Yes, sir. I'd give a year's seniority to know what that chap was going to say about a boat. I can't believe that he was referring to last night's fiasco." Kirk gently pulled the door shut, and the voices faded.

The two senior officers continued talking. "We'll get nothing more out of that one, John," Whitfeld-Clements remarked. "If he lets his friends discover that he said as much as he did, he's likely to be found behind some saloon with a knife in his back."

"D'you think this was a spur-of-the-moment operation, sir?" Commander Keen ground a fist into an open palm. "Or was it planned for some time?"

"The Fenians have a long and sordid history of border attacks, John," the captain frowned, "and they've never lacked for money, either." He paced back and forth, his hands clasped behind his back, "There may be more to come, and I'll not risk the ships in this sort of a frontier brawl. We'll take the squadron to sea. It's time for the men to get the shoreside rum out of their systems. Have the engineer officer raise steam, and signal Commander Knight that we'll tow him out on the afternoon tide."

The ebbing tide and a fresh westerly smacked HMS *Porpoise* along smartly in the screw corvette's wake. Juan de Fuca Strait was restless: the whitecaps of a choppy sea sprinkled the deep blue swell rolling past rocky headlands to crash a splintering white on the shore. Once clear of the land, *Calcutta* stopped her engine, banked the fires and set sail, swaying along gloriously ahead of the brig.

The ships cruised for five days among the intricate passages of the Gulf Islands, *Calcutta* taking *Porpoise* in tow twice through swift-running passes, before the captain ordered a return to Esquimalt. Under a lowering grey sky and scudding cloud the two ships raced southward along Haro Strait, just north of the disputed international boundary, carrying full sail in the brisk nor'easter. Helms were put up off Discovery Island, and the pair surged westward toward port.

"Sail ho!" Kirk looked up to the masthead. "A point to loo'ard, sir. She's a small schooner flying American colours and — she's towin' somethin', sir. Can't make out what." Instantly telescopes were levelled at the stranger.

"She is towing something, but damned if I can make it out," muttered the captain. "Go aloft, young Kirk, and see if you can do better."

"Aye aye, sir!" Kirk quickly fastened his jacket as he sprang for the rigging, then raced up the ratlines hand over hand. He was back in moments. "Sorry, sir. I can't tell exactly what it is, either. Looks like an iron barrel, but it's not bobbing about the way a barrel would. Seems to be heavy, sir. Look there, sir — you can just make it out now." He pointed at the mysterious object ploughing a turbulent wake through the rolling chop.

"Hmmm. Yes," the captain said shortly. "Yeoman. Make a signal to *Porpoise*: 'Investigate object towed by schooner'." He turned away, "We'll soon find out what it is."

Giles, his coat flapping in the wet wind, said apprehensively, "She'll be in American waters in half an hour, sir."

"I can see that, Mister Giles," Whitfeld-Clements bit out, "but *Porpoise* should have the legs of the schooner with this wind — especially with the schooner towing." Kirk watched interestedly, ignoring the biting wind, as *Porpoise* thrashed by carrying every stitch of canvas possible, from stuns'ls to royals. Gauging the distance by eye, Kirk saw that the brig should intercept the chase well before the quarry reached the invisible border. He stiffened, and whipped out his telescope. Staring for just an instant, he stuttered excitedly, "Sir! The schooner's slipped her tow!" beating the lookout to it by a scant second.

"So she has," agreed Commander Keen. "She's pulling away from it rapidly."

"Yeoman," ordered the captain without delay, "signal *Porpoise* to abandon the chase. Lieutenant Duncan, clew up the tops'ls and make ready to lower my gig. I want to have a look at that, whatever it is." Kirk, not intending to be left out of this, had already ordered the gig swung out even as the words left the captain's mouth.

Calcutta rounded up and hove to a cable's length to windward of the wave-washed object, mainsail aback and funnels belching smoke as sweating stokers frantically raised steam. Water splashed as the gig dropped on top of a crest, and the bowman shoved off with a flurry of spray and mumbled oaths.

"Lay us alongside that thing, Mister Kirk," the captain ordered, "but be careful — it may be some sort of infernal object." Low cheers accompanied them from the ship as the gig stuck her nose into a green swell and shipped a dollop of solid water onto the bowman.

"Aye aye, sir!" Kirk's heart pumped furiously with excitement. "Give way together." As the gig pitched over the seas, now high on a crest, now plunging sickeningly into a trough, Kirk stared at the nearing barrel shape; the bucking tiller lurched and strained in his hand. He could see that it was metal — rivets were wetly visible.

"Oars." He swung the tiller hard over. The gig rolled only a few feet away from the tossing object, high above or far below, as the long swells and short seas bounced the boat at will.

"Damn my eyes! It's some kind of vessel," exclaimed the captain. "Look there, lad — the part above surface is a hatch!" Kirk peered closer. Sure enough: a long, dark shape was occasionally greenly visible below the surface as the seas surged past.

"Get closer, Mister Kirk! You and I'll jump for it."

A sudden wave thrust the gig against the metal with a wail of tortured wooden gunwale, and Kirk, without thinking, leaped, arms and legs flailing as he reached for support. The ebb pulled the gig away, leaving the young officer perched like a seagull on a deadhead.

"Here, sub!" The captain threw a heaving-line, the weighted "monkey's fist" at the end nearly removing Kirk's cap as he grabbed the rope. "Pull us in."

Kirk strained on the line. As the gig surged closer, he made fast the line and looked around. Below him was a round hatch, with an opening wheel plainly visible in the foam swirling across the tiny tower. He spun the wheel, stiffly at first, then easily, and a thud announced Whitfeld-Clements' arrival. The captain looked on silently, then gave a hand as Kirk, balancing with difficulty on the pitching platform, swung the hatch open and fastened it. They peered down. Below, a flickering light barely dispelled the turbid darkness, faintly outlining rusty rungs leading to the bowels of the sluggishly rocking vessel.

Kirk glanced at his captain. The senior officer didn't waste time. "Follow me." His last word echoed hollowly, spectrally, from the interior. Kirk swung his long legs over the iron rim and followed, claustrophobic terror clutching at his imagination. His boots rang on the iron deck as he crouched beside the ladder, loathe to leave the feeling of safety conveyed by the pale round ring of light overhead. Curiosity got the better of his apprehension, and he looked at his surroundings. A lamp swung smokily from an overhead fitting, the oil flame faintly illuminating the sweating, round, rivetted hull. A convoluted crank, double-handled, led to a shaft disappearing into one end of the boat. Bow or stern — he couldn't tell. The shapes were identical. Amidships he dimly discerned a spoked wooden wheel and a binnacled compass. He grabbed the wheel as the strange craft rolled sharply.

"It's a submersible torpedo boat," said the captain slowly. "I've heard of these things, but never imagined that I'd be aboard one." He staggered as the craft lurched, and looked anxiously up the hatchway just in time to receive a splash of cold salt water full in the face. "Damn!" he muttered and hurriedly stepped back.

"Look forward there, sir," Kirk exclaimed. "There's a name-plate. I can just make it out — 'Holland Boat Works'."

"Yes. And right forward," the captain added, "must be the pumps to fill and empty ballast tanks." He looked up the hatchway again, a trifle apprehensively, "Time to go, young man. We'll take this craft in tow."

HMS *Calcutta* steamed slowly, the submersible riding heavily at the end of a short, thick, manila hawser. The weather had deteriorated and wind was shrieking savagely from the east, heavy seas breaking completely over the mysterious iron boat. Spray and an occasional surge of solid green water lashed the three men — Captain Whitfeld-Clements, Commander Keen and Acting Sublieutenant Kirk — who were clustered in a small soggy group on the warship's quarterdeck. Aloft, tops'ls, set to ease the deeply rolling ship, stood iron-stiff against the low grey cloud and churning billows of black funnel smoke. "Holland, sir," Commander Keen had to shout to be heard over the wind's banshee wail, "was involved with the Fenians. They raised money for him to build one of these boats, but apparently a disagreement sprang up between them, and the Fenians simply stole it. This might be the one!"

"A strange group, John," Whitfeld-Clements screamed back. "I've heard that another Fenian by the name of Train," he glanced nervously at the pitching submersible, then continued, "planned to build a bridge across these straits in order to invade Vancouver Island!"

"Steer small, dammit," the commander snarled at the straining helmsman, struggling with the huge, bucking wheel. "Mister Giles, put a second man on the wheel." He faced the captain again, "I'd surmise, sir, that this craft and last week's raid are not unconnected."

Kirk had been following the conversation with great interest, but in silence. He'd long since come to the conclusion that the less a junior officer spoke, the less could come back to haunt him. Something caught the corner of his eye and he snapped his head around, then shouted, "Towline's parted, sir!"

The captain cursed, then shouted a volley of orders to Giles, the wheel and the engine room. *Calcutta* rolled hugely as she turned, and a giant sea picked up the submersible, pitching it so that fully half of the rusty hull was exposed, then rolling it completely over. When the monster wave flattened, it was as though the submersible had never been.

The lieutenant-governor said quietly, "It may be as well that it did sink, Norman. Our possession of the Holland submersible could have led to diplomatic repercussions of a high — and unfriendly —

order. Over 50 Americans have, shall we say, voluntarily returned to their own country, and the United States government will be told quietly and unofficially of the events here. Let that be an end to the matter."

"Yes, sir," the captain agreed soberly. "Better to let 'sleeping dogs lie'."

"And Fenian submersibles sink," added the peer. "We'll have a toast to silence before you leave."

"Aye aye, sir. With pleasure."

"Such excitement," Kirk wrote. "British Columbia only stopped being a colony a few years ago, so it's like being on the frontier. We raided a Russian camp and chased them back to their own country, then the captain and I boarded a Fenian submersible boat and took it in tow, but we lost it when the towline parted.

"Now for the great news, which I didn't tell you before. I've been promoted to sublieutenant! and will be confirmed as soon as a Board can be set up, and am now Sub of the Gunroom Mess, which means I have to keep all the midshipmen in line. Van Dusen was promoted lieutenant, and is still the Schoolie or Snotties' Nurse as we call him, which means that he still has to teach the midshipmen as well as make sure their journals are up to date.

"With the next parcel could you send some more home-made jam and jelly as it's very expensive here and the mids gobble it up as soon as it's opened..."

With a faint sigh, Kirk scribbled his name and left the page open for the ink to dry, then resignedly picked up Norie's *Seamanship* and began to read. Overhead the Royal Marines stamped fore and aft, drilling, but the young officer didn't hear the heavy boots. In a few minutes his eyes blinked; he fought to keep them open but weariness won out, and he slumped over the open book, head resting on his arms, and fell asleep. His dreams, however, were not of sails, wearing and tacking ship, and laying out kedge anchors, but of Geraldine Willoughby, although her dark hair kept fading to a deep reddish hue, much the same as Jane and Janet MacKenzie — and why was she wearing a tartan...? She ran to him, arms outstretched as he opened his to meet her — then suddenly a huge vampire bat with the features of Mrs. Willoughby dove at them from a cliff and he awoke in a cold sweat, trembling. Rubbing his eyes, Kirk gathered his book and letter, undressed and fell into his berth and into a dreamless, heavy sleep.

Ashore, the admiral stared bleakly over his desk at Whitfeld-Clements. "His Excellency may believe that losing that submersible ends the Fenian threat, but I suspect there's more to it than that. On your next patrol I want a sharp lookout kept for any suspicious activities along the coast...."

Chapter Six

A Train of Trouble

HMS *Calcutta* rolled her 3,900 tons ponderously in the endless grey swell off Vancouver Island's bleak, inhospitable west coast, her three lofty masts and two athwartships funnels swaying widely — now rolling outward to the heaving empty ocean, now inward to the jagged, hazy shores. Great billows of voluminous black smoke churned from the funnels, forming a sticky fog with the low, scudding clouds and chill mist, while the bitter September gale drove stinging needles of spray past the teak rails into the numbed faces of the Watch on deck.

Aloft, the frigid lookout perched precariously in the maintop had long since heaved his breakfast into the seething wake, and was gnawing on a wafer of hardtack smuggled up inside his jumper. The oilskinned helmsman and standby sweated even in the chill, as they struggled with the huge spoked wheel. Lieutenant Derek Giles — gunner and Officer of the Watch — glanced into the binnacle, while a petty officer made his way across the heaving deck, crouched against the wind's force. Bracing himself, he grasped the lanyard and struck the ship's bell.

"Clang-clang, clang-clang!" Four bells in the Forenoon Watch — ten a.m. — thought Acting Sublieutenant Eric Kirk. Shivering, he thought wistfully of the Fijian sun they'd left just a short year ago. He glanced at Giles, who intercepted the look and nodded.

"Relieve the wheel and lookout," Kirk ordered. The petty officer scampered to the companionway and, leaning down, bawled out an order. Sailors scrambled up on deck, exchanging muttered scraps of information as they changed places.

Lieutenant Giles turned to Kirk when the petty officer had reported the relief completed. "Take over, sub. I'm going for a look below decks. Call me if the wind picks up any more," he paused. "I think we're in for a real blow."

"Aye aye, sir." Kirk, newly promoted to his acting rank from midshipman, felt a thrill as he surveyed the length of *Calcutta*, and reflected that he — he! — was in acting command of one of Her Majesty's men o' war. He strode to the wheel, stared into the binnacle while the helmsman and standby traded surreptitious winks, then growled, "Keep her up. Don't let her fall off in the troughs."

"Aye aye, sir!"

Kirk glanced sharply at the helmsman, Bloggins, his name was — a veteran seaman who would long ago have been rated petty officer had it not been for a huge appetite for rum — then decided to let the touch of humour in the man's response pass by. Sometime, he reflected, he might need the sailor's willing help, and discipline over a small matter was no way to gain loyalty. He winced mentally as he considered his early blunders, the icy wind for the moment forgotten. What had Clemmie told him? "Everyone makes mistakes, but those who learn from them become admirals!"

He grinned at the sailor, "I'm going forrard for a minute, Bloggins. Try not to lose the wheel overside!"

His friendly overture was returned. The helmsman shifted his tobacco to the other side of his cheek, and grunted back, "No, sir. Leastwise if I can keep Samuels here from droppin' it."

Kirk nodded and started forward, watching his footing on the bouncing, slippery deck. He exchanged a word with the petty officer of the Watch amidships, then went right forward to the bow lookout's position. The man was pale-faced and shivering, Kirk noted.

"Are you ill?" He studied the man closely.

"Nossir. Just cold." The seaman ducked quickly as a sheet of spray lashed over the weather bow.

"Very good. Keep a sharp lookout. Tell me at once if it gets too much for you."

"Aye aye, sir. Thankee."

On his way aft, Kirk went over the ship's officers in his mind, ignoring the rain rattling on his jacket. He'd been lucky to get *Calcutta*, a new ship with a good captain and capable officers. Clemmie was stern and somewhat aloof, but still friendly and helpful. The commander, John Keen — also aloof and very sensitive about his growing bald spot. Keen was getting a little old for promotion, Kirk mused. He could even be sent home on half-pay unless a last-

minute appointment saved him during this commission. The lieutenants: Giles, the first lieutenant and gunner, very proud of his 14
seven-inch rifled muzzle-loaders; Duncan, second lieutenant, tall,
aristocratic, his seamanship second only to the captain's, and
equally cool in action; Keith van Dusen, newly risen from the limbo
of sublieutenant and just a bit uncertain, although he tried to con-
ceal his misgivings; and Bullen, the engineer officer, lording it over
the nether regions of steam propulsion. Yes, Kirk concluded, he
could have done much worse!

Calcutta's engine was invaluable under conditions like this, he
thought, patrolling the deadly dangerous west coast of Vancouver
Island in search of a Fenian encampment. He shuddered as he
thought of the perils of doing it under sail alone.

In his spacious quarters, Clemmie — Captain A.N. Whitfeld-
Clements, RN, — leaned back in his bolted-down chair, feet firmly
braced against the hearth of the thinly glowing coal fireplace, and
read a book. Or tried to read. The wail and thunder of the wind and
the ship as she dropped and plunged kept interrupting. His mind
drifted to the curious experiences he'd had on this coast, encounters
which would bring him no great credit at the Admiralty, for all their
success. The failure of any, however, would have brought swift con-
demnation and probable retirement on half-pay, with little chance
of future employment. He shuddered as the vision of permanent
shore-life raced darkly through his thoughts. The attack on the Russian fort — if it had gone wrong, he might even now be facing a
bleak future. He shook the feeling off. It had cost poor Mudd his life,
but had gained acting ranks for van Dusen and young Kirk, both of
whom were far better officers than Mudd could ever have become.

A sharp knock sent his thoughts scattering. Midshipman —
Acting Sublieutenant — Kirk held the door open against the ship's
rolling and the wind's buffeting. "Mister Giles' respects, sir, and the
wind's freshening."

"Very good. My compliments to Mister Giles, and I'll be on deck
directly." He heaved himself out of his chair.

"Aye aye, sir." The young officer touched his cap and withdrew, gently shutting the door. His footsteps clattered on the deck
overhead as he reported to the Officer of the Watch. Sighing, the
captain stood, his massive body dwarfing the chair he'd been in,
and threw his boat-cloak over his shoulders. The wind grabbed at

the garment as he went on deck, snapping it straight as a man o' war's pennant.

Kirk, balancing inconspicuously by the binnacle — out of the way but available, he thought to himself — heard the lieutenant shout over the wailing wind. "Freshened very suddenly, sir. Thought it best to call you. Visibility's down to a mile, sir, and we won't see anything ashore."

"I can see that, Mister Giles," the captain roared back. "Are your guns double-lashed?"

"Yes, sir. I ordered it done at four bells." Giles staggered and clutched at a rail as the ship lurched.

"Very good." The captain shivered in an icy blast. "Relieve the wheel and lookouts every half-hour. Steer west by north. Put the engine at half-speed, and reduce to slow ahead if you judge it prudent."

"Aye aye, sir." Giles saluted and the captain touched his cap in return, then turned carefully and made his way across the pitching deck.

Kirk felt the ship's motion ease as Lieutenant Giles brought her on her new course, and slowed the engine. The wild rolling, transformed now into a sliding twist, was periodically punctuated by a thundering crash as the ship plunged into a trough and sent sheets of white water racing aft, driven by the screaming gale.

"You have the ship, Mister Kirk," Giles screeched into Kirk's ear. "I'm going for a prowl." He strode forward and disappeared into a companionway.

Once again jammed into his chair, the captain pondered his strange orders. More suggestions than orders, he reflected. The Fenians, Irish-Americans attempting to injure England by thrusting at Canada, were supposedly plotting again. O'Neill's nephew had been reported in San Francisco in the company of an erratic Fenian genius named Train, who had at one time harboured grandiose ideas of invading Vancouver Island by means of a wooden bridge spanning Juan de Fuca Strait. Whitfeld-Clements smiled at the thought: one storm such as this would have reduced Train's bridge to splinters. Faintly he heard the ship's bell — four double clangs. Noon. No chance of an observation in this weather.

His cabin door blew open and a gust of errant wind sent curtains and papers flapping and flying. "Dinner, sir. Fresh bread, potatoes and corn, sir, with boiled beef." Ashley, his steward, grinned gummily at him. His wife had insisted that Ashley accompany him, to "look after you and ensure that you eat properly," she'd stated firmly. Ashley must be in his sixties, thought the captain; he'd been a strapping country youth when I was a toddler.

"Put it on the table, Ashley, and rig the fiddles. I'll get to eat in a minute." He picked up some papers and pretended to study them.

"The missus said I wuz to make sure you'm eat well, cap'n," the old man insisted stubbornly, toothless lips sternly compressed. "You just sit down there an' I'll fetch your coffee." Surrendering with good grace, the captain moved to the table and lifted the tray's lid. The food looked and smelled good, and wonder of wonders, was still hot! Grabbing the tray to arrest its precipitate slide as the ship rolled, he began to eat.

Acting Lieutenant van Dusen, with a Dutch name but a Spaniard's dark hair and saturnine features, had relieved Kirk of the Watch. With him was the red-headed snotty, Reggie Perkins. Kirk paused on deck for a few moments to chat with them.

"Look there, sub," Perkins pointed, "the sun's breaking through." The ship shuddered as a huge sea thudded against her bows. "Crikey, that was a big one!"

The lieutenant scowled, "It's Lieutenant van Dusen, wart, and I'll thank you to remember it!" Kirk grinned to himself as the momentarily abashed but unsuppressible Perkins looked solemn.

"Oh, aye aye, su — sir! Sorry, sir, I forgot."

"Well and good," van Dusen's mouth quirked as he looked at the chastened midshipman. "Go and tell the captain that the weather's moderating."

Although the seas remained mountainous, heaving and subsiding in great welters of foam and white-streaked surges of dark green water, the wind had dropped to a moderate 20 knots when the captain came on deck. The hard blue in the sky warned of more bad weather in the offing, but for a time they'd enjoy a respite.

"Long foretold, long last," quoted Whitfeld-Clements, "short notice, soon past." He looked at van Dusen. "Have we suffered any damage? Has the well been sounded?"

The young officer wasn't flustered. "No damage, sir. Well is normal. The engineer officer reports that one of his coal bunkers shifted slightly, but his stokers are squaring it away."

"Very good. Steer nor'west by west — full speed ahead."

"Aye aye, sir." Lieutenant van Dusen crisply repeated the orders, and the ship resumed her coastwise search, steam rising like low mists from her drying decks.

Eric Kirk, off Watch and wisely out of sight in the mizzentop, watched the goings-on below him with amusement, glancing at his seamanship manual occasionally as the mast swung.

Captain Whitfeld-Clements was taking advantage of the fine weather. *Calcutta* surged along flaunting a glorious array of canvas: royals at the mastheads lording it over upper and lower topgallants and deep single tops'ls; huge courses on fore and main masts, cro'jack on the mizzen billowed wind-full in square-rigged splendour, while jibs, stays'ls and spanker heaved against taut sheets in the brisk westerly breeze. Dolphins gambolled in the bubbling bow-wave; on deck and aloft seamen overhauled standing and running rigging while in the 'tween decks the gunner exercised his gun crews. In the waist, drums and brass blared stirring martial tunes as the tiny contingent of Royal Marines marched and counter-marched heavy-booted on the teak decks.

"Well," remarked the captain to the cluster of officers on the quarterdeck, "I see that Mister Bullen has decided to let his stokers see daylight." A small group of grimy stokers, stripped to the waist, were scrubbing their clothes and themselves as they fended off good-natured jibes from passing seamen.

"Aye, sir," the ebullient engineer officer quickly responded. "Tisn't often they get the chance to laze about like the deck crew!"

"Score one for the worthy engineer," roared the captain, his voice carrying upward to Kirk. "What say you to that, Mister Duncan?"

"Even a troglodyte doesn't always shun the sun, sir."

Midshipman Perkins, also off Watch and leaning on a rail enjoying the sun by the quarterdeck ladder, turned his gust of laughter into a coughing fit as the engineer officer scowled blackly at him. Kirk chuckled as he enjoyed the byplay, feeling safely remote in his aerie.

"Deck there! Canoes coming out from shore, sir. Broad on the starboard bow," came a hail from the masthead.

"Heave the ship to, Mister Duncan," snapped the captain, his jocular mood vanishing like a sounding whale. "Furl royals, courses and cro'jack. Back the main tops'l and t'gallants. Ease stays'l sheets!"

"Aye aye, sir." David Duncan volleyed orders and men pounded over decks, up vibrating ratlines and out onto the swaying yards. Magically the flying white canvas became neatly rolled sausages along the yardarms, and the ship slowed as the yards swung aback. Kirk tucked his book under an arm and raced down the ratlines to the deck, all thoughts of being off Watch forgotten.

"Beat to quarters," ordered the captain. "Mister Kirk, my compliments to the gunner and I'll have the guns run out."

"Aye aye, sir!" Kirk disappeared instantly, and soon the rumble of gun carriages growled through the ship as the ports were triced up. Peeking through a gun port, Kirk saw that the three canoes, pitching wildly in the swell and tossing spray high in the air from carved bows, were nearing the warship. He spared only a moment to drink in the sight, then scurried back to his station just in time to hear David Duncan speak.

"One's a chief, sir. Or someone important," he steadied his telescope. "See his woven hat — much more ornate than the others." The captain grunted something noncommittal in reply.

The canoes bobbed alongside, Indians' hands reaching out to prevent the frail dugouts from crashing against the ship's massive timbers. "They seem to want to come aboard," commented the captain. "Here, Eric, you've bartered with natives before. Tell them we'll allow three aboard — the chief and two more."

"Aye aye, sir." Kirk ran to the rail and leaned over, hoping that his smattering of Chinook — the trade language — combined with English, some Russian and a few words in Spanish might get the idea across to the Indians. No sense protesting: "growl you may, but go you must" was the saying, with no praise if it worked, but immediate censure if he failed. His language conglomerate appeared to be effective, however, and he expelled a silent sigh of relief. The chief waved and issued an authoritative command, then he clambered up the ship's side, followed by two others, and stood on the deck with arms folded. All three were powerfully built, if short-statured, men, with intelligent dark faces under woven conical hats. They wore nearly identical bear-skin robes and cedar-bark capes, the chief's hat and cape more ornately decorated than the others.

The naval officers slowly gathered around the Indians in a curious semi-circle, until the captain called sharply, "Have you nothing better to do, gentlemen? I want only Commander Keen and

Sublieutenant Kirk with me. Mister Duncan, will you be kind enough to order my steward to bring refreshments? Biscuits and cocoa."

The men in the small group stared silently at one another until Ashley appeared with a laden tray of biscuits and steaming mugs of cocoa — "kye", in naval parlance. The Indians gave delighted grunts as they sampled it, then sat crossed-knees on the deck. The officers followed suit, sitting on convenient bollards or leaning on the polished teak rail.

"Now, Mister Kirk," ordered the captain, "I'll be obliged if you'll find out what brings them here."

Kirk, his mind racing, studied the Indians carefully before speaking. He'd decided that they must all be of high rank in their nation, and that he must be careful to avoid giving offence but that most questions must be addressed to the chief. He spoke slowly, gesticulating for emphasis, and waiting courteously for answers as the three discussed amongst themselves. He felt sweat running down his back when he finally stood, dusted off his knees, and said slowly, "As near as I can understand, sir, a number of their people have been captured by white men. Americans, I would say, sir, since the chief used the term 'Boston men'. The prisoners are being forced to build some unusual sort of boats — they don't know what for. The chief says that he attacked the white men once, but that two of the prisoners were shot in retaliation, and he was let know that further attacks would cause more slaughter. He's asking for help, I believe, sir. He says that he's always been at peace with us."

"I see," said Whitfeld-Clements after a pause. "Where are these white men?"

"I'll find out, sir." Kirk turned back to the waiting Indians, anticipating difficulty in translating, but found the chief had foreseen the question. Pointing at the sun, he swung his arm in an arc to indicate the dawn-to-dusk period, and made swift paddling motions. The chief then pointed at the shore and carefully said gutturally, "My village," then pointed to the southward and mouthed, "Boston men." He spat over the rail to emphasize the last words.

"I think, sir," Kirk said, "that he means that paddling hard, they can just make it to the renegades' camp between sunrise and sunset."

"I see," muttered the captain again. "So if they average five knots, that puts the whites' encampment some fifty miles away. Find out what sort of a guard the whites maintain, Kirk." The use of Eric's surname without the honorific "Mister" indicated the captain's misgivings.

Kirk spoke to the chief again, finding it easier to understand the multilingual parley, and also to make himself understood.

"He says that they keep only a careless guard, sir," he reported to the captain, "and that if they didn't have captives he'd have no trouble surprising them. He says that only a half-dozen are on guard, and that they're drunk most of the time." The chief, watching the captain's face closely, nodded vigorously and pantomimed lifting a bottle to his lips.

The captain smiled — the action like a ray of sun across a storm-swept sea. "Very good, Mister Kirk. Tell them that we are grateful to him for telling us of this breach of the Queen's peace, and that I will come to his village when I have made a decision. Get him to draw you a sketch of some sort of the enemy camp before he departs." He stood and bowed slightly to the chief, who returned the gesture with great dignity.

In his cabin, the captain studied a chart with Commander John Keen. "If we," suggested Keen, "send in a landing party, they'll have to be damned careful not to be seen, or we could cause a mass killing of the captives."

"Right, John, but I need information. We don't know who they are, or what their intentions are. The only thing of which we can be certain is that it's illegal."

"Yes, sir. D'you suppose it has anything to do with the mysterious Fenians?"

"I'll be very surprised if they don't have a finger in the pie." The captain thought for a few moments, the only sound Commander Keen's harsh breathing.

He straightened. "We'll take the chief with us," he said decisively, "and proceed under steam immediately to the Fenian — I'm assuming it is Fenian — camp, arriving well after nightfall. There we'll lie off with the ship darkened and silenced, and send in a landing party to scout the area." He paused to think for a moment. "The chief will have to go with the party to guide them, and young Kirk to interpret. Pick a reliable petty officer and crew for the cutter, and impress on them that they'll have to be back aboard before morning light, so we can get clear."

A knock came on the door, and as they turned to inspect the intruder, Lieutenant Bullen stuck his tired, soot-smeared face inside. "Steam's raised, sir. We can get under way whenever you wish."

Captain Whitfeld-Clements glanced at the bulkhead clock. "It's just past noon. We'll need four hour's steaming to get there, and it's dark by the Second Dog Watch at this time of year. Commander Keen, take the ship as close as possible to the native village, and send Kirk in to get the chief — what's his name, again?"

"Tooshka, sir."

"Right. As soon as Chief Tooshka's aboard, we'll steer for the Fenian area, showing no lights and running silently. Double the lookouts. I want no coaster to blunder into us and run grumbling and whining to his member of parliament. Belay all bells, and warn the hands there's to be no skylarking. Tell the carpenter to muffle the cutter's oars with marline or canvas, or whatever he has to hand."

"Will it be an armed party we send ashore, sir?"

"Cutlasses only. No firearms. I don't want an accidental discharge to put the Fenians on the alert. I leave it in your hands, John. Carry on with it."

"Aye aye, sir."

The shoreline was no more than a distant smudge freckled with spectral surf, only slightly darker than the encompassing murk, as HMS *Calcutta* lay still in the water, rolling gently in the easy ground swell. The captain peered at the barometer: still holding steady. He spoke softly to Commander Keen, "We didn't need a guide, it appears. Look at their huge fires."

"Yes, sir. But Chief Tooshka will know the best landing place, and perhaps where their sentries are posted."

"I suppose so," Whitfeld-Clements whispered savagely. "Dammit, how long have they been gone?"

"Just over two hours, sir. Not to worry — David Duncan's cautious and reliable, and young Kirk's shown his mettle."

"Petty Officer Peebles with them?"

"Yes, sir."

"Good. He's a dependable man."

A low whistle fluttered over the sea's oily surface.

"Show a light there, quickly," quietly ordered Keen. Midshipman Perkins whipped a hurricane lamp from under a tarpaulin shield, raised it quickly twice above the gunwale and as swiftly stowed it away. A blurred black blot appeared.

"Boat ahoy," called Lieutenant Giles softly, his voice barely audible above the velvety rustle of breezes in the rigging.

"Aye aye." The quiet response was only just discernible.

"Send Mister Duncan, Kirk and Chief Tooshka to my quarters as soon as they're aboard," ordered the captain. "When the cutter's hoisted in get under way for the Indian village. Maintain dark and silent status."

"Aye aye, sir."

Fumes from the swaying lamps and a not-unpleasant aroma from Chief Tooshka's robes filled the captain's cabin, as the heavy deadlights over scuttles prevented both the entry of air and the escape of light.

"A number of unusual floating constructions, sir," reported Lieutenant Duncan. "Four or five logs across and about one hundred feet long, with hand rails running fore and aft. They look for all the world like primitive floating bridges, but there are dozens of them, sir."

"With hundreds more logs stacked on the beach," added Kirk, "waiting to be used."

"Bridges!" Whitfeld-Clements exclaimed. "Bridges! I should have guessed. That Fenian Train, with his mad ideas of building a bridge from America to Vancouver Island. No one thought of a floating bridge. Well, I'll scotch his ideas!"

He stood and paced the deck, hands clasped and head bowed beneath the beams. "Mister Kirk, my compliments to all officers not on Watch, and I'll have them here forthwith. You too, to interpret to the chief." He smiled at Tooshka, who grinned in return.

HMS *Calcutta*, six high-prowed war canoes in tow, steamed silently through the gloom, her decks crammed with Indian warriors standing or sitting cheek by jowl with the ship's company. Off the Fenian camp she stopped, while the Indians slid sinuously — almost invisible in the darkness — down into their canoes. At the same time, two cutters were quickly lowered, filled with armed bluejackets and red-coated Royal Marines.

Smoothly the eight craft glided toward the indistinct shoreline, moving slowly to create no wash. Kirk, in the leading cutter, watched the flickering firelight closely as the boats and canoes neared the shore, then whispered quietly but savagely, "Not a word from anyone until the right moment, or I'll have your guts for garters! Right — Petty Officer Peebles, over with you and your men." Six shapes slipped stealthily over the side of the cutter and immediately vanished into the shoreside brush. Kirk waited as he mentally counted the passage of five minutes, then motioned to his remaining men and whistled softly. Indians and sailors moved furtively into the water and likewise vanished in the shadows, leaving one man with each boat.

As Kirk led his small troop through the scattered trees surrounding the palisaded log fort, he felt that the pounding of his heart must surely alarm the Fenians. Putting a cautionary hand behind him to halt his men, he stopped in the shelter of a clump of juniper and crouched to watch the fort's open gates, only a dozen yards distant.

A burst of raucous song shattered the night, "The Wearing o' the Green," and Kirk grinned involuntarily as six motley figures staggered out of the bush into the dim light by the gates.

"Who goes there?" A slurred challenge rumbled from a slouched figure leaning against a post, rifle casually resting in folded arms.

"Shure, an' don't ye have a dhrink fer ol' Paddy McGonigle an' his frens come all this way to sthrike a blow fer ould Oireland?"

"Shtep yez forrud an' let me be havin' a look at yez."

A couple of other figures joined the guard.

The newcomers howled, "Isn't that ould Jabez O'Rourke, now? Misther Train himself sent us to see yez."

"Me name's Jacob, not Jabez, but come up, lads. Is that a bottle I see yez wavin'?" The fellow peered out at them.

"Shure it is, Jacob. Here — be havin' a dhrink," and the brown bottle described a glinting arc through the firelight as the guards rushed to catch it.

Cutlasses flashed lightning as the small group charged the gate. Kirk leaped forward, qualms forgotten, shouting "Now lads — at 'em!" and whooping sailors and shouting warriors scaled the palisades and pounded through the gates.

100

Inside was a hellish inferno. Huge wood fires cast stark shadows on the walls and flickered redly on chained Indian men and women watching fearfully from crude, open-sided log shelters. Redcoated Royal Marines marched, halted, fired, reloaded like clockwork and fired again; warriors swept screeching on dazed, stumbling defenders, waving long knives and bloodied axes as yelling seamen charged with outstretched cutlasses and exploding pistols. Kirk felt sick as he saw an Indian axe thud deep into a man's head, then was himself desperately busy slashing at an upraised rifle that crashed flame into his face. Blinded momentarily by the fire and smoke, he felt his cutlass scrape viciously along metal and strike flesh and bone. As his vision cleared he saw his attacker reel and fall, his cheek laid open to the bone. The imprisoned Indians had come to life and were joining the battle: one huge warrior grabbed a Fenian, wrapped his wrist-chains around the man's neck and calmly strangled him; others attacked with burning stakes, rocks or whatever they could lay hands on.

The battle was short but bloody. Early dawn saw mounds of Fenian bodies piled in heaps, while a scant dozen battered prisoners were herded into a windowless cabin under Royal Marine guard. Kirk stopped a sailor staring grimly at the ruins, blood-light of battle still festering in his reddened eyes, and said, "Here. Hoist this on that tree." Reaching into his torn pocket, he pulled out a crumpled White Ensign and handed it to the seaman.

Captain Whitfeld-Clements was ashore in minutes after the flag was flown. Staring curiously at the shambles, he said curtly, "Well done. Now remove the wounded, have the Fenians bury their dead, and have our dead put aboard ship. You have an hour, no more."

Kirk saluted, "Aye aye, sir!" Looking through red-rimmed eyes for Petty Officer Peebles, he spotted him urging a hulking Fenian back inside the guard cabin with the point of his cutlass. The young sublieutenant ran over to Peebles, and repeated the captain's orders, adding, "Don't hesitate to use a rope's end or a cutlass point to urge them along."

The sound of shovels and picks slamming into the soft earth deadened the petty officer's reply, as a few random rain-drops spattered on Kirk's bare head. He looked up. Clouds were beginning to build ramparts on the horizon, and a crisp breeze began to stir tree tops. The captain beckoned to him.

"Keep the men at it, Mister Kirk. The glass is falling and I want to..." He stopped as Chief Tooshka padded over to him and stood waiting, then spoke hurriedly.

"He wishes to thank you, sir, and tell you he's leaving now." Kirk listened carefully to the chief's low voice, then added, "They'll just make it to their village if they go now. He says there's a big storm brewing and that you should be careful, sir. They've taken care of their dead."

"Tell him," the captain said slowly, "that I am happy to have been able to help him, and that he should tell me when other 'Boston men' do harm to his people."

The expressions of gratitude and farewell took only moments, then the canoes were pulling away, painted paddles flashing in the reddish morning light.

"Now, Mister Duncan," the captain asked quietly, "how many of our people did we lose?"

"Three men, sir. A petty officer and two ratings. All good men, sir."

"Have them taken on board, Mister Duncan. We'll give them proper burial at sea, not lay them alongside these scallawags."

"Aye aye, sir."

Duncan turned away to carry out his orders as the captain shouted to Kirk, "Mister Kirk, have these bridges and logs burned. Set a party to it at once. I want nothing left but ashes!"

Later that day, with the ship stopped and all hands at attention with caps off, Captain Whitfeld-Clements performed the short, poignant service for the three seamen lying under White Ensigns. Three splashes as the bodies were committed to the deep, and the ship slowly got under way, men returning heavy-footed to their duties.

The captain ordered the 12 Fenians brought before him in chains, Marine guards with bayonets fixed prodding them along. The captain glared at the scruffy mob. "Which among you is the leader?"

Silence. The rabble stared at the deck. One spat at the captain's shoes. He ignored the gesture.

"Very good. Pirates are hung. Petty Officer Peebles, reeve a whip with a hangman's noose at the lee main yardarm!"

It was ready in moments. The hush hanging over the decks was deathly.

"Mister Giles, hang these pirates one at a time until one decides that his dirty neck is worth more than silence. Start with that one," he pointed. "I'll be in my cabin. Report to me when one talks or the execution is complete, I don't care which. Tumble the bodies over the side — we'll not bother with a service for such rascals."

Kirk, eyes still red and sore from the night's action and the towering smoke rising from the ashes of the Fenian encampment, willed his aching body to be still and unobtrusive as he glanced at Lieutenant Giles. Giles' mouth opened slightly, then closed with a snap.

"Aye aye, sir!"

Nearby seamen stared at the captain's stiff departing back, and Kirk took a hesitant step after his commanding officer. He was brought to an abrupt halt by a savage whisper from Giles.

"Not one inch more, Mister Kirk!"

Giles turned blazing eyes on a group of men. "Chief Petty Officer Warfield! Start these men to work at once." His voice crackled over the soft sound of wind in the rigging and a gull's muted skreee overlying the chuckle of water below the main chains. The sailors turned to their duties listlessly, as Warfield blistered them verbally.

Strange, thought Kirk, the Fenians were not only unlawful invaders, but murderers whom any court in the land would order hanged without a second's thought, and last night's bitter combat had seen more than one of the bluejackets unflinchingly cut down a Fenian. Still, he mused, that was battle, not cold-blooded execution, and sailors were notoriously sentimental and soft-hearted — some would have it soft-headed — when away from duty.

The captain had just reached the companionway when Kirk's thoughts were interrupted by a hoarse shout, "Never moind, ye bastards! I'll not have ye hangin' me brave lads. 'Tis me, Tom O'Whelan, as is leader. Hang me, ye bloody scuts!"

The captain stopped and turned slowly about. He stared at the speaker, a scraggly-bearded ruffian with a dirty bandage over one eye. The renegade shuffled uneasily as the naval officer gazed silently at him, and opened his mouth to speak. He was peremptorily cut off by Whitfeld-Clements' harsh voice. "Right. Belay the hangings, Mister Giles. Have them locked below again. Sublieutenant Kirk, have Mister O'Whelan brought to my quarters under guard."

" 'Twas Misther Train's plan," the Fenian muttered sullenly, "to have our army gather on Stuart Island, on the American side o' th' straits. Then steam tugs would tow the bridges aroun' an' into position here, an' here, an' here," he pointed with a grimy, black-nailed finger, "from Stuart Island to Gooch Island, then to Forrest Island, an' then to Roberts Point on Vancouver Island. 'Tis no more nor six miles, an' as soon as th' bridges were in place, our lads would charge across — 'twould take but an hour or so. Then we'd march on Victoria, only a dozen miles away, before yez bloody bastards knew we wuz even comin'."

The captain stared wonderingly at the speaker, nose wrinkling at the stench of stale sweat and unwashed clothes emanating from him. "Obviously it was someone else's plan. There's not enough brains among this lot to boil a boot without burning it. Very good. Take him away and put him in with the rest."

Commander Keen and Sublieutenant Kirk stood silently as the captive was led away by the Royal Marines. Keen walked to a scuttle, rolling slightly with the ship's motion, and opened it to let a fresh sea breeze knife through the cabin. "Phew," he muttered, "the stench of them's enough to..."

He was interrupted by the captain, firmly closing the door and saying, "The amazing thing about all this is that their incredible plan could have succeeded. Given good weather for even a day, the bridges could have been in place — and when the Fenians were across, it wouldn't have mattered whether they broke up or not."

"Which they undoubtedly would have, sir, in the least bit of wind," commented Keen.

"And what do you think, young Kirk?" the captain grinned.

"Had they offered to employ Chief Tooshka's people instead of pressing them, sir, we might never have heard of it."

"Quite right." The captain grinned again. "But I think that we can now safely say that the Fenian Train has been de-railed!"

Chapter Seven

"Throw Him in the Brig!"

Eric Kirk, heavily burdened with titles — Midshipman, Royal Navy, also Acting Sublieutenant and temporary Third Lieutenant of HMS *Porpoise,* narrowed his eyes against the early October sun as the 800-ton brig beat out to sea. The full Watch was on deck. Commander Ira Knight, unlike Captain Whitfeld-Clements, was a strict disciplinarian who felt that any show of humanity toward seamen was "mollycoddling". Kirk privately felt that any officer with an insubordination obsession was inefficient and uncertain, but — he was only an acting subbie, and Knight was a full commander.

"Mark you, Mister Kirk," the commander had told him forcefully when the young man had reported aboard as a replacement for the third lieutenant, "I'll have no pampering of the ratings! Give 'em an inch and they'll take a mile. Keep 'em on deck and make 'em work during their Watch. Good hard work'll keep 'em warm."

"Aye aye, sir," Kirk had said, as he was bound to do, but secretly he began wondering whether his temporary appointment was as fortuitous as he'd originally thought. Perhaps Ames, with his broken leg mending in Esquimalt Hospital, was the lucky one.

The southeast breeze hadn't yet brought its normal drizzling cloud, so Vancouver Island was visible. Kirk glanced in the binnacle; the helmsman was precisely on course, west by north, 1/2 north, and the standby was at his elbow, standing properly at ease as the little ship plunged through the long rollers. He lapsed into daydreaming of the day when he would have his own ship, with a private cabin and steward, his own gig, and would be piped aboard —

"Mister Kirk! What is that man doing?"

Kirk shuddered to alertness. The captain had come on deck and was pointing, his eyes glaring and his face flushed, at a sailor who'd huddled his hands momentarily in his pockets to warm them.

"I'll speak to him, sir." Kirk started forward.

"Speak to him, goddam you? You'll do more than speak to him! Stop his grog for the rest of this week, Mister Kirk," snarled Knight, "and if he repeats it, throw him in the brig, sir. Throw him in the brig!" Commander Knight stalked down the companionway, ducking his bullet head as he left the flush deck, and muttering, "Insubordination, the mutinous bastards!"

"Master at Arms," called Kirk. The petty officer doubled across the holystoned deck and saluted.

"Sir?"

"Stop that man's grog until Friday and warn him to be more alert."

"Aye aye, sir!"

Idly Kirk wondered about Knight's use of the American term "brig", then put it down to a chequered background. A merchant captain originally, he'd heard; got a commission in the navy by way of a member of parliament who owed him a debt, or so rumour had it. Kirk shrugged. None of his business. If Knight was a capable officer, that was all that mattered. His mind drifted to wondering about their destination and task. Unlike Clemmie, this Ira Knight kept his own counsel, seldom talking to even his first lieutenant. Of course, Kirk reminded himself, he'd only been aboard a week and had much to learn. He'd keep his eyes open and his mouth closed, until he knew which way the wind was blowing.

"Standby," he said quietly.

The seaman came to attention, not easy on the heaving deck. "Sir?"

"My respects to the captain, and request permission to make it noon." Kirk smiled — inwardly — at the custom which required official permission for the time of day to be accepted.

"Aye aye, sir."

The little brig danced through the westerly swells, thumping and crashing as the southeast wind drove a steep chop over the swell, sheets of spray flying from her clipper bow. She leaned far over to port under the press of all plain sail, her hemp rigging creaking and whistling softly in the wind.

Kirk glanced aloft. Ira Knight was a seaman, no matter his other foibles. The brig's two square-rigged masts were carrying all the sail possible, and the captain had barked a flat "No!" to a request by Loyal Youngberg, first lieutenant, for permission to reef tops'ls. Wanting to compare the smaller vessel's abilities to *Calcutta* — five times her size — Kirk had remained on deck after his relief. He was pleasantly surprised at the manner in which the ship rode over the seas, where *Calcutta* ploughed ponderously through them, shouldering the waves aside with a shrug from her 3,900 tons.

The brig was rigged handily, he decided. Above her courses she carried both double tops'ls and double topgallants — no royals. Forward, three fore-and-afters billowed from her bowsprit and short jib-boom, outer and inner jibs and fore topmast stays'l, while on her mainmast a huge spanker balanced the forward three.

His gaze roamed forward from his position by the mainmast. Four muzzle-loading six-pounders to a side, a two-pound carronade fore and aft. Popguns, he thought, mentally comparing them with *Calcutta's* massive 12-pounders — but *Porpoise* could sail into shallow, narrow inlets denied the larger ship. He could understand now why their Lordships had combined such an unlikely pair into a cruising squadron. Gunpower, that was *Calcutta*. Handiness was *Porpoise's* strength. The young officer was obtaining a dim comprehension of the problems of the Admiralty.

A volley of crisp orders jarred his contemplation, as the captain squared the brig away before the southeast wind.

"Steer west-northwest," he snapped. "Master-at-Arms, take the name of the last man off the yards!"

The brig was now running heavily before the wind, her sharp bows plunging deeply into the troughs, noticeably slowing the ship as the stern lifted and green solid water churned through the hawsepipes. She'd do better with the topgallants clewed up, Kirk thought, but he wouldn't open his mouth for a month's pay! Not while he was off Watch, at any rate. The ever-present mist partly obscured a low, rocky coastline, splintered with breakers foaming white and tumbling in frustrated rage over offshore reefs and shoals. Kirk shuddered as he visualized being caught on a lee shore. *Porpoise* was small and handy; she might be able to claw her way off, but it would be a close thing.

"Sail ho!" The maintop lookout's shout, dulled by the wind, came faintly to the deck. "Broad to port, sir, about ten mile off."

"What's her course, dammit?" Knight scowled up at the hapless seaman. "Give a full report or I'll know why not!"

107

"She's close-hauled, sir. Course 'pears to be a bit south of east. She's a three-masted barque, sir."

Kirk peered in the indicated direction, trying to see but also attempting to stay out of the captain's sight. Nothing was yet visible from the heaving deck.

"Deck there!" It was the lookout again. "The barque's come about, sir. She's heading to close us now."

"Mister Kirk!" Kirk jumped as the captain bit out the order. "As you're on deck skylarking anyhow, get aloft and tell me what you see."

"Aye aye, sir." The young man leaped for the weather shrouds and climbed nimbly to the maintop up the shaking ratlines. He took the proffered telescope, studied the stranger closely and called down, "She's an American, sir, in distress. The ensign's upside-down and she's signalling, sir. I can't quite make out the flags," he added apprehensively.

"Dammit, Mister Kirk, use your eyes or must I look for myself?"

"Sorry, sir..." but Knight had already turned away.

"Yeoman. Hoist the answering pennant at the dip. At the dip, mind you, until Mister Kirk gets the sleep out of his eyes!"

Kirk, face flushed with repressed anger, bit down an angry — and unwise — retort and strained his eyes as the bronzed lookout eyed him sympathetically.

"NC, sir. 'In distress and require assistance'."

"Hoist the pennant close up, yeoman."

Kirk wiped a tear from his wind-whipped eyes, and stared at the American barque again. A new array of flags was being hoisted. "There's more, sir," he shouted down. "It's spelled out. 'Require food'."

"Lieutenant Youngberg! Bring the ship to the wind and heave to! Mister Smith!" Looking down, Kirk saw that the second lieutenant, woken from his usual torpor by the commotion, had emerged into the light. "Mister Smith," the captain roared again, "have two casks of salt beef, two bags of potatoes and a bag of onions swayed up on deck. A small cask of lime juice, too. Move, dammit!"

"Shove off, bows. Give way together." Kirk shoved the tiller over, feeling the polished wood smooth in his hand as the cutter rolled and pitched heavily alongside the brig. Weighted down by the half-ton of supplies, the double-banked pulling boat sloshed through a choppy sea toward the barque lying hove-to a half-mile away.

Kirk sprang into the main chains as the cutter eased alongside, and climbed on deck. He was shocked by the gaunt faces, and saw that the tell-tale swollen joints and missing teeth of scurvy were rampant among the crew. "Three men on deck, here," he called down to the cutter. "Reeve a tackle and get that food aboard smartly."

The barque's crew, staggering as the ship rolled, stared hungrily as the provisions were hoisted aboard. They lurched to the side and the hollow-cheeked mate ordered, "Bear a hand there, men. Don't let the limeys do it all."

"I'm the master. Daniels is the name." A frock-coated wraith stood at Kirk's side, looking up at the tall young man. He extended his hand, "Come to my cabin, sir." Kirk introduced himself as they walked aft.

Seated, the captain explained his predicament. "The barque, *Southern Cross*, Iquique toward Seattle with nitrates. We were becalmed two weeks in the doldrums, then contrary winds kept heading us — including this one. We went on half-rations ten days back, and ran out two days ago. We managed to catch a shark and a couple of gulls, but..." As the captain droned on, Kirk could hear the munchings and growls as the starving sailors tore into the uncooked vegetables and slurped the lime juice. He interrupted.

"Captain. Please wait." Kirk stood, walked quickly to the cabin door and shouted, "Leading Seaman Roberts! Bring some onions and potatoes here, quickly — and a pannikin of lime juice, too."

When the sailor appeared with the food, Kirk motioned to the table. "Set it there. Captain Daniels, please eat." He hesitated, "I'm sorry, but my captain wishes a signature for the goods... so that your company can be invoiced." He pulled a slip of paper from his pocket, heartily wishing he were elsewhere.

The merchant seaman's eyebrows rose slightly, but he found a pen and inkwell, and signed without comment, kindly ignoring the naval officer's embarrassment.

"Thank you, sir. I must return."

"Here, Mister Kirk," the American grasped his sleeve, "a glass of rum before you go. Plenty of rum aboard, and a good thing, too. Kept the crew from mutinying!"

The *Southern Cross* slowly fell astern in the mists as *Porpoise* proceeded on her way. Roger Smith, privately considered somewhat of a lout by Kirk, had the Watch. The captain, Kirk noticed, had begun popping out on deck like a jack-in-the-box, staring harshly around and then disappearing below again without a word.

Chewing on a plateful of cold beef in the tiny wardroom, Kirk asked Lieutenant Youngberg, "Do you have any idea where we're bound, sir?"

"Not a penny's worth," Youngberg grinned. "We never do until we get there."

"Clemmie always lets us know," began Kirk, "and it'd seem..." He hushed as he caught the other's warning frown.

The steward, short, black-haired, wearing a perpetual insincere smile on a round, oily face, bustled in. "Shall I clear the table, sir?"

Youngberg nodded.

Kirk's ears caught, faintly, the "ting" of the warning bell. "I'd better go on deck," he muttered. "I've got the Second Dog."

Youngberg rescued a platter of biscuits as the brig rolled heavily. "Yes," he grinned, "try not to put us aground."

"It'd be a change from this dull routine!"

"Careful," the lieutenant whispered, "everything he hears goes directly to the captain." He nodded at the steward, vanishing through the door.

Kirk walked up to the morose Smith. "Are there any special orders?"

"No." Smith gave him the course and went below as the bell sounded the change of the Watch.

Three days passed in the monotonous routine. Commander Knight seemed to have no schemes, or even desire, to keep the ship's company alert and interested, nor did he order his officers to take action. No fiddlers, no games, no practice shots. Just the incessant wheel, lookout, overhauling gear and holystoning already pristine decks. Kirk wondered, but wisely kept his own counsel. The brig left the treed, rocky shores of Vancouver Island dropping into the grey haze, and sailed into the open wastes of the inconstant North Pacific. Monotony continued: eat, sleep, stand Watch. Eat, sleep again, and back on Watch. Nothing to do during leisure time except try to read or watch endless grey Pacific rollers marching steadily across the grey horizon, or the very occasional backgammon game with Gosling in the gunroom. Only once was a spark of interest shown by the officers, when Kirk mentioned the Fenian bridge to Vancouver Island.

"What was their plan?" asked Smith, dull eyes momentarily lighting. "Were they planning to capture the entire island?"

"I don't know. Train — his full name was George Francis Train — sparked the idea, but didn't want to be directly involved. I doubt if the whole story will ever come to light."

"Oh," commented Smith, and forthwith lapsed into his usual apathy as Kirk wondered if Knight had driven out his spirit.

"Land ho!" The shout brought men tumbling on deck, looking excitedly about.

"Where away?" Kirk, leaning back and squinting at the maintop, shouted up over the hubbub.

"Broad on the starboard bow, sir!"

HMS *Porpoise* pranced through the long westerly swells, sharp stem slicing the waves like a hot knife through Devon butter. The sun, hidden for a week, glinted on the brig's sails as steam rose in twisting curlicues from her damp decks. The wind, southeast since leaving harbour, had finally veered westerly that morning, sending the low clouds scurrying over the horizon.

"Mister Kirk," Commander Knight had come on deck and was, strangely enough, smiling. "That is Cape St. James. Have the helm put up and steer east-nor'east. Call me when the cape lies on our port quarter." He padded below as Kirk shouted orders to lay the brig on her new course, and stole quick glances at the Queen Charlotte Islands.

Porpoise bounced along like a live thing, surging ahead in the following sea as her masts described great swinging arcs. In less than ten hours the cape's massive, mountainous bulk lay on their quarter, and Kirk reported to the captain.

"Very good, Mister Kirk," Knight didn't look up from his papers. "Have the helm put down and steer north. At latitude 53° 15' we will stand in toward shore. Should this wind hold, that will be about noon tomorrow. Notify your relief."

"Aye aye, sir. Captain, sir...could you tell me where we're bound?"

Commander Knight slammed his fist on the desk, sending papers fluttering to the deck. "You'll learn that in good time, Kirk! Carry on and don't bother me with goddam questions!"

All the following day the sun stayed bright, and the seamen brought tubs to the foredeck for washing clothes. Kirk was apprehensive about the captain's reaction to wet garments hanging to dry, but Knight said not a word. The brig reached up Hecate Strait past a myriad islets and inlets. Kirk noted a plume of steam rising from one, and pointed it out to the dour Smith, who remarked, "Yes. Hmmm," and lapsed into his usual silence.

Just before noon Lieutenant Youngberg showed a freshly shaved face on deck. He glanced around the horizon before opening the hinged mahogany box he carried carefully, and removing his sextant. As the sun approached its zenith, he raised the instrument to his eye and took several sights, calling his readings to Smith, who noted them stoically.

The captain came up, watching closely as the first lieutenant averaged his readings. "53° 14' 30"," he muttered. "Close enough. Mister Youngberg, bring the ship to the wind and steer northwest."

"Aye aye, sir." Crisply Youngberg barked the necessary commands, and the brig stood close-hauled toward a gaping inlet, leaning far to starboard as she drove through the short, steep seas.

Slowly the ship neared the inlet, which they could now see was protected by a long, low sandy finger stretching northward from the southernmost point. The sea, a lighter green in the shallow water, was dashing against the spit and splintering into grey-white foam as it receded bubbling and churning from the sand, leaving fading streaks etched momentarily. Dark green hills rose from the low shores. Smoke climbed skyward from a few scattered fires along the beach, while a rancid odour drifted from a ramshackle, weathered wooden structure at the head of a secluded cove.

"I will take over, Mister Youngberg." Commander Knight glanced at the menacing bar, foaming white now as seas crashed over it a scant cable to windward. "Send the hands to the braces, and stand by the main yards yourself. We will steer south into the bay after rounding the bar. When I give an order I'll flog any sluggard — officer or seaman!"

"Aye aye, sir." The response was automatic, but Loyal Youngberg's eyes flickered nervously at the treacherous sandbar.

"Mister Kirk, stand by the fore yards. Jump, damn you!"

"Aye aye, sir!" Kirk galloped forward, boots pounding a crescendo on the teak deck.

"Down helm!" The captain studied the bar closely as the brig straightened. Two seamen at the wheel spun the spokes frantically to port; the jib-boom raked past the shoreline as the ship came up into the wind, headsails booming.

Kirk stared at the thundering sandbar, now almost under the bows. He clutched the rail, feeling a touch of security from its sturdy smoothness. He cautioned his six sailors to be ready.

"Mainsail haul!" Sweating seamen cast off sheets and braces, hauling the huge main yards around. The brig swung faster and faster, ropes singing and creaking through blocks. She was through the wind's eye now, and the fore yards, fully aback, forced the bows to leeward.

"Let go and haul!"

"Jump to it, men!" Kirk shouted as he too heaved on a sheet, hearing a seam rip in his sleeve as he strained but paying no attention. Straining and cursing, the men heaved the fore yards around and the brig lurched, then gathered way on her new course, the raging bar now lying close to leeward, but falling farther astern as the brig raced for the sandy southern shore.

"Mister Kirk, clear away the starboard anchor! Smartly now — I'll be going about again shortly."

The brig's decks for the next hour were a frenzy of sweating, hauling, cursing, stumbling seamen and raging officers as the captain brought the vessel about, around a line of ragged reefs and tiny, rocky islets, then dropped anchor off the Haida village known as Haina, on Maude Island. Saturnine totem poles watched silently as the equally silent captain stalked to his cabin, and exhausted men fell to the decks without a word of reprimand from any officer.

Watching bronzed Haidas straggle down to the pebbled grey beach and ease their great carved cedar canoes into the rippled water, Kirk glanced back up Skidegate Inlet at the maelstrom of turbulent ocean cascading over the bar. He turned to Youngberg quizzically, "What now, sir?"

Youngberg shrugged. "We'll find out when he decides to tell us." He hesitated, "Call me Loyal when we're alone."

Eric grinned. "That's almost the first word of welcome I've had aboard this sorry tub!"

The first canoe came alongside, eager brown arms reaching out to clutch the brig's sides. It was followed by another, then another, until six of the canoes — each almost 40 feet in length — were rocking gently against the ship's hull.

Commander Knight's cabin door slammed as he marched out, closely followed by his obsequious steward struggling with a wooden chest almost as big as himself. "Mister Kirk, I understand that you have some knowledge of the native language. Tell them we'll allow ten of them aboard, including the chief."

"Aye aye, sir." Wondering how he'd been identified as a translator, with only the short contact during the Spanish treasure and the Fenian events to help his very limited knowledge, Kirk leaned over the gunwale and mustered every scrap of a foreign language he could. Fortunately, the chief was easily identified, so by using bits of English, Russian, Spanish and native dialect from Nootka Sound, he was able to convey the captain's directive.

During the parley, the steward had laid out an array of trade goods on deck — blankets, knives, old uniforms, muskets and beads — which started the Haidas chattering gutturally as they clambered over the ship's rail. At a quick word from Lieutenant Youngberg, seamen lined the ship's sides to forestall additional boarders.

Kirk was fascinated by the Haida warriors. Their glowing dark skin, and deep black eyes looking out of alert, intelligent faces impressed him. Woven hats, from cedar bark, he guessed, covered their heads, while some wore furs slung over muscular shoulders, and others had a kilt-like garment made from the same material as the hats. Bare feet padded on the unfamiliar deck as they inspected the trade items and one or two fingered a sailor's clothes.

The Haida chief majestically ignored the scattered goods lying on deck and, instantly selecting the captain, approached him. He passed close to Kirk, who sniffed at an agreeable scent of woodsmoke, dried fish and cedar as the Indian walked by. Ignoring all others, the chief spoke at length to Knight, waving an imperious arm toward the shore, and particularly in the direction of a magnificent cedar longhouse with a tendril of smoke rising from a hole in the roof.

Commander Knight raised an eyebrow at Kirk, who slowly said, half guessing, "He wants you to visit his lodge, sir. He calls it the 'house which always welcomes guests'. He wishes to do you honour, sir, and invite you to a feast." The chief looked at Kirk, and

114

with a trace of a smile, added a few more words. "He wishes all of the officers to come too, sir. He will give many gifts."

"Very good," Knight seemed to make up his mind suddenly. "Tell him that these presents are for him, and that we have more, but that we are looking for rocks such as this." He opened a tiny purse and removed a pebble streaked with veins of gold.

Kirk and the chief exchanged a few more words, with many gestures, then the young officer said, "He thinks it's funny, sir. They have lots of the rock. He says that they moved here from another shore, where there is much of this, and that they brought a lot of the funny rock with them."

"Tell him, Mister Kirk, that we'll accept his offer with pleasure — or whatever you think he'd like to hear."

Rattling drums and stamping, chanting dancers in the murky, smoke-filled longhouse shook the earth floor and vibrated the wood platters of smoking salmon and venison, as Commander Knight, with Youngberg, Smith and Kirk sat on benches cut into the soil. They nodded dreamily as they munched on continually filled plates of berries, clams, oysters, deer-meat and fish, watching the prancing, spear-waving dancers as they leaped. Midshipman Gosling had been left on Watch: the brig had only one snotty. Kirk wondered idly whether his friend was sorry to have missed the feast, or happy to be free of Commander Knight's irritable presence.

When at last Knight stood to indicate that the British must leave, Chief Taglis escorted the officers to the cutter, where the boat crew sat damp and shivering, even though a nearby fire threw flickers of warmth. Warriors bore the gifts of furs, fish and copper, standing while the chief made a gesticulating speech of farewell at great length.

In response to the captain's querying glance, Kirk translated, "The chief says we'll meet in the morning, sir, to trade for the gold."

"I see. Very well, Mister Kirk, tell him good night and offer our thanks."

A gentle rain pattered on the still harbour in the morning, as the cutter's wake traced triangles on the flat surface. In the stern-sheets, Commander Knight sat stoically at the tiller, while Kirk perched atop a bulky bundle of tarpaulin-wrapped blankets, and the captain's steward crouched in the bow. On the sloping beach, smoke curled upward, while Indians stood awaiting the boat's arrival. Women and children moved in and out of the longhouses, gathering firewood and readying the day's food, while the village elders, secure in years and respect, hobbled stiffly to the shore to join the younger men around the fire.

As four seamen strained to lift the bundle of blankets over the gunwale and carry it ashore, splashing through the shallow water, Knight snapped at them, "You four stay here with cutlasses. Remainder lie off in the cutter within earshot."

Kirk's eyes glazed as he saw the heap of gold ore piled in the deep, carved cedar chest. Gods — there must be a hundred pounds of it — much of it almost pure gold!

The captain strolled casually to the chest, sword tinkling as it touched a couple of pebbles, stooped and carefully picked up two nuggets. Studying them with pursed lips, he contemptuously dropped them and said to Kirk, "Tell them I'll give one blanket for the whole pile."

"Sir," Kirk exclaimed, "It's..."

"Shut your mouth and do as I say! Goddam your eyes!"

Kirk swallowed a savage retort that would have cost him his commission instantly, and laboriously began. His initial foray into the world of barter brought shock, then laughter, to the Haidas' faces, but the business developed, so that by noon an amiable bargain was struck. Chief Taglis signed that the naval officers should accompany him to the longhouse for the noon meal, and led the way.

"Cox'n," ordered Knight, "return to the ship and draw food from the galley and bring it here. You four," he indicated the armed seamen, "and you," to his steward, "remain here."

Halfway through the repast, a hullaballoo broke out, plainly audible even within the longhouse. Both Indians and whites, in considerable consternation, jumped up, crowding through the narrow entrance, and stampeding pell-mell to the beach, where they saw the steward writhing in the grip of two burly seamen.

"What's all this?" Knight's face was black with anger.

"Beggin' yer pardon, sir," the cox'n saluted, "we just come back an' this lot," he waved at the guards, "was helpin' us get the grub ashore when I sees this little rat stealin' some of the gold, so I grabbed the bloody Dago bastard."

Chief Taglis, scowling, nudged the captain, making a slicing motion across his throat with a gnarled finger. Knight shook his head as the captive cringed, whimpering.

"We'll return to the ship. Mister Kirk, express my pleasure to the chief for his company, and our sorrow that we must leave immediately."

The brig weighed anchor and sailed with the ebb tide, accompanied as far as the sandspit by a cluster of canoes. Commander Knight, with the steward, disappeared into his cabin immediately after the twittering bo's'n's calls had piped him aboard. He'd said shortly, "Take the ship out, Mister Youngberg. Return to Esquimalt. Call me when we're abeam of Cape St. James. Have the gold placed in my cabin."

Commander Knight came on deck only twice during the return passage. When told that the cape was abeam, he'd simply nodded and given curt orders to head southward; on the second occasion he'd come on deck, glanced aloft, and gone below again without a word.

Kirk made a few enquiries among the petty officers, found a pigtailed old sailor who was a fiddler, and daringly ordered hornpipes on deck during his Watch on a fine day. He half-expected Knight to arrive storming on deck to order the festivity ceased but nothing happened — even though Smith and Loyal Youngberg continually cast apprehensive looks at the captain's closed door and Gosling was obviously nervous.

HMS *Porpoise* entered Juan de Fuca Strait, beat up to Esquimalt against a spanking easterly, and anchored in the roadstead in a lashing rain squall late at night. "We'll wait for the morning tide," Youngberg decided. "I'll not risk trying to enter tonight." He added in a whisper to Kirk, "Especially when he refuses to take command!"

At first light, however, the captain appeared on deck. "Signal for a tug, Mister Kirk. We'll not dally out here with the gold aboard."

Two hours saw *Porpoise* snugged against a quay, and the ship's company scattered over the masts like a flock of crows, putting harbour furls on the sails and overhauling rigging. The captain had reverted to his accustomed abusive self during the tow: "Dammit Mister Youngberg, an old woman with palsy could handle the ship

117

better!" All officers and many seamen received the bitter vituperation, and a collective sigh of relief swept the brig when at last it was secured, and the captain stalked over the side to the high-pitched chirping of bo's'n's calls.

As Knight reached the brow, he snapped over his shoulder, "Mister Youngberg. Have the gold brought from my cabin. Mister Kirk, have the goodness to summon my steward. I'll have six armed men for escorts. I trust that you gentlemen can see to that without error — or shall I have my steward show you how?"

Lieutenant Smith had been standing by, even the bright sunshine failing to enliven his lacklustre face, waiting a chance to speak.

"What is it, Mister Smith?" The captain had halted in the middle of the gangplank. "Have you lost the anchor during the night?"

"No, sir," Smith mumbled. "Two seamen run during the night, sir. Able Seamen Abido and Tingle, sir, and your gig's missing."

As the captain opened his mouth, Youngberg ran up, boots pounding a tattoo. "The gold's gone, sir," he shouted, breathing heavily, "and..."

He was interrupted by Kirk, "Captain, sir, your steward's missing. I had the ship searched, sir."

Knight stood, face pale, mouth opening and closing like a stranded fish. Slowly his face purpled. "What!?"

Kirk watched, fascinated. He'd heard of men becoming livid, but this was his first actual experience.

"That treacherous bastard — I picked him starving off the beach, and this is what he — goddam thief!" Knight yanked off his cap and dashed it to the deck, where it rolled slowly along, teetered a moment, then slipped over the side. The soft "plop" as it hit the water was loud in the sudden silence.

Kirk stepped to the rail. The cap had landed smack on top of a particularly noisome mass of flotsam. "Looks like a new cap, sir," he observed brightly, knowing as he said it that it was most unwise.

Knight came back aboard. He marched up to Kirk, staring at him face to face for several interminable seconds. Kirk recoiled from the captain's breath. Shoving his face even closer, as the younger man tried to refrain from breathing, Knight shouted, "You may return to your ship, Mister Kirk!" He added, only slightly less raucously, "I am less than pleased with your efforts aboard my ship, and will tell your captain as much!"

118

Kirk stood, stunned, as the captain turned abruptly and entered his cabin, slamming the door behind him with a report that echoed through the ship. Kirk went slowly below and gathered his gear, a solitary tear mingling with a flush of rage. A tap on the door preceded Loyal Youngberg, who wordlessly picked up Kirk's seabag and carried it to the brow, then as silently shook his hand in farewell.

"Well, young man, are you happy to be back aboard?" His captain smiled at Kirk as *Calcutta* steamed past the jetty.

"Yes, sir! Very much. Captain, sir...what was the story behind the gold?"

Captain Whitfeld-Clements gave a quiet order to the helmsman, then looked at Kirk. "Knight didn't tell you? I suspected as much. Well, some 30 years ago the schooner, *Susan Sturges*, during the Queen Charlottes' gold rush, bought a considerable amount of gold from the Haidas. However, the crew became avaricious and attempted to raid the Haidas' mine, with the result that the Indians attacked the schooner, plundered and burned her, and took the crew captive."

He paused for a moment, studied the green shoreline drifting past, then noticed the small group of officers clustered nearby, trying to appear casual. "So, gentlemen, you're all interested. The crew, it seems, were unharmed, but the whereabouts of the plundered gold was never discovered, and it was thought that it had gone to the bottom with the schooner."

He turned his attention to the ship's course for a moment. "Starboard five, helmsman...steady. Keep her there."

The officers waited, and so, noticed Kirk, did the helmsman and a petty officer who had drifted within earshot. "Just a month ago," the captain continued, "word was received from a trader that a Haida village in Skidegate Inlet had gold to sell — but only to Her Majesty. Apparently they'd had their fill of Yankee traders. And the result was, gentlemen, that *Porpoise* was dispatched to recover the gold — with the unhappy outcome with which Mister Kirk is familiar."

"But wasn't the gold strike on the Pacific side, sir? Skidegate Inlet's on Hecate Strait."

"Correct, Mister Duncan. But when the Haida population began decreasing, a number of small villages moved, and this one brought the gold with it."

119

"If I may ask, sir," it was Commander Keen, "what will happen to Commander Knight?"

"I won't presume to anticipate the Admiralty Court's decision," Whitfeld-Clements smiled, "but perhaps Mister Kirk has an answer."

"Throw him in the brig, sir. Throw him in the brig!" Kirk's voice trembled with repressed anger and remembered humiliation.

"I suspect that your vehemence has an underlying meaning, Mister Kirk, but I think that we'll not discuss it at this time."

HMS *Calcutta* steamed on into the morning haze and mist, which turned Esquimalt's crude structures into faerie castles, and Sublieutenant Kirk's thoughts drifted away from Commander Knight and on to pleasanter subjects — Geraldine Willoughby. How could he ever-so-casually put the thought of a reception on board into the mind of Lieutenant Duncan? Who would then, he hoped, suggest it to the commander who would, in his turn, bring it up to the captain — and, of course, it was a foregone conclusion that the Willoughbys would receive an invitation. He smiled happily.

Chapter Eight

Money in the (Sand) Bank

Brow furrowed, chewing his lower lip, Eric Kirk groaned aloud in frustration and helplessness as he draped his long frame over the gunroom table. In front of him, below the dimly glimmering yellow light of the oil lamp, several sheets of paper were held firmly in place by his seamanship manual, and another, well spattered with ink blots and calculations, was the subject of his present concentration.

The ship was quiet. Only the gentle squeaking of manila fenders holding HMS *Calcutta* away from the Esquimalt jetty, and a soft slap of harbour wavelets against the wooden hull, disturbed the silence. Following Sunday Divisions, the church had been rigged for mandatory services, then liberty had been piped for all but the Duty Watch. First ashore had been the boisterous midshipmen, lightheartedly carrying with them Kirk's solemn injunction, as Sub of the Mess, to behave themselves and return on time. On deck, Midshipman Reg Perkins, standing disconsolate duty in the warm autumn sun, watched the ship's company rollicking down the road, dust hanging in the air behind them like a grey mist.

"Damn," Kirk muttered. "I get five pounds and three shillings every month — where does it go?" He lifted his head and studied the list from farther back, hoping that the different aspect would disclose a happy error. He searched his pockets again, finding nothing but a button and a piece of lint. His chair scraped on the wooden deck as he tilted it back to study the list from an even greater distance.

Written out, his list looked like this:

Messing	£1 10s
Wine	10s
Band	2s
Naval Club ashore	4s
Library	1s
Washing	10s
Servant	10s
Hammock-man	3s
Jam, cookies, etc.	10s
	£4 00s

"I should have a pound and three shillings left, but..." He thought about looking through his pockets again, but ruefully discarded the idea.

"Oh, well," he reflected, standing, and quickly ducking to avoid a stunning blow against the low beams overhead, "I might as well take a stroll ashore." Gathering the papers, he stuffed them into his battered oak sea-chest, and slammed the lid shut. Climbing through the companionway, he squinted momentarily in the sun's glare.

"Oh, sub," Reg Perkins called from his job of supervising seamen painting an overturned cutter on the jetty, "are you going ashore?"

Kirk tossed a salute as he crossed the ship's side, and walked toward the midshipman, "I believe I will. Why?"

Perkins extended his hand. "Would you like the five shillings I borrowed last month? I got some money from home in the post yesterday, along with the usual caution that it doesn't grow on trees."

Suddenly the sun shone brighter and the world was a better place. Kirk grabbed the coins from Perkins' hand and was gone, leaving the snotty staring after him, perplexed.

HMS *Porpoise* was berthed directly astern of *Calcutta*. Kirk strode alongside, nodded to the petty officer on duty and called through cupped hands, "Clarence!" A tousled head rose above the ship's rail.

"Oh, it's you, Eric. What d'you want?"

"Come for a stroll ashore and a glass of sherry at the Naval Club."

Clarence Gosling took a deep breath and a step, then he halted, face falling. "Sorry. Not much reason. I don't have so much as a penny!"

"Not to worry — one of the warts just paid me back five shillings!"

"Right! Wait one minute."

Actually three minutes elapsed before Gosling, newly risen to Temporary Acting Sublieutenant following Commander Knight's relief, hurried over the brow with a tossed salute, buttoning his jacket and grinning.

"Where away, my pecunious friend?"

"I think," said Kirk solemnly, "that we might honour the club with our presence for a sherry, then Ho! for the sights of Esquimalt."

In the distance a cornucopia of dust curled into the windless air, and slowly a horse and carriage appeared at its head. They recognized the captain, and as the rig drew nearer, stood to one side to give it room. Whitfeld-Clements pulled up beside them, and dust rose chokingly in the still air, then settled softly on leaves, grass and the two young officers. "Sorry about that," he grinned from beneath the canvas protection of the carriage's top, "and where are you two young fellows bound for?"

Saluting quickly, Kirk answered, "Strolling through the town, sir, and thought we might have a sherry at the club."

The captain looked at them. "Don't terrorize the natives, then. I wanted to speak to you two, and this is as good a time as any." He pulled gently on the reins as his horse moved uneasily, and rested his booted feet on the dashboard. "Give some thought to a pulling-boat race for the ships' companies. Perhaps you should discuss it this afternoon," he smiled, "while you're strolling. Let Commander Keen and Lieutenant Youngberg know what you decide, and what equipment is needed."

"Aye aye, sir."

"All right, then. Carry on." The captain shook the reins as the pair saluted, and the carriage moved toward the jetty, rattling and squeaking.

Later, settled in wicker chairs in a corner of the Naval Club, with paintings of ancient admirals frowning from darkly panelled walls, and as distant as possible from a pair of retired, crusty officers heatedly arguing tactics over port and ginger, the two discussed Captain Whitfeld-Clements' instructions. "I suppose that he's thinking about the men getting restless," Clarence mused, "but we've only had two weeks alongside."

"Hmmm," Eric stroked his chin, "although we've been cruising quite steadily, with a fair amount of action..."

"Ahh! You've had the action. *Porpoise* has been mostly lying off while *Calcutta*'s had the fun," Gosling expostulated. "But I suppose if Clemmie wants games, we'd better organize something."

"Right. You ask Lieutenant Youngberg if this coming Thursday is acceptable, and I'll sound out the commander."

"All right, Eric. Two whalers from each ship, d'you think?"

"Yes. Let's make it an event they'll remember. Clemmie will say there's to be no gambling, but you know what Jolly Jack is like — he'll bet on the sun coming up if there's nothing else. Let's have a *Calcutta* whaler race against one of yours, then repeat it with a second whaler from each ship..."

"Then," interrupted Gosling, "we can match the two winners against each other and the losers the same..."

"And then the final winner against the final loser?"

"Why not? And as a grand finish we could have all four boats in a sprint."

"And award points for each race to decide the champion boat, with extra points for the winner of the four-boat match."

Their voices rose as they grew more excited, planning details of the events, when they suddenly noticed the white-jacketed, skeletal-faced waiter hovering over them like an avenging hawk. He extended a silver platter with one clawlike hand, and nodded at the lone engraved card resting there.

"The h'admiral's compliments, sirs," he whispered huskily, "and 'e would h'appreciate a little decorum within the club."

The two youths stood, quickly if clumsily. "Our apologies to the admiral," said Kirk softly. "We're about to leave." Abashed, they sidled rapidly to the door and slipped out into the brightness of early afternoon.

"Would you be the starter, sir? We'll ask Mister Youngberg to officiate at the finish line, and the captain to award the prizes."

Commander Keen looked at the two sublieutenants standing anxiously before him on the quarterdeck. "I suppose so. Come and tell me where you plan the course." He turned, leading the way to his cabin. Inside, he spread a chart on a polished desk, weighting the corners to hold it in place.

Kirk touched a finger to the paper. "The start will be here, sir, right off the point so everyone will have a good view. They'll pull 'round a buoy two cables to the northeast — and they'll have to be alert," Kirk grinned at the senior officer, "or they'll go on the 'putty', because it shoals steeply a few fathoms inside the mark. Then they'll reverse course to the southwest and pull for the finish line — two buoys anchored a half-cable west of the starting line."

"What about the point system for winners?"

Clarence Gosling answered, "Five points for the winners of the first two heats, sir, another five for the winner of the third race..."

"Which will be the losers of the first two heats, sir," Kirk interrupted, "and..."

"Ten points for the first boat in, in the fourth race," continued Gosling. "We thought of awarding the prize then, sir."

"Which is?"

"This, sir." Kirk held high a sailor's brilliantly polished boot, into which was fastened a foot-high, varnished, crowing wooden rooster. "It's the 'Cock o' the Walk'."

Gosling interjected diffidently, "We thought perhaps something special for the winning team — a weekend liberty, sir?"

"I'll speak to the captain. Now, wasn't there something said earlier about a four-boat race?"

Kirk grinned. "Yes...we thought this should be fun, sir — a race with no holds barred. The crews could use sails, right-of-way tactics, whatever they can think up without causing harm to themselves or damage to the boats."

Keen chuckled, his voice like the rippling of water past the cutwater of a sailboat. Kirk wondered idly if people took on the characteristics of objects of long association, then snapped to awareness. Commander Keen had asked him a question.

Thinking comet-swiftly, Kirk realized that he'd heard "Entry fees" spoken, and guessing, answered, "We'd thought of charging an entry fee of six shillings per boat, sir — winner take all."

Keen frowned. "No, I don't like that idea. Some men send home all their pay except for a few pennies for tobacco and slops. It might create hardship, and that could engender bad feelings. I'll discuss this with the captain. Perhaps the ships will sponsor prizes. That'll do, then," he turned away, adding over his shoulder, "See the bo's'n about any ship's gear that you need, and tell him that I said you're to have it."

"Aye aye, sir. Thank you."

As Sublieutenant Kirk paced the quarterdeck during the First Watch, Commander Keen approached. "The captain will be the starter, Kirk, and I'll award prizes. He's personally donating two guineas as a prize for the last race, and approves the idea of a no-holds-barred event. The wardrooms have said they'll donate cash prizes for the other races, and oh, yes, the captain has agreed that guests will be invited. Does that please you? Thursday is suitable, weather permitting, and the master-at-arms should have defaulters lay out the course buoys and pick them up later. Tots will be issued ashore at six bells in the Forenoon Watch, and you are to see that refreshment tables are set up for guests of the officers and men. Tea and coffee only, with sandwiches. No liquor."

"Aye aye, sir."

"Very good, then. Good night, sub."

"Good night, sir." They exchanged salutes, and the commander padded away, slippers silent on the teak deck, alone with his enduring grief.

The gently sloping green of the grassy headland was black with sailors cheering, jeering, talking and laughing. One or two had laid claim to convenient stumps, while a few surveyed the quiet blue water of Esquimalt harbour from precarious perches in massive fir trees. A gentle breeze sent wavelets lapping at the clinker hulls of the four whalers, and tendrils of smoke from a hundred pipes curling and twisting overhead, blending with the softly vanishing morning mist and the hum of small talk from mingling guests.

Two of the boats, white hulls gleaming a rippled reflection in the water, drifted lazily well downwind of the starting line, which was marked by a red spar buoy to port, and a raised dais ashore. Captain Whitfeld-Clements stood on the latter, starting pistol in hand, eying the boats. The other two craft, varnished oars poised in the tanned hands of seamen alertly awaiting the signal for the first vital, heaving stroke, hovered only feet from the line — pictures of wire-taut tenseness. As the captain raised his pistol, the cox'ns firmed their grips on the tillers, warily watching each other and the captain.

The pistol cracked. Backs bent and oars dipped deep in swirling water, sending the boats surging ahead as the cox'ns hoarsely barked the stroke. Roars of encouragement and derision echoed and re-echoed off the low mossy cliffs on the opposite shore, then diminished to a rumble as the boats, neck-and-neck, rounded the half-way point. Cheering rose again to a crescendo; the sweating sailors, sunlight glinting on their bare torsoes and urged on by feverishly barking cox'ns, heaved and pulled for the finish line. A hush. Then a triumphant thunder of applause as Lieutenant Loyal Youngberg flourished his flag downward with a swoop, announcing with a somewhat rueful shout, "*Calcutta* wins!" A startled yelp arose from the winning boat, followed by a tremendous splash as the cox'n was thrown into the cold water. Surfacing, he started for the cutter, then thought better of it and swam easily for the nearby shore, where eager hands helped him out and restoratives were quickly but furtively poured down his willing throat.

Good humour and high spirits were everywhere throughout the ensuing three races. Number Two *Porpoise* whaler won a hands-down victory when *Calcutta*'s stroke oar caught a crab, tumbling into the whaler's bilges and throwing the rhythm out completely. *Calcutta* redeemed herself in the third event, finishing a full length ahead, but *Porpoise* won over-all honours when her Number Two boat edged in a nose ahead in the fourth race.

Commander Keen congratulated the perspiring winners, who exuberantly bore off their Cock o' the Walk trophy to the head of the line forming for tots.

Following the rum issue, and a half-hour Stand-easy, Captain Whitfeld-Clements again mounted the dais to announce the hitherto secret conditions for the fifth and final race. As he spoke, raising his voice over the growing chuckles and snickers of the men, Lieutenant Last, newly appointed second lieutenant of *Porpoise*, replacing the crippled Ames, walked grinning up to Kirk, where he stood protectively beside Geraldine. Touching his cap to the girl, he said, "A bet, sub — on the last race?"

"What odds, sir?" Kirk was suddenly cautious. "Your boat won the trophy." Geraldine glanced suspiciously at Last, but kept quiet.

"Fair's fair. I'll give you two to one — how's that?"

Kirk searched his pockets, recalling his impoverished state, and located three lone shillings. "This is all I have until our next pay — but I'll put them up."

"Done!" Last grinned at the apprehensive young pair, "I'll be back after the race to collect!"

"That remains to be seen, sir..." but Last had already disappeared into the crowd, chuckling to himself.

The sharp-sweet aroma of Navy rum drifted through the air now, mingling with tobacco smoke and the musty salt smell of the beach. The whalers lay by the shore, bows on the pebbled beach with painters made fast to nearby trees or boulders. A bo's'n's call shrilled, shattering the drone of conversations.

"Whalers' crews to your boats," shouted a chief petty officer. "Make ready for the final race!"

Within minutes the four boats, crews' faces flushed with rum and excitement, were ranged abeam near the starting line. A shot cracked out, and all seamen lifted from thwarts almost in unison, driving the hard-bending oars deep into the salt water, cox'ns shouting as the crowds ashore exhorted them to supreme efforts. Eric found Geraldine's hand, squeezing it in excitement.

Cries of astonished disbelief rose as Number Two *Porpoise* whaler drew rapidly ahead — first a length, then two, three and four lengths. The cries changed to laughter and subdued mutterings as the men realized that something was amiss. Petty Officer Peebles, cox'n of Number One *Calcutta* boat, suddenly stood up, stripped off his pants and jacket and dove over the stern. He emerged seconds later holding a canvas bucket and a short length of rope.

Roars of rage and laughter rolled over the assembled sailors, mingled with catcalls and hoots as they realized what the canny *Porpoise* crew had done — fastened weighted buckets to the rudder pintles of the other boats. Geraldine and Eric looked at each other, their shoulders shaking with laughter, tears rolling helplessly down their cheeks as they watched the furor and confusion of the other cox'ns stripping and diving into the chill water to cut loose their drags.

Porpoise Number Two whaler was now nearly upon the halfway buoy, with *Calcutta* five lengths astern as Peebles and his men strained to close the gap. Far behind, the last two boats lay dead in the water; hands helped the cox'ns clamber dripping aboard.

Shouts and jeers drifted back from the leading boat as it began to round the buoy, white water curling from the stem. The cox'n stood, turned half around, made a derisory gesture at Petty Officer Peebles and shouted — then suddenly pitched forward as the whaler's bow rose and stopped. Oarsmen were tossed like ninepins into the bilges, others made frantic grabs for oars drifting away on the tide, while two, quicker of thought and action, leaped over the side and tried to manhandle the two-ton vessel free.

"They're aground!" screamed Kirk, forgetting decorum and hugging the girl, who hesitated a moment before slipping free.

Peebles steered his command across the finish line, bowing left and right to cheers and applause. Two other whalers followed closely, with *Porpoise*'s Number Two boat limping in a sad last, to be met with gales of laughter and a few commiserating cheers.

"It was a good try," said Kirk to Gosling later, after returning Geraldine slowly home, "but the best-laid plans 'gang aft agley', as Burns wrote — and it was money in the bank for me." They were both basking in the knowledge of Clemmie's "Well done". He sipped his sherry thoughtfully. "Money in the bank." Kirk explained his bet with Lieutenant Last. "Actually," he concluded, "it was money in the sand bank!"

"Dear Mother, Father and Sister," Eric wrote, "We had a fine time yesterday with pulling-boat races. The *Porpoise* crews thought they had us beaten by tying buckets to our rudders, but were caught out when they got too excited, and ran aground. I won six shillings from Lieutenant Last, who has just been appointed to the brig. Please do me a favour. I'm wrapping up two shillings in this envelope, and I'd like father and Andrew to have a pint on me in the George and Dragon. Please do this, and don't forget to send some jam and jelly and maybe a little honey if the bees have made any with your next letter.

"Oh, I told you about Commander Knight and losing all the gold stolen by his personal steward and two seamen. Well, I just heard the other day that Knight lost his Court and was reprimanded and lost his ship, and I'm not sorry, although it's sad to see a man lose his career. I don't know who'll be given command of *Porpoise*.

"I'll close now to catch the mails, and please don't forget to send the jams and honey, etc. Love from your son and brother, Eric Kirk. (Sub-Lt.)"

Carefully stowing away his writing materials, Kirk stretched the kinks out of his arms, yawned deeply and went on deck, leaving his cap in the gunroom so no sailor would feel the necessity of saluting. Chuckles of male laughter rolled up from the lower decks, and from a few men gathered for a smoke and a gam near the foc'slehead in the evening twilight. Seeing Chief Petty Officer Ichabod Warfield leaning on the rail, wisps of smoke drifting from his stubby pipe, Kirk strolled casually toward him. More than slightly in awe of the drum-voiced, barrel-chested cox'n, the younger man emulated the older's position, nodding a good evening.

They stood in companionable silence for a few moments. Although Kirk didn't smoke, he sniffed the fragrant fumes with some appreciation. Warfield was first to break the silence.

"A good competition this morning, Mister Kirk."

"I thought it came off rather well." Kirk tried unsuccessfully to make his voice equally deep.

"Aye. The hands are in good spirits." Warfield leaned toward Kirk, his West Country burr dropping to a confidential rumble. "It's events like this, Mister Kirk, as makes a happy ship. I bin in a number o' ships in my thutty-two years — bad ones an' happy ones — an' 'twas always those as has good officeıs, such as yourself, sir, were the best to be in." He let the compliment hang in the air a moment while Kirk, flustered, hunted vainly for an acknowledgement. Perhaps sensing the youth's embarrassment, the veteran touched his cap casually, "Time to be turnin' in. Goodnight, sir."

Kirk watched him vanish into the 'tween decks; then, since he had the Morning Watch, beginning at four a.m., went aft to turn in as well, feeling strangely exhilarated. His joy was only slightly marred by the remarks he had overheard as two lieutenants talked idly during the festivities, about their time "on station" being almost up, and wondering where "their Lordships" would next send them.

"A stint in the Red Sea would suit me," one had said cheerfully. "Pleasant enough here, but a year or two of steady sunshine and cheap servants would do me fine!"

Chapter Nine

A Celestial Vision

"A junk!" The captain looked incredulously at the ruddy-faced merchant seaman sitting across the table, silently wondering if the prominent veins in the man's nose were the result of heredity, or a fondness for the bottle, then added, "How in the devil would a junk cross the North Pacific to this coast?"

"I dunno, cap. I'm just tellin' you what I saw. I was comin' down past Langara Island when it came on to blow, so I put the helm up and ran east through the pass. I wasn't payin' much attention to my position — a schooner's a real bitch to handle in a followin' sea with th' wind right aft — when th' lookout yelled he saw a ship on the rocks."

"Yes, I see. Ashley," the captain shouted, "another mug of hot rum for Captain Groenski!"

A grizzled head poked through the cabin door. "Yes, cap'n. Mebbe a tray o' pickles an' cold beef?"

The captain looked at the portly sealing skipper, whose porcine eyes lit at the mention of food. "Yes, Ashley, and close the door as you leave."

HMS *Calcutta* lay at anchor in Bull Harbour on Hope Island, just a few miles from the northern tip of Vancouver Island, snubbing to her chains as November gusts wailed through her rigging.

A light sprinkling of snow had dusted the decks, and Captain A.N. Whitfeld-Clements could hear the rhythmic swishing of brooms above his fireplace's cheery crackling. Cold eddies freshened the cabin air as they swept in through an open scuttle, carrying in an occasional wisp of crisp snow.

The captain's steward returned, silently setting food trays and a steaming pitcher of hot buttered rum on the table. He paused a moment to see if all was well, then quietly withdrew. A uniformed figure slipped in, shaking snow from his coat as the steward exited.

131

"Ah, John. Glad you returned in time to hear this." The captain stood, waiting as the blubberish sealer heaved himself to his feet with a wheeze. "Commander Keen, Captain Groenski."

Handshakes exchanged, the civilian immediately subsided jelly-like into his chair with a satisfied groan, echoed by the chair. Whitfeld-Clements looked apprehensive: his furniture wasn't built for tonnage such as Groenski's.

"Captain Groenski," he explained shortly to Keen, "is master and part-owner of the sealing schooner *Attu*. He came aboard to inform me of Russian harassment on the sealing grounds, which I explained is strictly an inter-governmental affair — the more so since the islands are claimed by both Russia and the United States of America."

"Hell," rambled the sealing captain, emitting a stench of foul breath flavoured with rum, "we been sealin' up yonder fer years, an' now them Russkies are tryin' to say we ain't got no more rights no more. Hell, fer two cents I'd mount a couple o' cannons on deck an'..."

"And be blown out of the water for your trouble," said the captain crisply. "No, Captain Groenski, taking the law into your own hands might have served a hundred years ago, but today you'd finish up in a Siberian prison, with no hope of release, ever."

"Well, what the hell are we gonna do?" The sealer pounded a fat hand on the chair's arm, as Whitfeld-Clements winced. "I got a crew to feed an' pay, an' if we don't get no seals they don't get no pay!"

"I shouldn't be surprised if sealing were outlawed in a few years," Commander Keen snapped. "From what I've seen and heard, you men have almost destroyed the herds!"

"Softly, gentlemen," cautioned the captain. "Here, Captain Groenski, let me freshen your drink." He leaned over and filled Groenski's glass brim-full.

Acting Sublieutenant Eric Kirk resisted the urge to stamp his feet to warm them, on the sure and certain knowledge that instant, bitter comments from the captain would blast through the skylight at him. His nostrils flared as a whiff of hot buttered rum wafted past. Although he was not one who actually liked the bittersweet flavour of the pungent drink, a hot mugful right now would certainly help to dispel the chill. He beat his arms against his greatcoat, envying the seamen forward who were clustered in a small group near the galley stovepipe while they had a short break. Fragments of talk drifting up diverted his attention from the unseasonal cold, and his mind wandered into daydreams of Chinese junks, seals and gallons of hot kye warming near crackling fireplaces....

Below, the burly sealer slopped a good half of his drink down, then wiped his bearded mouth with a grimy hand as the naval captain continued, "Captain Groenski was telling me a fascinating yarn about a Chinese junk wrecked on the north side of Graham Island, in the Queen Charlotte group, John. Perhaps you'd be good enough to continue, captain?"

"Sure." Groenski took another mighty draft of hot rum, belched, wiped his mouth again, this time with a greasy sleeve, and rumbled, "We was runnin' in a bad followin' sea when the lookout yelled he saw this here ship on the rocks. Well, there wasn't nothin' we could do, but I took a look through the glass in case it was worth while comin' back to — mebbe some salvage," he winked laboriously at the naval officers, "an' I saw it looked like a junk."

Commander Keen leaned forward. "No offense, captain, but have you ever seen a junk?" Keen had spent some years on the China Station.

Groenski stared at the commander. "Hell, man, I was 15 year in the tea trade afore comin' to this coast. I seen more junks than you seen swings o' the cat!"

"The cat has been abolished, but I see your point. Thank you." Keen pushed the pitcher of rum closer to Groenski, who nodded forgiveness and refilled his mug, slopping some of the warm liquor on the tabletop.

Whitfeld-Clements winced again, but asked politely, "Did you see anyone aboard? What I mean is, did the junk appear to have been there for days, weeks — or even years?"

"Jeez, cap, we was runnin' afore a gale, an' I just got a quick look at it through the spray. There wasn't no paint on it I could see, but them Chinks didn't use much paint nohow — just great big eyes on the bows so's they could see where they were goin' or so devils wouldn't get them — or somethin' like that."

"Was it a large junk? Could you see if it had one or two masts? And about how big was it?"

"One mast was still standin', but the mizzen or whatever them yellow devils call the one on the stern was gone by the board — just the stump was still standin'. Lemme see, now — it'd be about 90 to a hunnert feet on deck. An' that's all I can tell you. Gimme a chart an' I'll mark a position. Leastwise, close as I can."

"Certainly." The captain ruffled through a sheaf of flattened charts, then selected a well-used one and laid it on the table, keeping it clear of the rum stain.

The sealer stood, his belly forcing him to lean far over, puffing with exertion, to see clearly. He extended a bloated finger, nail permanently black-rimmed, and pointed. "Right about there, I figger. She was lyin' in a little cove behind a low reef. Must of drifted in on a high tide an' went aground. Lucky to miss the reef or there'd be nothin' left. Mebbe there's nothin' left now, but she seemed fairly safe."

"Thank you, Captain Groenski. I'm obliged for the information. Perhaps Commander Keen will put on his coat, have your crew called, and see you to your boat. Goodbye."

Kirk sprawled in the gunroom's most comfortable chair, a mug of cocoa at his elbow and a manual of navigation on his lap. The midshipmen, for once, were quietly studying and all was at peace. Lieutenant van Dusen poked his dark head in. "What's this? Are they all dead? It's as silent as the tomb in here. You must have put the fear of God and the cat into them, young fellow." Kirk was all of two years younger than van Dusen.

"No," Kirk grinned, "but the cold weather's a help. None of them want to be mastheaded in the snow, so they've been behaving quite well." A muffled snort came from one of the silent bodies, which was ignored.

"Good. Just thought I'd let you know that we're sailing in the morning — to the Queen Charlotte Islands."

Sublieutenant Kirk dropped his book. "Oh, no!" was all he said.

HMS *Calcutta*, 3,900 tons of Royal Navy iron screw corvette, smashed through the shallow steel-grey waters of Hecate Strait, tops'ls and topgallants drumhead-stiff as the southeast gale lashed sheets of icy spray over her slanting, slippery decks. Gale-chased mists mingled with wind-whipped smoke from her athwartships funnels and the wild wind howled banshee-screaming through the frozen rigging; Captain Whitfeld-Clements had cautiously ordered steam raised. Kirk, tanned face blue with cold, wondered numbly if the everlasting southeasters blew all winter long. He stamped his feet harshly on the icy deck, causing the two helmsmen to look around at him questioningly. Seeing the reason, they grinned tightly through chapped lips — Kirk was a popular young officer — and one said, "Never you mind, sir, summer's bound to come."

Kirk began an answer, but was distracted by Lieutenant Giles, gunner and Officer of the Watch, unshipping his long brass telescope and peering westward. He waved Kirk over, "Take a look there. Is that not Skidegate Inlet?"

The tall subbie shielded his eyes against the bitter spray peeling back from the plunging bows and stared. A long sandbar, dimly visible in the haze, was piled high with monstrous tumbles of white water hurled crashing into the air as the vicious sea assaulted the unyielding point.

"Yes, sir," Kirk shouted, "and Commander Knight took *Porpoise* around that bar and into the inlet!"

"Yes...well, I fear that Commander Knight won't be handling any more of HM ships." Giles paused, started to continue, then glanced at the helmsmen who were pretending not to hear, and changed his mind. "That's not the worst spot in these islands, I understand." Switching the subject smoothly, he waved an arm at the low green islands with their dusting of snow, "North of us lies Rose Spit — a hellhole designed by Old Nick himself!"

"Is that so, sir?" Kirk found it difficult to visualize anything worse than the raging shoal to the west. He glanced over to starboard. Out there behind the straggling mists, he knew, was the jagged British Columbia mainland coast. Invisible, but only 30 or 40 miles distant, and strewn with the splintered wrecks of ships forced ashore and destroyed on its hostile shores.

"Wind's backing slightly," it was Giles again. "Give my respects to the captain and tell him I'd like to steer a bit more to eastward."

"Aye aye, sir." The order terminated a friendly discussion between two professionals, and returned them to a superior and subordinate footing.

Whitfeld-Clements, shivering in slippers and bathrobe, studied the sky and cast a quick, professional glance around the ship. "Right, Mister Giles. Bring the ship two points to starboard. Keep a sharp lookout for Rose Spit and call me at first sight."

"Aye aye, sir. Hands to the braces!" Shouted orders brought *Calcutta* to starboard, heeling more as yards were swung to put the big ship quartering the wind, on the starboard tack. Derek Giles stayed by the wheel, balancing with difficulty on the pitching deck, while Kirk moved about the ship from handhold to handhold, directing a small pull on a brace here, an easing of sheets there, until the intricate lacework of hemp and canvas was balanced to his satisfaction. He paused to check the barometer as he returned aft.

"Glass is rising slightly, sir."

"Yes, sub, but — 'Short rise after low, oft foretells a stronger blow'," quoted Giles. "And at this time of year it's best to be prepared for the worst."

Kirk stared in awe at the maelstrom to leeward. Great crashing breakers savagely attacked Rose Spit, rumbling and thundering. Nature's furies sent rolling tons of salt water charging against the murderous sandbanks, splintering skyward in gouts of foam and surging irresistibly over the bar, their pandemonium plainly audible even through the screaming wind. For three or four miles the long, narrow spit was an appalling melee of oceanic fury in the fading afternoon light.

Kirk glanced aft. Lieutenant David Duncan had the Watch, with red-headed Midshipman Perkins as his "makee-learn", but both the captain and Commander Keen were on deck.

"Hands wear ship," called Duncan, his deep bass carrying clearly forward. "Lift sheets and braces. Up helm."

Calcutta straightened as her jib-boom raked the horizon from east to west, seamen hauling in or paying out sheets and braces, keeping her square sails full as she scudded momentarily, then heeled violently over to starboard and settled on the port tack. Her fore-and-afters — jibs, stays'ls and spanker — boomed and creaked as they filled, straining against the restraining sheets as the ship drove along on her new westward course.

"What do you think of that, sub?" Kirk looked around. Commander Keen had joined him by the weather main shrouds, and was looking at the frenzy of Rose Spit, slowly vanishing in the gathering gloom and omnipresent haze.

"Nothing could survive, sir," he said soberly. "Not even one of the new iron battleships I've read about."

"No," Keen agreed, "yet — there is a passage between the inner and outer parts of the spit. I once spoke to a fisherman who'd escaped a nor'west gale through it, but he was lucky to get away with it!" He put his hand on Kirk's shoulder, turning him gently and pointing with his free arm. "Look yonder — see the loom of a hill on the shore?"

Kirk strained his eyes. He could just make out the upthrusting mound.

"That's Tow Hill," said Keen. "Safe anchorage in southerly winds, but a lee shore otherwise. If you should see it in foul weather when you're not sure of your position, you'll know that Rose Spit is close by, so watch out!"

"Yes, sir, thank you." Kirk was grateful for the knowledge, but wondered why the usually taciturn commander had chosen him for conversation.

"Come in, John," the captain looked somewhat surprised but invited Keen to sit and chat.

"Thank you, sir. I needed to talk to someone."

Whitfeld-Clements' face softened. "It's very hard to accept, I know. No matter how much time passes."

"Yes, sir. He would have been young Kirk's age now." Keen accepted the drink the captain handed him, and tossed it down. It was refilled wordlessly.

"It's not just knowing that they're gone, sir. It's — not knowing what happened — and whether I could have saved them if I had been there."

"Yes," the captain said softly. "To lose both Mary and your son in a shipwreck when you're half the globe away. I can think of nothing more horrible."

Commander Keen stood, suddenly, his jaw unnaturally firm. "Thank you, sir," he said crisply. "I have control again. Good night, sir."

"Good night, John," the captain replied quietly, closing the door behind his tormented second in command and feeling helpless sympathy well into his throat.

A pale November morning sun, late to rise, but early to set, glinted from the snow-whitened rocky shores and the frigid rippled channel. HMS *Calcutta*, sails furled tightly in the near calm, steamed through Parry Passage, a constricted gut dividing Langara and Graham islands, at the northwest tip of the Queen Charlotte Islands.

Double lookouts, bundled against the chill, perched in fore, main and mizzentops, scanning the bleak rocks. Telescopes flashed brassily on the quarterdeck, and even sailors on duty cast frequent glances toward the land. Hours passed. The captain squinted anxiously at the barometer. Virago Sound, bounded by Capes Naden and Edenshaw, drifted past, indistinct in the low haze. Telescopes scanned the inlet's recesses, but the captain had wisely decided not to enter. "It would take a full week to search it all — too long to spend on what might be a will o' the wisp, particularly with a storm brewing."

Cape Edenshaw came abeam. A low, misty, wooded shoreline led eastward to Wiah Point. Smoke, mingling with the mist, drifted lazily upward from campfires behind two small islands, and the shore curled away to the southeast and disappeared in a blend of land and sky. The sky's light blue had hardened to a glaze, and from astern a freshening breeze picked fitfully at the rigging.

The captain studied the sky and felt the wind, then stared hard at the water, now choppy, with the promise of a greasy swell. "Mister van Dusen!"

The swarthy young officer ran to the captain's side. "Sir?"

"Send the Watch Below below decks. Tell the engineer officer I want steam for full speed in one hour. One hour — not a second more, mind you, and have the Watch on deck batten down everything and secure all loose gear."

"Sir?" Van Dusen looked at the sky, the sea and the peaceful horizon as the afternoon sun sank toward the horizon, then habit took over. "Aye aye, sir!" He saluted and turned. "Midshipman, on the double, go and tell the captains of the tops to secure for a blow. Go below yourself and see all is secured. Warn Mister Giles that double lashings are to be put on the guns. Lively now!"

In 30 seconds the ship, above and below decks, was a swarming medley of noise and confusion. The captain turned to Commander Keen, "I've seen this weather before, John. The wind will veer northwest and be blowing a full gale in less than two hours, or I'm a son of a sea-cook!"

"Deck there!" The cry drifted down from the maintop lookout. "Somethin' in sight, sir, bearin' northeast. Looks like a hulk, sir — just off that lone hill."

Whitfeld-Clements jammed the telegraph to "full speed ahead". Billows of ink-like smoke pouring from the funnels became thicker, heavier, and the decks began to vibrate. A curling wake rolled away from the sharp bow, growing higher and breaking at the top into flurries of tumbling green-white as the ship's speed increased. "I'm going aloft." The captain stepped on the rail and started up the ratlines, his ease and familiarity 20 years and three rank-stripes behind him. The lookout moved over when the captain puffed his way clumsily onto the top, and unlimbered his telescope. As he steadied the brass instrument, he noticed that in spite of their speed to the northwest, the funnel smoke was now blowing nearly due south, and a new humming was whining through the rigging.

He focussed the glass with an effort and sharply drew in his breath. Rolling hugely in the growing sea was a junk, a war-junk, to judge from the number of medieval cannons on her deck. He studied the vessel. Only the splintered stubs of masts remained, the foremast stump canting steeply forward. She'd be on the spit in an hour, more likely less. The ebbing tide was already setting strongly across the steep northwest side of Rose Spit, aided by a growing lump of sea even now crashing whitely over the sand.

Suddenly he stiffened. A figure had appeared on deck! Was it a man, or perhaps a sea lion which had somehow crawled aboard?

"Take this," he thrust the telescope into the seaman's hands, "and tell me what you see!"

The sailor looked long and steadily, swaying with the ship's motion. Finally he handed the instrument back. "There's a man on the hulk, sir."

The captain scrambled down to the deck, shocked at how wind and sea had grown in the short time he'd been aloft. "Mister van Dusen," he yelled, "there's a man on that hulk! Clear away a cutter for lowering, and have the tops'ls set at once."

Calcutta pounded through the growing gale, shuddering deck awash as she pitched and rolled amid a heavy beam sea. Whitfeld-Clements sent leadsmen to the chains while the stricken junk grew nearer, and was forced to reef the newly set tops'ls because the screaming wind threatened to blow the sails right out of their bolt ropes. A quarter-mile to windward of the hulk, which itself lay a scant cable's length from the madly frothing overfalls, he rounded up and furled tops'ls.

"Get that cutter over the side, smartly now! Drift it down on a long painter." As he watched the boat being lowered away, Kirk dashed up, throwing a fast salute.

"Let me take the cutter, sir," he puffed. "I have a volunteer crew ready." The young man braced himself against the suddenly bitter wind, and waited.

The captain frowned. "Mister Kirk, use your head! No crew on earth could pull a cutter away from that bar. Look at that!" He waved a navy-blue arm at the surging surf. "Even this way there's hardly a chance of success."

Kirk stared at the bar, now visible only by the tumult along its length. Great tumbling masses of white water were streaked with green and brown as the seas physically picked up slices of the spit and hurled them high.

The cutter was drifting down on the wreck, both of them gyrating frenziedly on the huge, breaking swells lashing through the surf. Through the spray and foam the lone figure on the junk was barely visible as he crouched by the splintered rail, watching the small boat. Suddenly a giant sea picked up the two-ton cutter as though it were a twig, snapping the line like string and sending the cutter tumbling end over end until it smashed into kindling against the junk's teak planking. Seamen fell sprawling and cursing as strain came off the taut line, slipping and sliding on the drenched, heaving deck.

"No time for another boat," the captain barked, his body tensing. "Float a life-ring down to him. Slow the engine so we make a little sternway! Get that broken line clear before it fouls the screw, Mister Kirk!" As Kirk stumbled aft, Whitfeld-Clements cocked an ear to hear the leadsman.

"By the mark, five!"

Thirty feet of water, he thought apprehensively. Little enough at the best of times — touch and go with the ship plunging as madly as she now was.

A crash like thunder interrupted his concentration. He spun to see Kirk leading a motley group of sailors and Royal Marines forward at the double. The second cutter had broken loose from its

140

chocks, and its stern was splintering and bashing against the deckhouse.

Unable to watch two problems at once, the captain returned his gaze to the doomed junk and realized his attempt to assist was hopeless. "No — we can't do it," he breathed aloud, then shouted, "Full speed ahead!" He opened his arms in helplessness to the Chinese as *Calcutta* gathered way.

The other seemed also to realize the situation was hopeless. He waved once and disappeared below decks. The derelict rolled and heaved in the savage breakers, vanishing completely from sight as it plunged into canyon-like troughs. The captain swung to watch Kirk and his gang of sweating men; they had managed to get a line on the careening cutter, and were straining to make it fast. Other men were swarming toward the boat to help. Whitfeld-Clements turned away and missed the near tragedy.

Kirk, both hands straining on a coarse-fibred manila rope, hauled with five others to tame the wild cutter. Suddenly the next man's foot skidded on the slippery deck, and he lurched into the young officer. Kirk let go of the line as he stumbled backward, tripped and, arms flailing helplessly, fell over the rail. His cap dropped off and was instantly snatched away by a welter of foaming green-white water. Incongruously he thought, "Three shillings gone...", then felt his left ankle clutched as he swayed upside-down. A surging sea filled his mouth and nose with frigid salt water, and his left ear crashed against the ship's timbers, stunning him momentarily. He choked, then felt eager hands hauling him roughly back aboard. Safe on deck, he leaned over the rail, retched up what seemed like gallons of brine, then shakingly turned to thank his rescuers.

"Thought you was a goner, sir," a red-coated Royal Marine husked, "but the chief," he nodded at Chief Petty Officer Warfield, "clapped a hand on yer leg an' hauled you up. Yer ear's bleedin' like a stuck pig, sir," he added. "'Ere's a bit o' rag t' staunch it."

"Thank you." Kirk accepted the cloth with a nod of appreciation, then looked straight at Warfield. "I won't forget this."

A shout from the quarterdeck snapped their attention to the foundering junk. Commander Keen, telescope to eye, had bellowed, "Look there!"

The doomed Chinese had returned on deck, but transformed. His brilliant metal breastplate reflected the scant sun, as did a plumed metal cap. His ornate scarlet tunic and trousers contrasted with the junk's weathered grey timbers, and a long, curved sword was in his hand. Maintaining his balance with difficulty, he raised the weapon high, then threw it into the boiling surf. Scrambling up on the shattered poop, he again stood, bowed ceremoniously in *Calcutta*'s direction, and then as the British watched aghast, stepped calmly over the side. His armour took him down before anyone aboard the man o' war could so much as blink. Captain Whitfeld-Clements removed his cap — for a moment only — and bowed his head.

Kirk, dripping and shivering, drew in his breath as the junk was lifted high on a giant sea so that the entire bottom was visible, then crashed down on the hard sand of Rose Spit, breaking her back. The vessel was gone in seconds — only a few splintered planks marking her passing. As he turned to go below and change into dry clothing, he faintly heard the captain.

"Very well, Mister van Dusen. Send the ship's company to cruising stations and steer northeast."

The captain contemplated the inlaid backgammon board, laid away in his sea-chest since leaving Fiji, and smiled at the discomfited young officer seated across the table. "You'll learn to avoid playing a 'back-game', sub. No matter how often you blot my men, you must get your own all 'round the board, and that gives me the opportunity of bearing off before you. Another game?"

"No, thank you, sir," Kirk shook his head and stood. Clemmie's habit of inviting all his officers in turn for a social evening was pleasant, but somehow it was always a bit of an ordeal. "The commander's scheduled a meeting of all officers to plan the ship's Christmas party."

The captain stood also. "I gather there'll be more than the usual plum duff and extra tots?"

"Yes, sir. The youngest seaman will be 'Captain of the Day', of course, and the petty officers are organizing a comb-and-whistle band."

"Good. Well, carry on, then..." The captain paused as a thought struck him. "Wait one minute. This might interest you." He rummaged through his desk, then straightened, extending an intricately carved wooden box about a foot square by three inches thick. Kirk

142

took it, curiously studying the ornately molded solid brass dragon-hinges, and the encrusted white salt-stains on the mellowed varnish.

"Open it, sub."

The young man's fingers, roughened by two years of hauling on stiff, coarse manila rope and the other manual tasks that regularly came to midshipmen, plucked unhandily at the catch. Eventually, at the expense of a torn fingernail, he pried it open and stared at the contents. A book, leather-bound, encompassed by a faded purple ribbon, neatly filled the space. He opened the heavily carved cover, with great care and wonder. "Is this Chinese, sir?"

"Yes. Captain Groenski, the sealer who first saw the junk and told me about it, discovered it on Rose Spit. I told him of the junk's fate, and I suppose he sailed up there in the hope of finding something of value cast up on the sands." The captain looked grim. "I told him that if he got into trouble...," he didn't finish the statement.

"He was taking a chance, wasn't he, sir?" The storm-wracked picture of Rose Spit flashed before Kirk's eyes.

"Yes. Not often the weather is quiet enough, especially at this time of year, to even get near the spit, but he was lucky. He landed on the sand with a few men, and found this half-buried under some kelp. When he returned he presented it to me." The captain chuckled. "He didn't volunteer any further information about what he found, nor did I ask. I'd surmise that his venture was profitable," the captain grinned quickly, "or else this wouldn't have left his hands."

"Do you know what it is, sir?"

Whitfeld-Clements hesitated. "Don't let this get to the snotties or the hands. I don't want the knowledge to leave the ship, but it's apparently a communication from the Empress of China to Her Majesty, Queen Victoria, offering an alliance between our two nations. The lieutenant-governor spent some years in China as an attache, and even now retains some Chinese staff. This is written in Court Mandarin, so that it was difficult to translate even without the water stains and smeared ink. The bearer was a high court official, and there were gifts of silks and jewels accompanying it — which now are presumably on the ocean floor."

"Or possibly in Captain Groenski's holds, sir," suggested Kirk, greatly daring.

"Possibly, but we'll never know. He wouldn't have brought anything unusually valuable into a customs port."

"I see, sir." Kirk was frantically curious, but managed to restrain himself — barely — from asking the obvious question.

The captain eyed him narrowly. "This will be forwarded to Her Majesty along with my report to the Admiralty. And who knows — we may be ordered to the Yangtze next year. That is," a black look flashed over his face, "if we don't have to teach the Frogs another lesson first!" A smile replaced the scowl. "That answer the question you were dying to ask?"

"Yes, sir. Thank you, sir." He flushed, realizing that the captain had read his face like a book.

"Very good, then. You may carry on — and remember my caution."

"Aye aye, sir. Thank you." He slipped out the door, already inventing a "red-herring" yarn for the midshipmen.

Chapter Ten

Convoys and Cunning

Captain Whitfeld-Clements, Royal Navy, commanding officer of the iron screw corvette HMS *Calcutta*, eased his spindly chair a trifle farther from the musty smell of the ancient, black-clad, funereal-featured man perched creakily behind the cluttered roll-top desk. As the wheezing voice rasped and crackled its tremulous tale, he studied the austere office. Stained wallpaper faded into obscurity as the lone kerosene lamp's flickering light fought and lost a battle to penetrate the gloom. Late afternoon sunlight, attempting to filter through the single fly-specked window, also gave up the unequal struggle, so that only a few faltering rays streaked the linoleum.

"And so," the complaining monotone whined on, "I feel that it is the navy's responsibility to offer protection to my ships."

Whitfeld-Clements stood, his action causing small flurries of dust to rise near his feet. "Very good, Mister Etherington, I'll take the matter under consideration." He strode to the door, escaping before the old miser could impale him with more complaints. The crisp March air was bracing and he inhaled deeply to rid his lungs of the stale office dust. His boots clattered along the planked boardwalk as he marched past false-fronted frame buildings.

In the sun-glinted harbour to his left, smoke rose in a lazy curl from the tall single funnel of a sternwheel ferry about to depart, while tall spars speared loftily from two full-riggers discharging cargo at the jetty. He stopped for a moment, searching for the "Etherington & Co., Traders and Merchants" vessel, and blinked as a dray, drawn by a pair of enormous Clydesdales, squeaked and rumbled past in a turmoil of dust and noise.

Watching his chance to cross the road, he saw a break in the unusually heavy horse-drawn traffic and walked quickly to the seawall, lifting his hand in semi-salute to a passing acquaintance. There she lay, the *Yukon Girl*, a black, brig-rigged sidewheeler, decks cluttered with oddments of cargo and gear. He studied the ship carefully. Strips of peeling white paint fluttered from her deckhouse, a gaping vacancy indicated the home of her lost figurehead, and a multitude of Irish pennants adorned the rigging. The captain shuddered: he wouldn't care to cross the harbour in such a ramshackle old tub.

Jamming his hands into his pockets — the wind was chilly even though the sun took a little of the bite from the cold — the captain headed toward the livery stable to retrieve his horse and carriage. He thought about old man Etherington's request — almost a demand, dammit! — for a naval escort for the decrepit old *Yukon Girl* on her voyages to and from San Francisco. Impossible, of course, yet a cruise would do no harm to the ships' companies; they had been a long time in harbour. So long, in fact, that he'd overheard a dockyard matey referring scornfully to them as "depot ships". A withering glance had sent the man scurrying, but the comment stung.

Calcutta and *Porpoise* bustled with activity as he drew up nearby. Fiddles scraped lustily in the waists of both ships as dozens of seamen pounded heavily or skipped lightly to hornpipes, and on the heel of *Calcutta*'s bowsprit a comb-and-whistle band screeched and tooted. Whitfeld-Clements grinned. It was four months ago, almost to the day, that young Kirk had told him about this band being formed, and it had become immensely popular with the hands. Almost every day in the Dog Watches it could be heard making raucous harmony. Enough to drive a person mad, at times, but the men liked it. It was a good thing. There was little sulking or lollygagging in the ship, but plenty of skylarking.

He watched the officers keeping a weather eye on the capering sailors, and the midshipmen by the brow keeping a weather eye on him. Even as he flapped the reins and clucked to his horse, he saw the snotty aboard *Calcutta* send the messenger scurrying away, for the Officer of the Watch and side boys, no doubt. Well, they could cool their heels for a time. He was in no great hurry to go aboard.

No! Procrastination over a decision about Etherington would not do. He pulled up the horse and threw the reins to Ashley, who opened his mouth but closed it as he saw the captain's black brow; gruffly, the captain ordered him to put the rig away and feed the horse, then stalked stiff-legged toward his ship.

146

Bo's'n's calls shrilled as he climbed the brow — it was a high tide — and both Lieutenant Duncan and Sublieutenant Kirk saluted as he came aboard. He touched his hat in response, but said not a word, although they were favourites. Red-headed Midshipman Perkins, seeing the captain's frame of mind, scuttled out of the way toward the main chains, but he was too late.

"Mister Perkins! My compliments to Commander Keen and I'll be pleased to see him in my cabin. And brush your uniform. You're a disgrace to the fleet!"

"Aye aye, sir." Perkins doubled unhappily away.

In his cabin the captain's mood improved. Ashley had a coal fire glowing and flickering in the fireplace, and — by Jove! — there was a steaming pitcher of hot coffee on the sideboard. He sniffed. Yes, there was a faint aroma of rum wafting up with the delicious smell of coffee.

A diffident knock came on the door. Keen had apparently been warned of his ill humour. Whitfeld-Clements grinned. He'd surprise both his commander and the one who had warned him.

"Come in, come in, John!" The door opened, and a mystified commander stepped through, bringing a draft of cold air with him. "Have a cup of coffee, John, and sit here by the fireplace. It's too chilly a day to let a good fire go wasted. I need your advice on a minor puzzle, but we might as well be warm."

Seated and sipping, he began. "Etherington, of the trading company, sent a note asking to see me, pleading infirmity for not coming here. His firm owns the *Yukon Girl* — that rundown tub of a sidewheel brig, and a couple more like her — and trades between here and San Francisco. South with canned salmon, furs or lumber, north with any old kind of cargo he can pick up — bricks, pottery, vegetables, fruit and so forth. On the last two passages his ships have been fired on off the Oregon coast, and chased by a black schooner of about 200 tons, but managed to escape. No name or port of registry on the schooner."

Keen's forehead crinkled, "Strange that a schooner couldn't intercept one of those ships, sir."

"They were in luck both times. Had the wind right aft — a schooner's slowest point of sailing, as you know. That gave them time enough to raise steam in their rusty old kettles. If they'd been reaching or close-hauled, I daresay the story would have been different."

"Another 'Missing, presumed lost', I suppose."

"Exactly. At any rate, Etherington wants an escort for at least part of the way on his next passage. He obviously has influence, as a note came from His Excellency asking me to 'extend all consideration' toward the old skinflint."

"That sort, is he, sir?" Keen chuckled.

"Yes. That's not what concerns me, however..."

"D'you think the Fenians are up to their old tricks, sir?"

His captain frowned. "Frankly, I don't know. They've been quiet for quite some time, but with the murder of Lord Cavendish by Fenians in Ireland, and our problems with them in British Columbia, I tend to think that they're fomenting another of their bloody uprisings. Or," he added, "at least a continuation of harassment."

"Have ships other than Etherington's been attacked, sir?"

"That's what I'm going to find out, John. Tomorrow I want you to send young Kirk around to all the shipping offices, with orders to find out about any untoward occurrences. Tell him to keep his mouth closed — I don't want to be swamped with demands from every owner of a teredo-eaten tub clamouring for a naval escort!"

Eric Kirk, returning to the ship after a pleasant Saturday evening at the Willoughby home, had little thought for naval matters. His mind was full of remembered young people's chatter, gathering 'round the piano to sing as Geraldine played, and then the inevitable cookies and tea as the Willoughby Witch indicated it was time for the young guests to leave. He had been the most popular one during the entertainment, singing carefully purified sea chanties and "forebitters" as the half-dozen others applauded and even Mrs. Willoughby (he had to stop thinking of her as the "Witch") had smiled faintly.

Humming softly as he marched up the brow, tossing a salute casually to the quarterdeck, he felt that all was well with his world.

"About time, young fellow." The crisp words sizzled through the gloom as Commander Keen moved out of the shadows. "I've been waiting to talk to you. Come to my cabin, if you please." Kirk followed him numbly, searching his mind for anything he had done — or left undone.

Keen held the door ajar for Kirk to precede him, then stepped quickly to the small sideboard. "You'll join me in a glass, sub." Since it was perceptibly a command, not a question, Kirk murmured acquiescence. His gaze, drifting about the cabin, came to rest on a painting of a young woman with a baby in her arms.

"My family," the commander said curtly. Kirk was startled. He suddenly realized that Keen was standing in front of him, holding out a ruby-coloured glass of wine.

"Thank you, sir. Your health." He judged it best to remain noncommittal about the painting. If the commander wanted to talk about his loss, he could initiate the subject.

They drank, and again Kirk let his eyes roam about, since the commander remained silent. The cabin was furnished in much the same manner as the captain's, but was considerably smaller.

Commander Keen tossed his drink down, refilled his and Kirk's glasses, though the sublieutenant had barely touched his, then began his instructions....

Three double clangs of the ship's bell — three p.m. — on Friday afternoon heralded Kirk's return to *Calcutta*. He approached the captain in his cabin. "Several instances of sighting a black, two-masted schooner, sir," he held out a sheet of paper. "I've listed them here. Three vessels reported being chased, one was fired on, and — "he paused, "the schooner, *Czar*, expected two weeks ago, is unreported."

"I see," said the captain thoughtfully. "Thank you, Mister Kirk. My compliments to Commander Keen and Mister Youngberg, and I'd be pleased to see them at their convenience."

"Aye aye, sir." The tall young officer left quickly, boots rattling on the deck as he hurried on his mission. Full well he knew that "at their convenience" meant "immediately"!

"Here's the situation, gentlemen," Whitfeld-Clements explained when the two officers had reported. "The *Yukon Girl* sails on Monday for San Francisco and, as Etherington said, will use her engine only if wind and tide are dead foul. However, on this passage, I intend to stipulate that steam must be used until past Cape Flattery. From there, he may proceed southward under sail if he so desires. *Calcutta* will stay hull down to seaward of *Yukon Girl* once past the cape, to be out of sight of the schooner should she make an appearance. If *Yukon Girl* signals we'll come to her assistance."

"And *Porpoise*, sir?" Lieutenant Youngberg's face was worried. In acting command of *Porpoise* until a new commanding officer arrived, he knew all too well that his performance on this cruise could enhance or jeopardize his opportunity for promotion.

Whitfeld-Clements grinned slowly. "Lieutenant Youngberg, you will proceed southward independently as far as Mendocino, making every effort to appear a British merchantman. Should a strange schooner pass near, keep most of your men below decks, so as not to look like a man o' war. Fly the Red Ensign, and keep the ship less than neat. For example, have washing drying on a line, and dress the ship's company in ordinary clothes."

"We've a couple of 'Queen's Hard Bargains' aboard *Calcutta* if you'd like to borrow them," laughed Keen. "Make your deception more real with them floundering about."

It was an indication of Youngberg's concern that he failed to rise to the commander's pleasantry. His gaze never wavered from the captain. "Yes, sir. And if I'm attacked I'm to beat to quarters and take the schooner as a prize?"

"If possible. She'll probably have the heels of you to wind'ard, so if you make contact you should try to disable her rigging. Shoot away a mast if you can."

"What if she gets inside the three-mile limit, sir?"

"Follow them! The principle of 'hot pursuit' is recognized internationally — but don't enter an American port. Obtain all the information possible, then find *Calcutta* and report to me."

"Yes, sir." Youngberg grinned hugely. "With your permission, sir, I'll be gone and start getting the brig ready for sea."

"One moment, Mister Youngberg. You may proceed immediately that your ship is ready. With the tide this evening, if you wish. Is *Porpoise* complete with stores?"

"All but for water, sir, and I'll have that today."

"Very good. When will you sail?"

"With the morning tide, sir. With your permission I'll send Lieutenant Last to arrange for a tug from dockyard."

"Granted. I'll send you written orders this evening."

"Thank you, sir." Youngberg slipped out the door, and a few moments later could be faintly heard, shouting for his new lieutenant.

Sublieutenant Kirk grinned to himself as a burst of male laughter splintered the chill night air. Far down the road he could dimly see a group of shadowy figures walking, or rather wobbling, in the general direction of *Calcutta* and *Porpoise*, preceded by drones of conversation spasmodically erupting into snatches of bawdy songs.

"Appears the men had a good time in Esquimalt," he remarked conversationally to Midshipman Perkins, now painfully neat. "Good thing that Mister Duncan's on Watch. He'll just slip them below quietly before the commander hears them."

The snotty nodded. "If Keeners or the captain got woken up, there might be a few matlows on charge in the morning."

"Right," Kirk agreed. "Let's get out of it, now — in case any of them are too exuberant." They moved away, two shadows on the dark deck.

The men were wary, however. Jubilance diminished as the sailors neared the ships, and the last thing that Kirk heard as he dropped off to sleep was the soft shuffling of shoes tip-toeing down to the lower decks.

"But, Captain Whitfeld-Clements," the voice whined, "my expenses would be ruinous, and it's little enough profit I make each voyage, what with wages, new gear, repairs and docking fees..."

"Mister Etherington, Her Majesty's ships will not be kept waiting while *Yukon Girl* dithers about the high seas under sail! I repeat, your ship will proceed under steam until well past Cape Flattery, or else she will sail unescorted."

"Oh, very well then," the old man wheezed resignedly, reaching for a quill pen, "I'll inform Captain McInnes he's to follow your orders. Perhaps you'll be good enough to give him this note when you go aboard his ship."

Whitfeld-Clements nodded brusquely, waited while the scrap of paper was blotted and folded, then pocketed it with a curt "Good afternoon", and left the dank, gloomy cubicle.

He arrived aboard *Calcutta* later in high, black dudgeon. "My God!" he bit out to Commander Keen, "between Etherington and that lumbering rum-pot of a skipper on his ship, it's a flaming wonder that the old tub ever completes a passage at all!"

Keen raised his eyebrows. "Sir?"

"I went aboard to tell the master my plans, and the damned ship stank like a distillery! McInnes, the so-called captain, was so drunk and dirty that it was all I could do to breathe, and I could hardly understand a word he mumbled. I finally gave my orders to the mate, Baird, who seemed to have a small glimmer of intelligence. At least he wasn't too drunk to talk."

Whitfeld-Clements surveyed his ship as the bitter words poured out, "Make preparations for sea, commander. I intend to sail at noon Sunday, so as not to give anyone the impression that —" he waited a few seconds as a party of seamen lurched past, carrying a length of hawser on their shoulders, "—that the *Yukon Girl* has an escort when she blunders out Monday morning." He stalked away, leaving Keen's "Aye aye, sir," hanging in the dusk.

Kirk, Sublieutenant of the Gunroom Mess, irritably sipping his kye, looked down his nose at the snotties gobbling their afternoon "tea". Crumbs and smears of jam littered the wooden table as the midshipmen, hunched along the hard benches, crammed their mouths full under the swaying oil lamp.

"Easy, you lot," snapped Kirk. "Suppose you were invited to a levee at the lieutenant-governor's mansion some evening. Would you be stuffing your pockets full of roast quail and your greedy mouths full of cake there? Suppose His Excellency asked you a question in tactics, or the captain told you off to dance with Her Ladyship — would you spray crumbs over his dinner jacket or go galumphing about the ballroom with your mouth stretched like a walrus's with a fish in it?" Kirk slammed his fist on the table, wincing slightly as he did so, to the unconcealed amusement of the midshipmen. "Straighten up and treat this as a mess instead of a hog-wallow, or I'll give you something to remember!"

Sheepishly the boys sat erect, faint grins on a couple of faces. *Calcutta* was hove to off Cape Flattery, rolling heavily in the long, slow swells, and the gunroom bore a faint but pungent odour of vomit: the ceaseless movement had overcome one of the youngsters. The old *Yukon Girl* had not yet showed her rusty funnel above the horizon, nor had *Porpoise* been seen. The captain had assumed, and his notions had filtered down to the men, that the brig had made a fast passage and was even now southbound along the American coast.

Kirk stretched. "I'm going on deck for a look-see," he announced. "You warts see that the mess is clean before leaving."

Calcutta rolled and pitched ponderously in the steel-grey seas, making bare headway as Kirk arrived on the wet main deck. To the southeast the snow-capped, dark bulk of the Olympic Mountains fell precipitously into the ocean, while to the east, the treed mountain ranges of Vancouver Island slumbered beneath a scattering of low clouds. He looked around. David Duncan, Officer of the Watch, waved and called a cheery greeting. Kirk returned the wave and continued looking around. Aloft, the maintop lookout unceasingly scanned the mist-blurred meeting of sea and sky; forward and aft, seamen stamped their booted feet as they peered into the haze. A leading seaman — Blake, Kirk thought — supervised a trio of shivering sailors pushing snow-laden brooms along the decks, while scattered groups of seamen knocked ice from the standing rigging. He looked up. Wisps of smoke curled from the funnels, showing that Lieutenant Bullen had steam up, and the galley stack was belching smoke, indicating the cook was baking bread.

"Well, sub, too warm below?" He turned quickly. The captain stood beside him, bulky in a wool-lined cloak.

"No, sir. I wanted to see the entrance to Juan de Fuca's Straits, and fix the picture in my mind."

"Good." Whitfeld-Clements studied the subbie's earnest face. "There's been no chance to convene a Board to confirm your promotion, but I hope that Miss Willoughby hasn't entirely halted your studies."

Kirk recognized the question wasn't idle. "No, sir. Mister Duncan's giving me lessons in navigation, and the snotties' nurse — sorry, sir — Acting Lieutenant van Dusen has..."

"Sail ho!" The cry snapped to the deck from the maintop, shattering the relative silence. "A brig, sir — bearing sou'east, about ten miles."

The captain's face brightened. "Good! Go up, young Eric. See if the *Yukon Girl* has finally blundered into us."

The ratlines swaying under his feet, tiny icicles tinkling to the deck as his pounding hands and feet shook them loose, Kirk scuttled to the top. Clambering onto the slippery platform, sending more ice chips downward to splinter, glinting, on rail and deck, he accepted the lookout's help to steady himself. The distant ship was a brig — a ratty-looking thing, too. He watched carefully as it rose to a swell, and asked the lookout, "Is it missing its figurehead?"

The sailor squinted for a moment, steadying himself as the ship rolled deeply, then answered positively, "Aye, sir. Yon packet's got no figurehead. Got a bloody great gap where 't should be, sir."

"Right. Thank you." Kirk leaned far over, clasping a shroud for support, and shouted to the captain, a small dark figure against the white deck, "It's the *Yukon Girl* right enough, sir. She's missing her figurehead. Winters here confirms it."

"Very good. You may come down."

Yukon Girl was abeam in slightly more than an hour, gouts of steam surrounding her weatherbeaten hull like a haze. Her paddles dipped deeply as she rolled, and her patched sails were iron-stiff when she plunged her barren bows under, her squat stern lifting to a following sea. As *Calcutta*'s people watched, the paddlewheels slowed, then rotated freely. Captain McInnes was saving coal. "To buy rum with," Whitfeld-Clements commented wryly.

"All right, Mister Duncan," the captain said shortly, "you may put the ship under way. Keep five or six miles to seaward of her in good daytime visibility, and keep her masts in sight at all times. At night we'll close to within two miles — although I don't foresee any attacks after dark."

The brig rolled past, gouts of greasy smoke trailing to leeward from her single funnel as her fires burned down, and *Calcutta* took station to starboard. Kirk interestedly watched the patrician Lieutenant Duncan experimenting with various combinations of sail in order to maintain position, at last settling on all fore-and-afters, in combination with all three tops'ls and the main topgallant as a control. The smaller sail could be reefed or set when the corvette was found to be headreaching or falling astern of the merchantman. Kirk admired Duncan's skill: no orders were wasted, but very quickly *Calcutta* was on station, six miles astern of the ramshackle brig.

By the third day the two ships had weathered a short but vicious southeast gale; all hands in *Calcutta* were called on deck to force in reefs with numbed fingers as the leaning corvette smashed through huge seas, sending icy spray high into the rigging to shower masts and men. The storm had lasted only a few hours, from four bells in the Morning Watch, through the gradual greying of the sky until seven bells in the Forenoon Watch — five hours of fury and frustration. Following the frenzy, the wind veered westerly, dropping to Force 5 and bringing clearing skies of a cold, frosty blue.

"I'm damned happy to see a westerly," the captain remarked to Commander Keen as they paced fore and aft, leaning slightly into the wind. "We'd have had a rough time of it beating to windward to save that brig, if the schooner had appeared."

"Yes, sir," Keen agreed soberly, thinking that a captain's berth wasn't all wine and roses. "Even with an hour's notice for steam it might have been touch and go."

"Precisely. And I doubt whether McInnes would have been sober enough to put his helm up and run down to us."

"Well — not to worry, now, sir." The commander looked over at the brig, plunging along five miles to leeward under courses and tops'ls, "We can be alongside in a half-hour under sail if need be."

"Deck there! The brig's turning toward us, sir. She's close-hauled and just set her t'gallants — and she's raising steam."

"See to it that the lookout's given an extra tot of rum, Mister Giles, and square the ship off toward the brig."

"Aye aye, sir! Shall I beat to quarters?" The light of battle and the thought of using his beloved guns glinted in Giles' eyes.

"Not yet. I don't trust McInnes. He may be running from *Porpoise*."

"Or he could have run short of rum, sir," Keen murmured sardonically.

Calcutta straightened as she came before the wind, the sound of the air in her rigging diminishing to a low hum as she ploughed through a following sea. Brass glinted on the quarterdeck; telescopes were trained on and past the brig.

"Deck there!" The officers stared aloft again, to where the lookout was gesticulating. "There's a schooner beating up toward the brig, sir. 'Bout two mile off, I make it!" Telescopes swung to leeward once more, but the stranger's spars still lay below the shrouded horizon.

"Mister Kirk!" The captain shouted, even though the young officer was scarcely ten feet distant. "Have the drummer beat to quarters. Mister Giles, I'll thank you to have the guns loaded with chain-shot and ready to run out."

The Royal Marine drummer took his stance in the waist. A rapid tattoo brought men tumbling on deck and the rigging shook as sailors scrambled monkey-like to their posts. Wisps of smoke from the twin funnels became billows as stokers frantically shovelled coal onto banked fires. Muffled shouts drifted up from the gun deck, where the seven-inch muzzle-loading guns, the ship's main armament, were being loaded.

155

"There she is, sir!" Kirk screamed, remembering at the last moment to lower his voice, so that the "sir" came out artificially deep. He pointed at two toothpicks swaying along on the far side of the *Yukon Girl*, barely discernible against the muted gloom of the coastal mountains.

The captain's face brightened with a momentary grin as he said calmly, "Very good, Mister Kirk. Set the upper and lower t'gallants — smartly now. Mister van Dusen, clear away the forrard carronades and Mister Duncan, have the armourer issue pistols and cutlasses to a 30-man boarding party." Bedlam filled the air as officers called orders, petty officers repeated them and men scurried to obey. The brig was closer, only a couple of miles away, but the strange schooner was a scant two miles past that and closing rapidly as she plunged along, heeled far over under a massive press of canvas. *Calcutta* rolled more heavily under the force of her topgallants, now straining full of wind above tops'ls and huge courses.

Kirk, momentarily free, wondered why the brig didn't haul to one side, instead of staying in line between the schooner and the man o' war. Probably frightened out of his wits, he thought, recalling his captain's scathing indictment of Captain McInnes.

"Messenger! My compliments to Lieutenant Giles, and I'll have the guns run out." Whitfeld-Clements turned to David Duncan and Kirk. "The brig's a mile off, and the schooner barely a mile past her. In ten minutes I'll bring the ship to larboard so that our line of fire will be clear — unless that sot of a McInnes gets in the way! — and give Mister Giles a chance at a broadside. We'll be lucky to get a hit with chain-shot at this range, but we might deter him. Go below, sub. Tell Lieutenant Giles what I intend to do. And tell him to aim high — I want to cripple that fellow, not sink him."

"Aye aye, sir!"

Puffing slightly, Kirk ran back to the captain. "Mister Giles' respects, sir, and all's ready."

"Very good. You will take command of the boarding party if we get alongside. Now, have the ship shortened to fighting sail immediately that we turn."

"Aye aye, sir." Kirk skipped down the short quarterdeck ladder into the waist.

"Sheets and braces," the captain shouted, "down helm — hard down, dammit!" *Calcutta* yawed hugely and leaned far to leeward as she spun on her keel, the decks a medley of organized confusion as men hauled on lines to swing the great yards about.

"Clew up the t'gallants," Kirk yelled, "double reef the cro'jack and furl the foretopmast stays'l!" Sweating sailors scrambled out on yardarms, balancing precariously on swaying footropes, fisting the finger-ripping canvas into rolls of furled material, hauling on downhauls and straining on halyards as the ship rolled back to windward and a cloud of acrid smoke exploded from the starboard battery with a deafening crash.

"Up helm," ordered the captain, "bring her back before the wind. Great Flaming Gods of War, I believe we hit her! Look there, Mister Duncan — is her foretopmast falling?"

Duncan strained to see. "Yes, sir — and the sail's blowing into ribbons."

"Mister Kirk! Have all sail set to the royals."

"Deck there! The schooner's bearing off, sir. She's running."

Kirk's "Aye aye, sir" was lost in the confusion, but in seconds the ship's rigging was alive with men as *Calcutta* became a thundercloud of canvas. Seldom-set royals strained above upper and lower topgallants, which in turn lorded their slim splendour over deep-bellied single tops'ls and the ponderous courses and cro'jack.

Bulky billows of coal smoke churned and choked between the masts, entrapped by the towering piles of sails, as petty officer stokers exhorted seamen stokers. Coal-laden barrows crunched and trundled between hold and furnace, shoved along by near-naked, sooty, sweating imps, whose sweat-cloths served only to smear grime and soot on pasty faces. Equally grimy stokers, sweat dried instantly by the blazing blast from open furnace doors, swung shovelfuls of black coal into white-hot maws in a monotonous blasphemous ballet, choreographed by crouching, shouting officers. Reigning over the miniature Hell was the engineer officer, frisking like one possessed between engine and boiler room, his once-white boiler suit smudged blackly.

The *Yukon Girl* surged past with, as Kirk remarked scornfully to Midshipman Perkins, "All sail set to the Old Man's drawers", her crew staring astern at the threatening schooner. Her bedraggled captain shouted through cupped hands at *Calcutta* as the corvette drove imperially past, but finding himself totally ignored, McInnes lurched to a bollard and sat, extracting a dark bottle from a voluminous pocket.

All aboard *Calcutta* stared ahead at the schooner, with the exception of the lookouts, who well knew the captain's bitter tongue when he saw inattention to duty. David Duncan paced the decks, ordering a haul on a brace here, a sheet eased there, every command obeyed with alacrity. The seamen were infused with the thrill of the chase.

Kirk remarked cautiously to Keen, "He seems to be making for that fogbank lying offshore, sir."

The commander nodded and began to answer, when a shuddering flap from overhead brought all eyes aloft. The main royal hung limply. Even as they watched, the courses sagged, followed in ascending order by tops'ls and topgallants. The captain swore, and personally jammed the engine-room telegraph from "half" to "full speed ahead".

"Furl all sail," he ordered curtly. "Mister Bullen will have to move the ship whether he's got a full head of steam or not!"

The decks and yards again became a confused tumble of reaching, shouting, straining, bending bodies, obscenities blazing through the noise like lightning flashes, as great grey clouds of canvas were clewed up, hauled down or brailed. Officers, petty officers and seamen worked side by side to keep the ship a fighting entity.

Perched alongside Kirk on the weather main tops'l yardarm, Perkins turned his freckled face toward the sublieutenant. "The schooner's still got her sails full, sub, and look — she's even setting a raffee squaresail. How's it that we lost the wind?"

Kirk glared at the snotty as he tied a reefing gasket. "Use your bloody loaf, wart! We were moving under steam as well as sail, and in this light air the ship's speed equalled the wind."

Perkins had the grace to look abashed, his ruddy features turning even rosier.

The schooner, a bare half-mile ahead, became shadowy, then clear again as it ghosted into the fringes of fog. "Mister van Dusen," called the captain, "try a shot with the carronade. We'll most certainly lose him if I turn for another broadside," he muttered to Keen, standing tensely at his side.

The carronade banged — its report like a firecracker compared to the seven-inchers' thunder — and a tiny waterspout grew from the water just short of the schooner's rounded counter.

"Cease fire. All officers muster on the quarterdeck." Whitfeld-Clements waited impatiently for them to gather, their footsteps muted by the soft snow which had begun falling, then spoke.

"Mister Kirk, muster your boarding party amidships — I'll try to lay alongside the schooner. Mister Duncan, have grappling irons ready, and Mister Giles, hold your fire until I give the order. I won't fire unless he seems to be escaping — you'd blow him into splinters at close range. No one except the boarding party is to go over unless I give orders, but all hands are to be armed. Second Sergeant," he turned to the Royal Marine standing slightly back, "station your men in the tops to fire down, but they're to hold their fire when the boarding party attacks. Clear?"

When the sergeant nodded understanding, the captain looked around. "Do you all understand your orders? Very good, then, go to your stations and explain to your men."

"Gather 'round, lads," said Kirk tightly, not noticing the smiles of a few seamen double his age. "We'll have three jobs. Leading Seaman Blake, you will cut the schooner's halyards — take these five as your section." Kirk indicated five ratings with a wave of his hand. "Petty Officer Peebles, take six men and secure the poop. These six." He selected another half-dozen sailors. "The remainder of the men will stay with me as the main party, to overwhelm any opposition. Blake, take your section forrard after boarding. PO, you move aft. I will head for the mass of men. These are likely Fenians, so be ready for anything, and show no mercy." A low growl rumbled through the men and they fingered their weapons.

"What d'you suppose the schooner'll do, sir?" asked Petty Officer Peebles, eyes glinting as he tested the edge of his cutlass.

"Probably head for the nearest port if she gets away," Kirk said. "For certain she'll not try to outmanoeuvre a steamship. Well — there they go — into the fog. It's up to Lady Luck now."

Commander Keen watched the chase slip wraithlike into the mist. "The wind's dying, sir. We may catch her becalmed."

"Right," answered the captain — not cheerfully. "Take over now, John. Engine at slow ahead and warn all hands to be silent." With that, he scrambled to the top of the midships house, where he could be seen and heard by all aboard.

Calcutta silently entered the cotton-thick white dampness, a ghost drifting through the pale stillness. Immersed in a soft circle of semi-visibility, the hush was near-absolute; even the clank of stokehold shovels was stilled as the engine chuffed softly on the available steam.

Kirk jumped as a hand clutched his arm. "There, sir." He stared — there was a faint thickening of the fog. He turned, waved to attract the captain's attention, and pointed.

The ship listed gently as the wheel was put over, then suddenly they were on the schooner, bows almost touching, sterns narrowing together. Shouts and crashes marked Duncan's men heaving grappling irons. Kirk's stomach turned as he saw a schoonerman impaled with the brutal hooks and pinioned screaming against the gunwale, but he screeched, "Come on, you sons of sea-cooks!" A crackle of Royal Marine musketry drowned his yell, but the men saw his wave and followed him over the side in a cacophony of shouts, screams, threats, clanging of bells and a sudden explosion. The schooner's guns, Kirk thought as he swung onto the rail and fell heavily on the strange deck.

He went flat as a boot landed in the middle of his back, but was up in an instant, firing his pistol directly into an enraged purplish face. He quickly fired twice more; the face gurgled and dropped, and then he parried a pikepole with his cutlass. The deck was a mass of heaving, slashing bodies punctuated with pistol shots and clanging cutlasses. He ducked to avoid a swinging blade, parried a second and ducked again as a blaze of light and a burst of powder-smoke singed his eyebrows. A flashing blade impaled the cutlass wielder. He collapsed like an unstuffed rag doll, bubbling softly as he fell.

A small group of Fenians shouting brogued defiance clustered around the mainmast, then disappeared as the huge mainsail collapsed over them, and the massive gaff crashed, splintered, to the deck. A muffled shriek about "limey bast—" was cut off short.

As suddenly as it had begun the fight was ended. Petty Officer Peebles and his party held three officers at gunpoint on the small poop, while seamen, following Kirk's hoarse orders, grinned as they wrapped lines around the canvas-encompassed group by the mainmast. Bodies, most still, a few twitching or moaning, were strewn randomly on the schooner's rough pine deck. Curses and threats stopped suddenly as cutlasses were lifted.

Kirk staggered at a shuddering crash. He looked around, hefting his cutlass, and blinked as a horde of bluejackets stampeded over the schooner's other rail — from HMS *Porpoise*! Lieutenant Youngberg explained, as the prisoners were herded below, "I heard gunfire, and climbed to the maintop for a look. The schooner was firing at the *Yukon Girl*, but their gunnery was worse than their strategy. I immediately turned and..." He stopped as Whitfeld-Clements held up a restraining hand.

"So, Mister O'Whelan," the captain walked over to a surly oaf pinioned by two seamen, "you needed another lesson!" He turned to the seamen, "Put this man in irons with a Marine guard. Take him to my cabin. Shoot if he attempts to escape."

In conference with Commander Keen and Lieutenant Youngberg, after the prisoners had been secured and the ships restored to order, the captain said, "It's a quandary, gentlemen. Technically, they're pirates and deserve hanging. But they're also American citizens. Hanging them — no matter how richly they warrant it — could precipitate troublesome diplomatic relations between the two countries."

"Could we take them into an American port, sir, and turn them over to the authorities?" asked Keen. "Let them look after their own, as it were."

"Or let them swim for it," interjected Youngberg.

Whitfeld-Clements grinned tightly. "Worthy of consideration, but sympathizers could start trouble, and the press could exaggerate things."

"Sir," Youngberg suggested deferentially, "perhaps they could be released in their own boats with enough food and water to see them to shore, and the schooner could be retained as a prize?"

"Ashley!" the captain roared.

A head poked into the cabin. "Sir?"

"Hot rum, and quickly, damn your eyes!"

The servant was uncowed. "Aye aye, sir." He withdrew, but was back in seconds with a steaming pitcher. "Thought as you might be wantin' some, sir."

"Your health, Mister Youngberg," the captain toasted after pouring the hot, pungent rum into mugs. "I believe that you hit upon the answer. Now, who shall have command of the schooner?"

"Young Kirk, sir," Keen said positively. "He took the vessel, and it's time that he had a taste of command. Too," the commander added — he liked Kirk — "it'll look well when he faces the Board."

"Very good, John. That's what I'll do, then."

Youngberg sipped his fiery rum. "Did you get anything from O'Whelan when you questioned him, sir?"

"No — he's just a pawn. Since the floating bridge fiasco, he's apparently not been entrusted with more than the bare minimum of information. There may be someone aboard with more knowledge, but I'll not waste time looking for him." He drained his mug. "Thank you both. Lieutenant Youngberg, proceed independently to Esquimalt as soon as the Fenians are in their boats and pulling for shore. Commander, please have young Kirk report to me."

Keen leaned over the rail to call to Kirk, who was supervising three seamen splicing the schooner's cut halyards. "The captain wants to see you, sub, and," he made it a carrying whisper, "better brush your uniform and look your best."

Kirk looked apprehensive and nodded his thanks, wondering what he'd done. "Thank you, sir," he muttered absently, thinking that the schooner capture had come off well and not one in his party had been hurt, barring a few scratches on faces and arms. Well, he'd better hurry. No sense delaying and putting Clemmie in a foul mood.

The captain was standing, cap on, as Kirk knocked, entered and saluted. He spoke, thin-lipped, "Sublieutenant Kirk, are you pleased with this morning's action?"

Kirk thought swiftly once more. He'd done nothing wrong. "Yes, sir. I think everything went well." As he spoke, his memory flashed back over the past few days. No — he was relatively blame-free.

The captain grinned. "So do I, young man. You may have a petty officer and ten seamen to man the schooner."

Kirk stared. "You're giving me the schooner, sir? But the lieutenants..."

"Will have enough to do without worrying about you. You'd best select your ship's company — we'll leave as soon as the Fenians are in their boats."

"Aye aye, sir. And — thank you."

Five days later, on a bleak, cold Wednesday with spatters of rain drumming on his oilskins, Eric Kirk sailed his first command into the harbour. Unconsciously emulating Lieutenant David Duncan, he kept his orders short and precise, studiously avoiding unnecessary shouting or giving further orders to men who were already doing their jobs well. Faintly his voice echoed across the slate-grey water as he rounded up into the wind, and let go the anchor with a splash. The schooner gained sternway and the sails came down with a run and a great slatting of stiff canvas. Although he'd seen Whitfeld-Clements' oilskinned figure watching closely from *Calcutta*'s quarterdeck, Kirk had managed, with some effort, to keep from looking in the captain's direction.

As he walked forward, giving a quiet order here or a word of commendation there, from the corner of his eye he noticed a signal hoist climbing up the flagship's halyard. He ignored it, knowing that Peebles would soon report, and at that instant, the petty officer was at his elbow.

"Signal from *Calcutta*, sir. 'Captain to captain. Come on board and report'."

"Acknowledge," Kirk answered briefly. "Call away a boat."

"Aye aye, sir. Boat's alongside now."

"Very good." Kirk walked slowly to the rail, sad that his adventure in command was all but done. He came to an abrupt, surprised halt when Peebles said softly, "Sorry, sir. This side, sir." Kirk changed direction in mid-stride, then stared.

Four seamen stood rigidly by the gunwale, and Petty Officer Peebles was at attention by the entry port, bo's'n's call at his lips. They were giving him — a lowly acting subbie — the honours due a captain! Mistrusting his voice, and feeling an emotional tear welling at the corner of each eye, Kirk silently raised his hand to the salute and stepped over the side, hardly hearing Peebles holding the single, high, shrill note of the "Still". Only when the young officer was seated in the gig's stern-sheets with tiller in hand, and had ordered "Give way", did the petty officer pipe the warbling "Carry On". Kirk was so choked with emotion that the passage to *Calcutta* seemed like a dream.

The captain met him at the entry port. "Well, sub," he asked cheerfully, "any problems on your passage?" He led the way to his cabin as they talked.

"No, sir. I couldn't find any identification on the schooner. Her official number had been planed off the main beam and her log was missing. Even her name had been planed off the stern and bows, sir."

"Not to worry, then." The captain waved him to a chair and poured out two glasses of Madeira. "We'll leave her for the local authorities to look after." He raised his glass. "Your health."

Kirk lifted his glass in return, "Thank you, sir." Then, bursting with curiosity, he asked, "Leave her?"

"Yes, Eric. Orders came this morning. HMS *Inconstant* is replacing us on this station, and we're sailing for England tomorrow to go into refit." His face showed compassion as Kirk's face whitened in shock.

"Call all hands to man the capstan,
See your cables run down clear;
Hoist away, and with a will, boys,
For old England we will steer."

The nostalgic strains of the homeward-bound chanty came to Kirk's drowsy ears at six in the morning — four bells in the Morning Watch. Grabbing his uniform, he hurriedly dressed and tumbled on deck as the entire Watch roared out the chorus:

"Rolling home, rolling home,
Rolling home across the sea,
Rolling home to Merrie England,
Rolling home, dear land, to thee!"

as they heaved round on the huge capstan, weighing anchor. He looked astern toward the jetty, seeing a slim figure standing alone and forlorn. Running to the rail, he waved, and saw her return wave, then she slowly faded into the morning mists as the ship vibrated and gathered way.

In an hour the tug had slipped *Porpoise*'s tow-cable, and both *Calcutta* and *Porpoise* were glorious in clouds of white sail, rolling along Juan de Fuca Strait as the deep green water tumbled and surged into white foam under their bows. A tear slipped down Kirk's cheek. There had been only time enough for him to run to the Willoughby house, where he had managed no more than ten tearful minutes alone with Geraldine before her mother, still suspicious, had appeared, narrow-eyed and watchful. Suggesting that it was quite late, she had offered — more like an order — tea and cookies "before you return to your ship," and had stayed with them even during their final, frustrated farewell. He watched the forested mountains slipping into the mist astern, and promised himself that he would return — some day.

164

Shrill yells and an uproar of scuffling from the gunroom suddenly banished Geraldine from his mind. Boots drumming across the deck, he yanked the door open, shouting, "Avast, you warts! Into the tops with you, smartly, and stay there till I tell you to come down!"

Commander Keen exchanged an amused glance with his captain. Their awkward midshipman was well on the way both to overcoming his first love affair, and becoming a responsible naval officer.

A Glossary of Sea Terms of this Era

Aft	At, or toward the stern.
Astern	Behind a ship; or, to go astern.
Avast	Stop, or hold.
Aye aye, sir	Response to an order.
Barque	Three-or-more-masted sailing vessel, with aftermost mast fore-and-aft rigged.
Beat to Quarters	Action stations.
Belay	Stop, or make fast a rope.
Bells	Ship's time is divided into bells; one stroke every half-hour.
Bibles	Small stones used for cleaning tight spots.
Boarding netting	Netting hung about a ship's side to hinder boarders.
Brig	A two-masted vessel square-rigged on both masts.
Bulkhead	A vertical partition.
Buntlines	Pieces of rope used for sail.
Cable	Measure of distance; 600 feet.
Carronade	A short gun firing a heavy shell for a short range.
Catch a crab	A mis-stroke while rowing.
Cells	Ship's prison; "brig" in U.S. terms.
Chanty	A working song, chorus sung by all hands.
Chart	A sea map.
Close-hauled	Sailing as close into the wind as possible.
Clew up	To furl or reef a sail.
Companion	Access to lower decks.
Cutter	A ship's boat; larger than a whaler.
Deckhead	The ceiling, below decks.
Dog Watch	A "half-watch" two hours long; intended to ensure that no one stands the same Watch two days in succession.
Forebitter	A relaxation song, sung in the foc'sle.
Furl	To shorten sail; to roll a sail tightly.
Give way	Command to start rowing in a pulling boat.
Grapeshot	Small shells intended for use against men.
Grog	Rum, diluted three parts to one with water.
Gunroom	Ship's mess for midshipmen and sublieutenants.
Halyard	A rope for raising sails.
"Heart of Oak"	The Royal Navy's March Past.
Heave to	To set sails so the ship is motionless.
Heaving line	A light rope attached to a heavier one.

166

Holystone	Large stone used for cleaning decks.
Log	A daily journal of ship's activities.
Looard	Sea pronunciation of "leeward"; to the lee.
Matlow	Royal Navy slang for a sailor.
Masts	Vertical spars in a ship.
Monkey's fist	Weighted knot on a heaving line.
PO	Petty Officer.
Plain sail	All ordinary sail, without stuns'ls, etc.
Port	The left side of a vessel.
Putty	Slang term for sea bottom.
"Queen's Hard Bargain"	A poor sailor; a rumpot.
Ranks	Officers' ranks are: Admiral, Vice Admiral, Rear Admiral, Commodore, Captain, Commander, Lieutenant-commander, Lieutenant, Sublieutenant, Midshipman, with Acting ranks between.
Ratings	Chief Petty Officer, Petty Officer, Leading Seaman ("Killick"), Able Seaman, Ordinary Seaman. Petty Officer and above ranks have First and Second classes.
Rattle	Slang term for being in trouble, or in cells.
Sculling about	Slang term for being "on the loose", idling.
Scuttle	A porthole.
Ship	A sailing vessel with three or more masts, all square-rigged.
Snotty	Slang term for a midshipman.
Soogieing	Cleaning material.
Starboard	The right side of a vessel.
Tar	Slang term for a British sailor.
Up Spirits	The command for an issue of rum or grog.
Wardroom	Mess for lieutenants and above, not including the captain, who had to be invited in.
Watch	A period of duty, either four hours or, in Dog Watches, two hours:

First Watch	2000 - 2400
Mid Watch	0000 - 0400
Morning Watch	0400 - 0800
Forenoon Watch	0800 - 1200
Afternoon Watch	1200 - 1600
First Dog Watch	1600 - 1800
Last Dog Watch	1800 - 2000

Weigh anchor	To raise anchor before sailing.
Whaler	A pulling boat, smaller than a cutter.

Printed in Canada